Just Follow the Money

by

Jinx Schwartz

JUST FOLLOW THE MONEY
Published by Jinx Schwartz
Copyright 2017
Book 9: Hetta Coffey series
All rights reserved.

In loving memory of Robert "Mad Dog" Schwartz
April 18, 1937—March 8, 2017

If tears could build a stairway, and memories a lane, I would walk right up to Heaven and bring you back again. —*Anonymous*

You were my heart, my rock, my best friend, and you made me a better person. We literally weathered storms, shared adventures, and made a wonderful life together. Without your patience, encouragement, and willingness to dive into this strange world of publishing, I would never have written a book; and but for your tackling the technical mysteries, none would be published.

Our thirty years together were the best in my life.

Thank you, Mad Dog, and give God a run for his money on that heavenly golf course of His.

JUST FOLLOW THE MONEY

Cherchez la femme: look for the woman; the cause of
the situation must be a woman

Chapter One

JAN SLAPPED A newspaper in my hand. "Here! Read it and weep."

I gave the evening copy of *Le Parisien* a look and was dismayed to see a photo of Po Thang front and center, caught red-pawed in the act of pulling a white tablecloth laden with china, cutlery, crystal, wine, and obviously gourmet fare, from a dining table. The background made it clear the setting was in a first-class restaurant.

"Oh, no."

"Oh, yes. I got the gist, but you translate it, okay?"

I sighed and began to read aloud. "***Faits divers***. That means the news, but also means *various things*. Kinda like *this and that*. It's a social page featuring local happenings."

Jan circled her hand. "Get on with it, Hetta."

"Alright, alright. Hold your horses."

"***American dog faces deportation for theft!***"

I gave the perpetrator the evil eye and then read on, translating as I went.

"Several incidents of vandalism and thievery at some of Paris's beloved premier dining establishments have gone mostly unreported, and it is rumored that the crimes were hushed-up by persons in high authority. However, once a YouTube video taken by an assaulted diner was posted on the internet, reports by other eyewitnesses quickly emerged. As one victim, who asked not to be identified said, "Before I could shout au voleur! *(Stop, thief!) my* magret de canard *(duck breast) had disappeared down the beast's gullet."*

While the restaurateurs, chefs and staff remain discreetly silent on the issue, it has come to our attention that this is possibly the same dog that made headlines in the South of France last month while in the company of three American females boating on the Canal du Midi. These women are bruited to have ties to an alleged domestic terrorist taken into custody at the Port of Lauragais on the same night Charles de Gaulle airport was evacuated. The abandoned luggage that sparked the incident in the airport was traced back to this unidentified Frenchman (who was somehow associated with the three aforementioned American women) and we suspect a cover-up of epic proportions.

We have also learned through unimpeachable sources that this diner-terrorizing dog, and his mysterious entourage of women, will leave France tomorrow on a privately chartered Air France flight.

We may never know the extent of the havoc unleashed by these four, but at least Parisian diners will now be safe from this foreign canine with questionable table manners.

Chapter Two

"GAWD, THE FRENCH are such drama queens," I griped as I handed the paper back to Jan.

She chuffed a razz and flipped *LeParisiene* over her shoulder. The newspaper sailed through open French doors, where it landed with a plop and skidded across a gleaming checkerboard black-and-white marble floor.

Po Thang—the badly-mannered foreign canine of mention—lifted his head and watched the paper's flight as though considering giving it a chase, but changed his mind and snuggled back into his own blankie. This uncharacteristic laissez-faire attitude made me wonder if he'd slurped some of my champagne when I wasn't looking.

Jan, my dog, and I were sitting on our balcony, bundled up in feather duvets against December's chill.

"Judging by today's gossip headlines," Jan drawled, "we've not only been outed," she frowned at Po Thang,

"I think we've plumb worn out our welcome here. You lookin' forward to headin' home, Hetta?"

I had to think about it. Was I?

Just as she posed the question, the Eiffel Tower went into sparkle mode like it does every night for ten minutes every hour on the hour. Because Christmas loomed, the lights featured a lot of red and green. I raised my glass in a toast, "*Vive la France.*"

Jan held up her own flute of champagne between us so the glittering tower and golden bubbles in her glass reflected through the sparkling wine, throwing a disco ball-like shower of light on us. "Jean Luc showed me how to do this."

"Jean Luc?" I croaked. "He was here?" What I didn't ask was, *At night? In your bed-sitting room? Drinking champagne?*

"Well, duh. He, like, *owns* the place, ya know. You jealous?"

"Don't be ridiculous," I spluttered. "I just didn't know that he...uh, I thought it was just you and Rhonda staying here."

"He doesn't *stay* here. He has much finer digs nearby. This joint is just for visitors."

I swiveled my head and looked back into the "joint" we were occupying thanks to the generosity of Jean Luc. Our guest room, on the third floor—he owns the whole building—was a sumptuous one-bedroom plus sleeper couch affair with a small kitchen area and a spa-like marble palace of a bathroom, all of it a perfect blend of old-monied French aristocracy and modern convenience.

Probably only France's Minister of Finance knew its worth.

Annoyed with myself and embarrassed by my inappropriate reaction to news of Jean Luc's nocturnal visit, I changed the subject. "So, where is Rhonda, by the way? I haven't seen hide nor hair of her since I got here this morning."

"Today's a spa day."

"Rhonda has spa days?" I tried, and failed, to envision our frumpish friend at one of those Parisian glamour salons frequented by petite and oh-so-fashionable French women. It was Rhonda who was responsible for all of us being in Paris in the first place; there was a bit of truth in that newspaper article. Okay, maybe more than a bit.

Hearing a tap on our apartment door, Po Thang growled, sprang to his feet, shook off his blankie, and loped toward the noise.

Jan yelled, "Enter if you dare, but fair warning, Hetta's here."

Po Thang's growl changed to a friendly whine and I turned, half-expecting to see Jean Luc. Dreading it was him, if the truth be known.

I was trying to think of something fitting to say to a man who had, quite literally, changed my life for the worse once upon a time, when my jaw dropped. "Rhonda? Holy Moly, what have they done to you?"

She spun around, put one hand in a vamp stance upon the waist of a designer frock, and fluffed her newly jet-black French coif with the other. "*Aimez-vous ça?*"

Stunned by her transformation, I was atypically short on words. Just weeks ago, when we first met, Rhonda was, to put it kindly, plain. Dowdy. A Hollywood stereotype of a frumpy schoolmarm who was about as street smart as a nun. She was, at the time, under the lovesick spell of a slick Machiavellian-like Frenchman whom Jan and I were convinced was scheming to steal her newly acquired inheritance. The femme fatale in front of me was akin to the metamorphosis of a caterpillar to a butterfly.

"*Chat* got your tongue, Hetta?" Jan teased.

"Wow." Sometimes my eloquence is downright astounding.

Rhonda rushed over and gave me a hug, which I tolerated even though I usually save hugs for dogs and verrry good friends. "I can't thank you enough for saving my life!" she gushed.

"Yeah, if Hetta wasn't such a nosy, meddling busybody, you'd be in tall doo-doo about now. Want a glass of champers?"

"Can I have one?"

"Of course you can, Rhonda," I huffed indignantly. "Rousel *le Roué* is no longer around to tell you what to do. You can have anything you want."

"Oh, it's not that, Hetta. Jan is keeping count for me. I've lost ten pounds in two weeks, thanks to her. Alcohol contains empty calories, you know."

Annoyed by that prissy-sounding insult to what I considered the nectar of the Gods, I downed a couple a hundred empty calories instead of verbally blasting her off her high horse.

Jan, attuned to my piques, picked up on my irritation and smirked. "That's so, Miz Rhonda, and congratulations for grasping a concept *some*," she gave me a meaningful look, "never do. However, tonight is a special occasion, what with it being our last night in Paris and all." She picked up her cellphone and tapped it. "Whoa, you *deserve* a reward. Your Fitbit says you walked ten miles today?"

"Yep, before I went to *Dior Institut*," Rhonda said, further vexing me by pronouncing the spa's name perfectly as *Deeor Ansteetoo;* after all, *I'm* the one who speaks French, here! I took another mouthful of liquid ambrosia as she continued. "I walked from the tower, across the river, looped the Louvre, then zig-zagged back and forth across the Seine bridges to the Plaza Athénée."

"Impressive," I said, albeit a bit grudgingly, not only meaning the miles walked; the *Institut Dior* at Hotel Plaza Athénée is *the* number one—read expensive—spa in Paris, and a far cry from Aline's Warsh 'n' Set back in my Texas high school days. "I remember the first time I visited Paris and walked so much I had huge blisters on the bottoms of my feet."

Rhonda raised what I recognized from times gone *way* by as a silk-stockinged leg, and flaunted what might have been considered a rather clunky shoe had it not been patent leather with a faux zebra inset. "*Arches*," she said, pronouncing the pricey brand of shoe perfectly as, "Arsh."

You've come a long way, Charlie Brown, I thought, but said, "Very chic. I see Jan has been busily spending your inheritance."

"Oh, yes. Bless her heart, we are having *so* much fun."

I almost laughed out loud. I knew Rhonda meant it as a compliment, but in Texas, when we say, "Bless her heart," what we really mean is, "Bless her heart, the bitch."

"Well, God love her," I drawled, adding my own back-handed Southern slur to Rhonda's unintended insult. What the hell? A few weeks back Jan wanted to throttle Rhonda and now she's her new best friend?

Jan tilted her head at me and gave me a, *F-you and the horse you rode in on* smile, but none of these subtleties registered on Rhonda as she prattled on. "And now, thanks to Jan, men, even *French* men, are ogling me! *Me!* Well, as long as Jan's not with me."

She was so enthralled with her new self that I didn't have the heart to tell her that libidinous looks were the French male's national pastime. We did, after all, have a common bond; I've spent the past twenty-some-odd years as the invisible woman when in the company of the tall, lanky, blue-eyed blonde, Jan.

Rhonda did deign to share a glass of champagne with us. I couldn't stop staring—okay, with no small amount of envy—at the new Rhonda. "You two have worked wonders. Well done, girls. Not only do you look spectacular, Miz R, you seem to have successfully washed that rat, Rousel, right out of your newly styled hair."

"Amazing, isn't it, that I was so naïve? I mean, ever since I graduated from college, I've done nothing but take care of Mom and teach school. No social life outside the occasional movie and pizza night with my limited friends. When my mother died and I found I had a considerable amount of money— "

I cut her off. "Which, if you hang out with Jan much longer, she'll divest you of even faster than Rousel could have stolen it," I teased.

Jan stuck her tongue out at me and Rhonda giggled. "Thank goodness for you two." She raised her glass. "To Jan, for helping me enjoy my wealth," I rolled my eyes, "and to Hetta, for your...tenaciousness,"—Jan snorted in the background at the word, probably thinking *bullheadedness* more appropriate—"in protecting me from that despicable lout. Speaking of, have you heard anything about what the cops did with him? There has been absolutely nothing about Rousel, or his part in that terrorist scheme, in the news."

I returned her toast. "And hopefully there never will be, thank goodness. I sure as hell don't want to be fingered as one of the people responsible for nailing his smarmy ass, although *someone* in this room seems to have put us on the media's radar."

We all glared at Po Thang who moaned and buried his snoot in his blankie.

"That dawg," Jan declared, "will be the death of us someday. Anyhow, according to Jean Luc, who has contacts in the know, the only official report was the one issued by the French Minister of Defense in his press conference. Orly Airport was evacuated only as a safety measure when an unidentified female tourist," she jerked her head toward Rhonda, "*innocently* left a pile of luggage unattended in the airport terminal while she walked outside to look for her boyfriend, who was late for their flight. That set off all kinds of built-in security measures."

I barked a laugh. "I liked that 'innocently' touch. When we watched the press conference, the minister's facial expression made it clear he really wanted to say, 'stupidly,' but he refrained. At least he added the incident was thoroughly investigated and proved to be a false alarm. Period. End of story."

Rhonda, who had not witnessed the minister's television dog-and-pony spin, shrugged. "Hey, as long as he didn't use my name he could have gone ahead and called me stupid for all I care. Anyhow, Jean Luc said Rousel was told he was arrested because of something in the luggage that identified him, and now he's in the custody of some CIA-type group who will probably make him disappear for-*ever*. Fine with me."

Flouncing toward the door, one expensively clad foot in front of the other like a runway model, hair glistening and swaying, she stopped and threw us an over-the-shoulder smolder. "Let me know what we're doing for dinner, okay?" Then she added, "Not that I'll eat much," before sashaying off to pack her bags—which she made a point of letting me know were Louis Vuitton—with several thousand Euro's worth of designer duds and overpriced underwear.

Compliments of Air France, we were all flying on a private charter to New York the next day. And not because our dog was on the deportee list; it was their way of thanking Jan, Rhonda, and me for being key players in foiling that terrorist plot against the airline at Orly.

After the door closed behind our newly minted diva, I shook my head. "I think I liked her better when she was just plain pitiful instead of pitifully sanctimonious."

Jan nodded in agreement. "I am afraid I have created a monster."

At that moment the Eiffel Tower shimmered and caught my attention. "Right on the money. I could get used to watching this every night, all night."

"I kinda have," Jan said. "I love leaving the drapes open and falling asleep with this view. What do ya figure it'd cost to actually live here in Paris, in an apartment like this one?"

"More than *we'll* ever be able to steal."

Jan grinned. "Not that we won't try. You, at least have a shot at it."

"Yeah, right. Who do I gotta mug?"

"Don't play dumb with someone who knows you so well, Chica. You could marry, or at least live with, Jean Luc, and ya know it. He's nuts for you."

"He's just nuts then. I'm in love with Jenks." A deep sigh escaped me and Po Thang unearthed himself from his cocoon and rested his head on my knee.

"What's with the glum, Chum? Even your dog can tell you've got a touch of the blues."

"Well, for starters, Jenks left for Dubai this morning and I'm stuck in Paris, on my last night in France, with you and a dawg."

"Po Thang, I think yo mama just insulted us."

"Sorry, I didn't mean it that way. It's just that we head back to Mexico tomorrow, then I'll be in La Paz, alone, for Christmas *and* New Year's Eve, no less. I was leading a pretty lonely existence there before I landed this job in France. Now that it's wrapped up, I'll be back to scrubbing decks and other boat work."

"Gee, thanks for reminding me. Hell, I'll be relegated to a fish camp, no Santa in sight, flipping tortillas for the research crew. But at least I'll have Chino, *when* he can tear himself away from those damned whales of his."

We fell silent, each thinking our own thoughts while admiring the glowing resplendence of the City of Light at night.

Po Thang gave me an icy nose nudge so I scratched his ears and leaned over to kiss his snout. "How about you, Dawg, you ready to head back to Mexico?"

"*Wouf.*" In the past few weeks he'd picked up a lot of French.

Jan harrumphed. "That hound doesn't give a dang where he is, so long as you're with him and there's food involved. I think he'll miss his new French pal, Charles, though." She pronounced it, "Sharles." Po Thang's ears twitched and he whined when Jan mentioned his buddy. "But I gotta say, I think some of that poodle's elegant good manners rubbed off on him a tiny bit. Last night at the restaurant, Po Thang didn't even eye-beg *too* much."

"Are you kidding? Did you *read* that article?"

"We oughta sue 'em for slander, huh, Po? Okay, so there was a little tablecloth thing or two, but the rest of the time he *almost* behaved himself."

"Thanks for keeping him while Jenks and I toured the South of France for the past week. Dog friendly as France is, hauling this big galoot around in a Fiat Cinquecento is a pain in the butt."

Jan jerked a thumb at the newspaper lying on the floor behind us. "Which, by the way, wasn't easy. It isn't like when he stays with me at the fish camp, where he can run loose and steal all the fish tacos he wants. You owe me, big time. Thank goodness Jean Luc knows everyone who is anyone in Paris, or you'd be bailing me and that rapscallion pooch of yours out of a Parisian jail."

"I thought you said he almost behaved."

"I forgot to add, 'for a stray with questionable training'. "

"Hey, I've done what I can. I guess it will be a relief to be back in a country where my dawg, should he choose to behave so badly, will end up as taco filling."

We laughed, me trying to picture us even being allowed in an upscale Mexican restaurant with a dog, much less him getting his own place setting like he does in France. My moment of amusement passed quickly, however, replaced by that annoying malaise, a grinchy slap shot to the spirit, that had plagued me all day, ever since seeing Jenks off that morning.

"Saying goodbye to Jenks, once again, isn't all that's bothering me. Truth be known, I've been thinking about other things lately."

"Like?"

"Like, do you ever worry about ending up as a bag lady?"

Jan pointed at my empty flute and raised a perfectly plucked eyebrow. I nodded, and she refilled it. "Bag lady? Where on earth did that come from?"

"I dunno. Lately it's occurred to me that we have, like, twenty years to prepare for retirement."

"Twenty? I'll probably have to work until I'm eighty if I keep hanging out with you. But on the bright side, I wouldn't worry too much about it, Chica. Our lifestyles don't bode well for achieving long and healthy lives."

"There is some truth in that. But practically speaking, just in case we miraculously outwit the odds and live normal lifespans, we really don't have that many earning years left to make some big bucks for retirement, and judging by our past performance, and present for that matter, things just don't look all that rosy."

"Might I remind you that I am your accountant? You are not all that broke."

"I have a unpaid-for boat that is the epitome of the old adage, 'a hole in the water into which one pours money.' Scads of money. And a dog that eats his weight daily, and to make matters worse, I am most likely unemployable."

Jan smirked. "And yet here you sit, in a bazillion euro apartment, drinking very expensive champagne while watching the Eiffel Tower from your let-them-eat-cake balcony," she drawled ironically. "You *po* thang."

Chapter Three

IN ALL HONESTY—which Jan says I'm a mite loose with—if I hadn't formed my own company, I probably wouldn't even *have* a job. I am not a team player, and therefore not exactly corporate material. Unless the corporation is mine, and even so, if my resume came across my desk, I definitely wouldn't hire me.

I am CEO, CFO, president, and sole employee of Hetta Coffey, SI, LLC. The SI stands for Civil Engineer, in an ode to peepull who are educated to spell fonetically. I am chronically single and recently turned forty; the *forty* part actually escapes my lips now without the aid of waterboarding.

A civil engineer by degree, I actually specialized in Materials Management: a kind of drawing-to-field concept for the stuff required to build mega projects for global engineering/construction firms. That was before I went rogue on one of them, namely Baxter Brothers, and ratted them out to the client for getting even greedier than usual, and got myself sacked.

I presently stay employed by virtue of a willingness—a downright eagerness say some—to engage in more or less unorthodox undertakings, so long as they pay well.

Jan, my best friend and often cohort in these endeavors, says this tendency to tread upon a felonious path less taken by saner folks will eventually land us both in the penal facility of some country or another, but who is she to talk? She's an unemployed CPA who acts as chief tortilla patter and fish fryer in a whale camp run by her *amour du jour*, world-renowned marine biologist, Doctor Brigido Comacho Yee, aka, Chino. Whoever heard of an accountant who works for free? Unless it's for me, of course.

I finally have a wonderful man in my life now, but Jenks is just as perpetually absent as I am single. His work as a security specialist—so he says, but I personally think he might run a black op or two on occasion—takes him all over hell and back. Most recently he's been headquartered in Dubai, which is why Jan says we stay together; we are not around each other long enough for me to scare him off.

When Jenks and I *are* able to spend time together, all is magic. Then he leaves me on my own, and that is when I teeter on the brink of screwing up the closest thing to a normal relationship I've ever had.

By virtue of my pigheadedness, along with a Texas temperament that can turn as fiery as my hair right after a touch up, I manage to somehow find trouble that threatens to piss off even the seemingly unflappable and patient Jenks.

Jan says I'm stubborn, incorrigible, and morally corrupt, which is why she likes me so much.

I prefer to think of myself as self-governing.

Po Thang and I were still sitting on the balcony, enjoying the Parisian landscape, when Jan returned, fresh from a shower. "Hey, there, future bag lady, ya wanna go rummage in the trash bins in the back alley? We're hungry, ain't we, dawg?"

"*Wouf.*"

"Very funny. Thanks for being sooo totally unsympathetic to my concern for our futures, Miz Jan. You might want to think a bit about where you're going to end up one of these days, yourself. However, being the kind of friend to you that you should be to me, I shall address your immediate concerns. Since going out for dinner," I scowled at my dog, "is out of the question, let us raid that giant fridge and larder in the main kitchen and see what scraps we find."

The three of us left our apartment and went upstairs to the penthouse floor, and its luxury kitchen. An ode to the French culinary arts, the appliances and accoutrements were fantabulous, so I figured the fridge had to be stocked with a treasure trove of goodies. One look inside told me I was right.

"Okay, I've got it. Grilled cheese."

"What? Our last night in Paris and you want grilled cheese sandwiches?" Jan threw up her hands in disgust.

"Just trust me on this one, okay? You and Po Thang go fetch us at least three, make that four, baguettes while I get dinner going."

Jan looked doubtful, but leashed Po Thang for his last walk of the night. She took a poop bag with her, even though she was probably the only person in Paris who picks up a dog's leavings. Walking the sidewalks of Paris is a perilous undertaking.

I rummaged through the kitchen and found everything I knew I'd find. After all, this was Jean Luc's building, he's a great cook, and my first clue was that half-round of Livradoux I spotted in the industrial sized refrigerator.

Putting tiny potatoes on to boil, I pulled out all manner of *entremets* and put them in heavy crockery bowls on an antique country kitchen table that was no doubt the real deal. French elite do not go in for reproductions.

As I was placing a bowl of paper thin *viande de grison* slices on the table, Rhonda entered the kitchen. "Hey, what smells so good?"

"I'm making dinner while Jan went out for bread and to walk *le* dawg. Can you grab a bottle of Pinot Gris from the wine chiller?"

"Want to spell that?"

"W-i-n—"

She cut me off with a laugh. "Smarty. Which wine?"

I told her the labels to look for while I tested the potatoes and found them perfectly done. I'd fired up the *raclette* machine and the cheese was starting to bubble. Jan and Po Thang arrived, both sniffing the air and making approving noises. "*À table!*" I announced. "Grab a chair."

Placing a few potatoes, thin slices of *viande de grison*, and a *cornichon* onto each plate, I then scraped a blob of bubbling cheese on them.

"Smells divine, but what is all this stuff?" Rhonda asked. Then she turned to Jan and added, "Can I even *have* any of it?"

"I think so," she pointed to the tiny *cornichon*, "at least the pickle. And this is beef, right?" Jan forked a slice of transparent, air-dried beef known as *grison* and waved it in the air.

"Yep, and the cheese is basically Swiss, so somewhat low fat. Even though it originated in Switzerland, this is a traditional French *raclette*. As a matter of fact—"

The door flew open and Jean Luc barged in. "Do I smell *raclette*?"

Before I could stop myself, I said, "*Merde.*"

Jan whacked me lightly with the back of her hand and growled, "Play nice, Hetta."

Jean Luc acted as though he hadn't heard my expletive and bent down to pet my ecstatically wiggling dog, the fickle little turd dropper. Is there no loyalty left in the world?

"Take a seat, Jean Luc. I'll get you a plate and a glass," Rhonda gushed. She does that a lot.

"Merci, *mademoiselle* Rhonda. My, don't you look *ravissante* tonight?"

Rhonda blushed the color of my hair. I doubt anyone had ever called her ravishing in her entire life. I know the feeling.

Jean Luc went on, "As do all of you ladies. And Hetta, you have prepared the *raclette*? And just the way you know I like it. Merci, *ma petite chou-fleur.*"

Rhonda's ravishing and I'm his little cauliflower? And thanks for the reminder, you jerk, that twenty years ago I made you anything *the way you liked it, and for all that I got kicked to the curb without a fond* adieu.

Jan piped up before I showed how ungrateful I can be when living in someone's house, drinking their wine, and eating their food. "I happened to run into Jean Luc downstairs and invited him up to join us, of course."

I stuffed an entire potato in my mouth when he pulled a chair way too close, scraped cheese onto his plate and then turned to face me. "I am so pleased I had the opportunity to see you once again, and say goodbye before you leave tomorrow."

Better than you did all those years ago, I wanted to say, but with that potato in my throat, all I could do was grunt. Probably just as well, for I had several retorts I longed to deliver, none of them pleasant. I was actually surprised at my reaction; I thought I'd buried the hatchet with Jean Luc d'Ormesson, or Jean Luc d'Rat, as I called him. His nickname had by now devolved into a simple one-word aspersion: DooRah.

Clearly, I was not totally immune to the effect DooRah still held over me, evidenced by the state of nervous agitation I found myself in with this drop-dead gorgeous charmer sitting by my side. One who had once permanently wounded my heart.

I choked down the potato and jumped to my feet. "My phone's ringing."

"You can hear it from across the building? My, I know you have superb hearing abilities, but that is downright amazing," Jan drawled dryly.

Shooting her a murderous look, I scurried out of the room. Po Thang, torn between following me and remaining in a room full of food, took the low road. Two-timing cur.

Back in our apartment, I threw cold water onto my fiery face and took several deep breaths. "Hetta Coffey," I said to myself in the mirror, "grow up! Jean Luc is twenty-year-old history. Pull on your big girl panties and go be gracious, for cryin' out loud."

Which I did, just as soon as the Valium I downed hit my system.

I sailed back toward the kitchen and picked up the unique scent of caramelizing Calvados. As I entered, Jean Luc was spooning gelato into peach halves he'd sautéed and then set ablaze with apple brandy.

Waggling my phone in the air I said, "Sorry, it was Mom, so I had to take it. Oooh, *les pêches flambeés!*"

Jan's eyes narrowed as she leaned forward to get a better look at me. A smirk told me she was onto that Valium fix. I ignored her and dug into the creamy gelato, even disregarding Jean Luc's comment that he'd made the dessert especially for me because he knew it was one of my favorites. Like *every* dessert isn't?

Rhonda, who was eating peaches only, couldn't keep her eyes off Jean Luc, who couldn't seem to keep his eyes off me. Thank goodness I'd be out of France and out of sight *tout de suite*. My phone vibrated and caller ID said it was Jenks. I mentally crossed myself and thanked every saint I am aware of, and I'm not even Catholic.

Excusing myself from the table again, I walked into the living area, answering the call on my way. "Jenks, I miss you!"

"I miss you, too, and I only left this morning. We just took off from Lille."

"Oh, how I would love to be with you on that plane. Can Po Thang and I come to Dubai instead of going back to Mexico?" He hesitated, which didn't set well with me. "Never mind."

"Hetta, I would like nothing more than to have you with me, wherever I am, but it won't work right now. However, I do have some very good news for you."

"I could use some about now."

"Is everything alright? What's wrong?"

I sighed. "Nothing, really. I get this way when I have to leave almost anywhere. Gimme the good news."

"For starters, you don't have to leave France just yet. Unless you want to, and it doesn't sound like you do. Someone we know has asked for a big favor, and since you and Jan are already in France, I thought we could work something out. It's actually a job."

My heart did a dance. "Anything!"

"Don't you want to know the details? Or how much money is involved?"

"Not really. I need a job, any money is better than none, and since I know this one has your stamp of approval, we're in."

"Shouldn't you ask Jan first?"

"Are you kidding? She was just saying she wasn't looking forward to going back to the Baja and that whale camp. This time of the year she hardly sees Chino anyhow, he's so busy counting whales and their babies."

"Okay, then. I'll get the ball rolling."

Evidently the Valium was a little too calming, for I generously asked, "Uh, what about Rhonda? Can she get in on this?"

"I don't see why not. You'll get an email from—"

The call dropped. I scowled at the phone, "From who? Whom? Oh, well, who cares?" Chemically-enhanced tranquility still prevailed, so I literally skipped back into the kitchen.

"Guess what? We're staying in France! Jenks has a friend who's hired *all* of us! Well, except you, Jean Luc."

Everyone started talking at once, so I held up my hand for silence. "I don't know what, for how long, or where, but if Jenks thinks it's okay, it must be, so who's in?"

Jan and Rhonda chorused, "Me!"

"*Wouf!*"

Jean Luc took a large swig of brandy directly from the bottle. "*Mon Dieu! Aidez la France.*"

Chapter Four

JEAN LUC'S PLEA for God to help France in light of my tribe staying on in his country for a while longer struck us all as funny, but he was probably serious.

Of course, he was way too polite to suggest we vacate his guest quarters, but I told him we'd most likely be moving out as soon as we heard from our new unnamed mentor.

We cleaned up the kitchen, even though Jean Luc insisted the staff would take care of it in the morning. Raclette is yummy, but messy, and if you leave the cheese to harden on plates overnight, a jackhammer might come in handy. Kinda makes one wonder what it does to one's innards, *n'est-ce pas* ? I drank a liter of water.

By the time we got back to our apartment, Jan and I had speculated on all kinds of scenarios as to what we were going to be doing next, but Jenks hadn't given me a hint because I hadn't even asked.

"Well for crying out loud, you nincompoop. The suspense is killing me. Why didn't you let Jenks tell you anything when you had him on the line? Call him back," Jan demanded as we resumed our posts on the balcony after dinner.

"I tried. Goes to voicemail. Betcha Jenks is catching some sleep before arriving in Dubai for work in the morning. They keep him pretty busy."

"Well, gee, glad *he'll* snatch some Zs. I won't be able to sleep a wee-unk until I know what to tell Chino. He still thinks I'll be home in a couple of days."

I checked my iPhone again. "Okay it's after ten here, so he's probably still out in the boat doing his whale thing. Maybe we'll get some info by midnight. Oh, oh, incoming email!"

"Read it! Who's it from?"

"Don't recognize the address, but it's from Mexico. Mexico? What the hell? Okay, here we go. 'Dear Miss Coffey, you do not know me, but I have heard many good things about you.' "

Jan scoffed, "He is obviously misinformed."

"Hush. 'I am forever grateful for your willingness to aid me in a very private matter. My team leader will be in contact with you very soon. I am offering each of you involved a ten-thousand dollar fee, plus expenses, which will be deposited where you wish, no matter the outcome. I thank you from the bottom of my heart and hope we meet one day. Juan'. "

"Read that again, especially the money part."

I did, then said, "I wonder if Agent Po Thang gets the ten grand, too?"

Po Thang yawned. He has little use for cash, only what it can buy in the way of treats. Jan and I shared a yuk, but I was serious and sent an answer to clear up the fact we had four on our team, and asked what the "plus expenses" covered. I am the queen of padding an expense account, but a girl has to plan ahead.

Another email came back almost immediately, from a different address, but still originating in Mexico. It wasn't signed.

"Whoa, get this. They, whoever *they* are, want us to be ready to roll day after tomorrow. A car will pick us up here and drive us to Nice. The driver will know which hotel we'll be in, and further instructions are to follow. We're to keep a low profile while in Nice, order meals from room service and not leave the hotel."

"Yeah, like that'll work. Who's gonna walk the danged dawg?"

"I'm sure the hotel has people for that. Unless they dump us in a dump, which I doubt, since they expect us to order room service. Interesting. Mystery trip, coming up!"

"I'm gonna call Chino right now so he'll probably be still out counting those whales of his. That way I can leave a message without getting into a row of some kind, but what will I say? Hey, Chino, I'm staying in France indefinitely doing God only knows what?"

"Wing it."

She hit a key on her phone and waited. I leaned in to listen and after a few clicks and weird noises I heard the distinctive Mexican ring. But only once. "*¡Querida!* I miss you."

Jan mouthed, "Crap."

I twirled my finger for her to keep talking so he couldn't ask too many questions.

"Oh, hi, Chinito," Jan cooed, using her personal diminutive for him. "I miss you, too. But, uh, I have to tell you something."

"Do not worry, *mi corazón*, I already know you will be delayed."

"You do?"

"Yes, but we cannot discuss it on the phone."

They talked about whales, the weather, and then started some mush talk, so I quit listening to his end. Finally they exchanged sappy lovey-dovey bye-byes in English and Spanish before she ended the call and stabbed a finger at me. "Just what the hell have you gotten us into this time? Chino can't discuss it on the phone? What? The NSA gives a big crap what I'm doing?"

"Got me. Jenks was also cryptic. The only defense I have is that it was he who told me about it, so it must be safe and on the up and up. Right?"

She did a double head tilt. "Yeah, I guess so. And Chino certainly wouldn't agree to anything that would put me in danger. That's *your* job."

I let that jab slide. "Curiouser and curiouser. Let's hit the sack, we've got one more day in Paris and I want to get in some power shopping, then we gotta pack up and head south, to Nice of all places. I was there once and it's *très* cool. Not as chic as Cannes, in my opinion, but as an international destination, it's way up there."

"Yeah, it should be pretty damned excitin' from our hotel room window."

"Oh, please. Since when did we start following orders? What are they gonna do, lock us in and post a guard?"

By the time Po Thang and I dragged ourselves back to the apartment the next evening, my feet were sore and my bank account had taken a hit, but when I arrived a pile of delivered packages already waited. Service in France can be iffy, but when it comes to upscale restaurants and stores, they excel.

Jan was sorting through a pile of elegant, shiny boxes and gift bags when we arrived. "Jeez, you two. Is there anything left to buy in Paris?"

I headed for the couch and kicked off my shoes. "Two words inspired me: plus expenses."

She eyed several unopened boxes. "Does 'expenses' cover all this wine?"

"But of curse," I said in my best Inspector Clouseau accent. "We are, after all, in France, and in danger of being under house arrest in a hotel for who knows how long. We must prepare for the worst."

"Makes sense to me. What's in this one?" She picked up a large box labeled, *la moustache*, Paris. "Dog food, treats, shampoo, and," I leaned over, removed the bow and opened the box, "check this out! When I dropped *le dawg* off for a spa day of his own this morning, I found this treasure." I held up a black doggie hoodie printed with an "I Heart Paris" logo. "And, since it's getting chilly out, I bought one for each of his humans, as well."

"And what's all this?" She picked up one of many shiny chic bags.

"Look inside. You shoulda come with me."

"Seems like it. Oh, well, Rhonda and I went for a massage and I'm all packed to go, at least." She opened the large bag and pulled out an assortment of tee shirts. "Souvenirs?"

"Thought I'd take some back to the Baja for the guys who work on the boat. They love this kind of thing."

She grabbed a pink and black bag with an F logo and peered inside. "Oooh, Fauchon foody stuff. The French really know how to market expensive treats. We've got your *pâté de foie gras*, truffles, jelly— "

"Puleez! That's fig *confiture*, you Barbarian."

"Okay, let me rephrase that. *Expensive* jelly. All this is making me hungry. What do you say we go out tonight instead of messing up the kitchen?"

"Sure. Where?"

"I've heard about a place nearby that sounds good."

"Count me in. Rhonda coming?"

"She said she used up all her calories for this week last night."

"I may have to garrote her. There is nothing worse than hanging out with a reforming chubbette."

"Oh, yes, there is. Hanging out with a *perpetual* chubbette."

I whacked her on the head with a wad of tissue paper. "At least she hasn't gone vegan. Yet. That would be the very last straw."

"Cut her some slack, Hetta. She's looking good and feeling great about herself, probably for the first time in her life. And, quite frankly, there is nothing worse for someone on a diet than hanging out with you."

"Fine, I'm due a good dinner without a calorie Nazi at the table anyhow. I walked my ass off today."

Jan bent and peered around me. "Looks the same to me. Big."

This set us to giggling, so Po Thang did his little wiggle dance around us to show his support before sticking his nose into another slick-looking bag with dog bones printed all over it. I snatched it away, took out a box of *bisque de caviar*, which is French for overpriced dog biscuit, and gave him one. "I'm taking this out of your paycheck, you know."

"Ha! You're taking his *whole* paycheck."

"I'm his guardian."

Jan plucked out another *bisque* and dangled it in front of Po Thang. "What do you think, Boy? Do you want your Auntie Jan to take care of your finances? I am a CPA, after all. Your so-called guardian here? She'll rob you blind."

"*Wouf.*"

"I'll take that as a *oui*. I'll get your paw print later, as soon as I draw up some papers for you to sign. In the meanwhile, let's just shake and seal the deal with another treat." Po Thang raised his paw.

"Clear cut bribery of a minor! He wants his lawyer."

"And I want dinner. Let's go!"

Chapter Five

AFTER LOTS OF back and forth about taking Po Thang with us, we figured since we were leaving town the next day anyhow, we'd take a chance and bring him along. Hopefully the eatery Jan picked hadn't heard of him yet.

As we made our way through a thick fog of smoke thanks to the usual complement of cigarette puffers gathered right by the front door, I covered my nose with a new cashmere shawl I'd thrown around my shoulders to ward off the chill. France finally got around to outlawing smoking inside their restaurants and bars, but judging by the crowds outside, a law hadn't put a dent in their habit.

The small café was almost empty, due to the fact, I figured, that everyone was outside smoking between courses. One table however, had a single occupant: Jean Luc d'Ormesson. I glared at Jan, who tried to look innocent, while my dog made a tail-wagging beeline for DooRah. I guess two-timers stick together.

Jean Luc stood. "*Quelle surprise!*"

"Yeah, what a surprise, indeed," I snarled.

"Please, join me. I have not ordered as yet." Three waiters materialized with chairs, including one for Po Thang, and place settings were added with speed and skill.

Jean Luc ordered a bottle of champagne just as Jan's phone rang. Checking caller ID, she said it was Rhonda and answered. "Hey, what's up?" She listened for a minute, then said, "I'll be right there."

Putting her phone away, she said, "Sorry, you guys, gotta run. Rhonda's having some kinda crisis, and I *am* her support system, so you two have a good time. I'll take Po Thang with me if you like. Oh, and bring us both a doggie bag, *s'il vous plaît?*"

I was contemplating following my traitorous friend out the door when the champagne arrived, along with a small plate of delicious-looking canapés. Oh, well, what the heck. Might as well finish off the *pâté de foie gras* and chase it with ice cold bubbles, I figured, losing my never-ending battle to unearth a scruple or two I was almost certain lurked deep down inside of me. They are slow to surface in the face of fabulous food and expensive wine.

"Go ahead, you Jezebel. And take the mutt."

"I have no idea what you're talking about, Hetta," Jan said loftily as she turned on her heel and dragged a very reluctant Po Thang with her. He loves *pâté*, as well.

Coquilles Saint-Jacques arrived, wiping out any hint of moral uncertainty, and I dove in. I hadn't realized how hungry I was, and the scallops in a lemon-wine-butter sauce were perfect. I almost forgot I was breaking baguettes with the enemy.

"I remember all your favorite foods, you know. And many other things about you, as well," Jean Luc said in that oh, so sexy French accent of his.

My ears heated as I chased a juicy scallop with a sip of very dry champagne. "What is with it you, Jean Luc? You know I'm in love with Jenks. Why do you insist on setting me up like this?"

"My heart holds hope?"

"You ever heard of stalking?"

He threw his hands up in a very French gesture that encompassed our table and the cafe's charming interior. "I do not think having a meal with an old friend qualifies as stalking. And I do want to be your friend. It is possible, *non?*"

"Well, gosh, sure. I mean, how can I possibly resist being buds with an adulterer who lied to me, used me, and—" I stopped myself short before saying, "and shattered my heart." That was something I certainly did not want to admit to him.

His ironic smile, part of his *almost*-irresistible charm, *almost* made me forget the *almost* part. "Might I remind you I was not as yet married when we met, therefore not an *adultère.*"

I resisted an urge to whop him one with a scallop shell. "Might I remind *you* that you were hopping out of *my* bed every morning and rushing off to plan *your* wedding to someone else? Don't you think you might have mentioned that?"

"*Mais non!* I was in love with you."

This convoluted line of reasoning caused me to snort a laugh, and he joined me, the two of us wiping tears at the blatant absurdity of his statement.

I was still dabbing my eyes with my napkin when I spotted a cart being rolled our way. "I really should walk out on you after that ridiculous piece of Gallic justification you just laid on me, but what the hell, I see steak *au poivre vert* coming this way, which you well know is my all-time favorite."

We watched as the waiter seared the steak *bleu*—still cold in the center—and set it aside on a warm platter. Adding brined green peppercorns from Madagascar, and a *soupçon* of cognac to deglaze the pan, he then added heavy cream. Transferring the steak back into the sauce, he expertly added more cognac and lit it. One practiced twitch of the wrist doused the fire.

The ritual and aroma aroused unwanted fiery recollections of many a *dîner romantique pour deux* two decades ago, but I was way too hungry to let the memory of the two of us seated at a small table in my tiny Left Bank apartment, candles and wine in abundance, ruin *this* meal.

I scarfed down my food in record time, drawing disdainful sniffs from a couple of scrawny French broads nibbling tiny morsels at a nearby table. They were probably wondering what such a handsome and obviously refined one of theirs was doing with a *Néandertal* like me. Let them eat cake.

When I finally came up for air, Jean Luc was watching me and grinning.

"What?" I asked.

"I'd forgotten what it was like to watch a woman enjoy her food like you do. French women are...."

"Anorexic?"

He guffawed loudly, catching the women's attention again. They pursed their lips, obviously annoyed that such a fine Frenchman found me *très amusante*. He caught their ennui and said, much louder than is polite in a French restaurant, "Darling, it's late. I suppose we should get home to the children before the nanny puts them to bed."

I giggled. Jean Luc has a wicked sense of humor that matches my own.

"Yes, let's forego the *crêpes* for now," I suggested in French. "I will make them for you at home. Shall we walk, *mon chéri?* It is so nice out this evening. Send the chauffeur home."

He picked up his phone and pretended to alert our driver that we would be walking home tonight. By now the women were trying to act like they were ignoring us, but their body language fairly screamed of jealousy.

Much to my relief, Jean Luc walked me to the front door at his apartment building, passed on the traditional cheek kisses, and said, "*À la prochaine, ma chérie.*" He turned to leave, then stopped and reached in his pocket. "I brought you a little gift. Actually I bought it twenty years ago, but was afraid to leave it for you when I...left."

"What? You've kept it for twenty years?"

"It was a goodbye gift I was too cowardly to give you, but please, do me the honor of accepting it now."

He reached over, tied a small bag to my wrist and rushed away.

I murmured, *"Au revoir,"* in a voice low enough so he probably didn't hear me. Once inside, I leaned against the wall and thought, *No, Jean Luc, not until next time. It's goodbye forever. I can't be friends with you, at least not without inevitable benefits.*

"So, how'd dinner go?" Jan asked when I walked in and handed her a bag the chef packed. *TO GO* is not normally in a fine *restaurant français's* vocabulary, but they did it for Jean Luc.

"Just the way you planned it. I should be mad at you for setting me up, but I had a fantastic dinner and said a final goodbye."

"Too bad in a way. I know you love Jenks, but Jean Luc and you have a bond. I can feel it."

"Yeah? Well, how bonded would you feel about someone who swept you off your feet, moved in with you for a month, and then disappeared to marry someone else the very next week? In a society wedding that had been planned for a year, I might add?"

"I know, I know. But he's asked your forgiveness and it's obvious he regrets what he did. My guess is he would jump at the chance to re-ignite the flame. He's been divorced for a long time."

"Too late. Being around him makes me...uneasy. I feel disloyal to Jenks."

Po Thang nosed the food bag. "Okay, okay." I moved into the small kitchenette, set the table, and opened the carefully wrapped packages to reveal a cold dinner of all kinds of wondrous goodies, including crab legs, *pâté de foie gras*, and *crème brûlée* . "Geez, if I wasn't so stuffed I'd dive into this."

"Have some wine. Hey, what's that around your arm?"

I worked at untying the tiny box from my wrist, but with one hand it proved difficult. "Oh, I forgot. Jean Luc just gave it to me. Whatever it is, he said he bought it for me as a goodbye gift twenty years ago, but was afraid to tell me it was *adios,* the coward."

Jan loosened the ribbon and slipped the tiny velvet box over my hand, opened it, snaked out a glittering bracelet, and held it up for inspection. "Ooh, a tennis bracelet."

A lump formed in my throat as a memory flooded my eyes. Jean Luc and I were walking along the Champs Elysées one balmy evening just days before Jean Luc disappeared from my life. As we strolled hand in hand, we window-shopped. In one elegantly decorated display, this bracelet sparkled under carefully placed lighting, and I'd commented on its beauty. There was no price on it, which immediately told me I'd never be able to afford it.

"Oh my," I said softly. Mesmerized by the gleam of diamonds glittering in the light of candles Jan lit on the tiny dining table, I sighed deeply. I had once coveted this very piece of jewelry, and was shocked that Jean Luc bought it and held onto it for twenty years. "Jan, this isn't a tennis bracelet. It's a belle époque Cartier. I can't keep it."

"Of course you can't. It's almost Christmas. Give it to me."

We were on the road to Nice before dawn.

Jan and I downed a *pain au chocolat* and coffee before leaving. Rhonda had tea, of course, for chocolate stuffed croissants have at least two-hundred and fifty calories each. Jenks and I'd traveled the French autoroutes recently, so I knew the rest stops along the highway offer mediocre road food, so we stuffed a picnic basket with goodies for the nine or so hour trip. Even with pee-and-stretch stops for human and beast alike, I figured we'd be in our hotel room for dinner. I hoped their room service grub would be decent, but for ten grand I'd live on food scraps.

Okay, *French* food scraps.

Chapter Six

NICE'S HOTEL HOTEL Negresco has been irresistible to the great, rich and notorious for over a hundred years. The likes of HRH Queen Elizabeth stayed there. James Brown and his wife got into a scandalous row. Rumor has it Bill Gates wanted to buy it but was told he didn't have enough money.

One is greeted at the front entrance by men who, although decked out in blue frock coats, red knee britches and top hats boasting red pom-poms, manage to carry off the frilly livery with dignity. The hotel decor is antiques-meet-whimsy, with the art work from the best and wildest like Dali and Chagall, the furnishings pure Madame de la Pompadour.

Unfortunately, we only learned all of this intriguing info from the internet, since we were whisked by our driver through a service entrance, into a freight elevator, and then into our fifth-floor suite as though the paparazzi were hot on our tails.

Once safely inside—but safe from what, one might ask—my phone rang.

"Yes, Jenks, we're in our suite, and no, we were not seen by a soul, as far as I know. Is there something you'd like to share with me? Like, why in the hell are we being treated as though we're in a witness protection program?"

"How's the suite?" he asked, ignoring my question.

I looked around, taking in the opulent decor. "I just hope to hell Po Thang doesn't lift his leg on something silk."

Jenks chuckled. "He won't. He's a good boy."

"Never, ever, trust a dog. That's my motto. So how long are we to be under house arrest in this gilded Bastille?"

"You'll be moved out pretty pronto. For now, we don't want you to be seen around Nice. Don't worry, you'll be happy with your next move."

"*We* don't want us seen? We who? How about this? Since the four of us are being treated so crappily, *we* want twenty grand. Each."

"Hetta, you are in a five-star hotel. Besides, the money is not my call, and you already agreed to the deal. Just relax, rest up, and order what you want from room service, but don't answer the door unless whoever it is knocks 'shave and a haircut'. "

"You have *got* to be kidding me."

"Nope, them's the rules, and I'm just the messenger. Oh, and if you go out on the balcony, cover your hair or wear a hat, and sunglasses. All of you."

"Po Thang left his hat and sunglasses at home."

"Keep him off the balcony."

"Jenks, we're on the fifth freakin' floor. Who can even see us?"

"I know it sounds like overkill, but there's a reason. And by the way, I'm told the fifth floor is *the* floor to be on if you want great security. And we do. All will be revealed soon enough, then you'll be free to roam at will. I promise. It'll be a ball."

I grumbled something like, "I'll have yours if this keeps up," under my breath, but he'd already hung up.

Jan, who had sidled over to eavesdrop, asked, "What did Jenks have to say? All I heard was, 'you'll have a ball.' So, when does said ball start?"

"He said soon. Until then we can't even go out on the balcony unless we're in disguise. Oh, well, let's get settled in and order something expensive from room service."

"Well, ain't that just the pits. I saw on the internet that Richard Burton got drunk in the *Le Bar Negresco* downstairs. I wanna do that."

"Not tonight, Chica. We're stuck."

"I know. There's a guard on the door."

"You're kidding."

"Nope, I peeked."

"What does he look like? Can we take him?"

"Sure. You got a gun?"

"You know the French cops still have mine. Why?"

"Cuz that big dude outside the door does."

"So, one has to wonder if he's our bodyguard or our jailer."

"Ya wanna test him?"

"Nah, too tired. Where's that room service menu. Order from the right side."

Back in the main salon after showers and a change into sweats, we raided the minibar while perusing our food choices. We were evidently in some kind of VIP suite, as we had two bathrooms, an office, three bedrooms, a balcony—the one we were forbidden to use freely—a spectacular ocean view, a kitchenette with a quickly emptying minibar, and all of it in over-the-top luxury.

"What can I have for dinner, Jan?" Rhonda asked.

"I suggest the fresh salmon salad, and you can have a glass of wine."

"Gee, what can *I* have, Jan?" I sneered.

"Anything you want. You're a lost cause."

"Hey, watch it! I consider myself Rubenesque."

"Kinda like these cherubs decorating our abode?" Jan asked, sweeping her arm to encompass gilded-winged chubbettes in abundance. "Although, there is absolutely nothing cherubic about you."

"How about me? What would my description be now?" Rhonda asked.

"Hmmm." I had to admit her transformation was incredible. And even though I was annoyed with that diet of hers, I decided to be as angelic as charged. For now. "Anne Hathaway-ish. Although not as tall or as thin. She's too skinny, anyhow."

Rhonda glowed. "Anne Hathaway? Wow, thanks."

Jan gave me a look of approval. Since I was on a roll, I said, "And you, Jan? Guess Botticelli-ish. Although not as...white and rounded."

We all shared a giggle and Po Thang jumped up in my lap, wanting in on the fun. I grabbed his ears and looked into his eyes. "You, my fine furry friend, are very...dawg-ish. I wonder what you'd look like with a poodle cut? I mean, we *all* need a disguise, according to Jenks."

"Oh! I saw something on the internet you gotta see." Jan left and returned with her laptop, did a search, and showed us the screen, which we all found funny. Except Po Thang. He snorted derision, somehow sensing he might not like what we thought so amusing, especially when the video entitled "How to give your dog a lion cut," soundtrack buzzed with an electric clipper.

After learning a king of the jungle "do" would take at least five hours and some hair dye to transform Po Thang's coat into a lion-look, we ditched that idea and decided to order dinner instead.

As we were trying to make up our minds, someone tapped, "Shave and a haircut, two bits," on the door. Po Thang charged the door, growling like the lion he would be had it not been too much work. "Friend," I told him, and he sat, but still grumbled. "At least they have the secret knock, so they must be."

I opened the door to a guy dressed similar to the doormen in the full livery we'd seen photos of on the internet. I craned my neck, but couldn't spot our keeper anywhere. "Dinner, *mademoiselles*," our visitor announced.

"Now *that's* what I call room service," Jan said. "We haven't even ordered yet, and here it is."

I stepped back for the man to push in a large cart. "I guess the staff here is so good all you have to do is *think* of something, and they deliver."

"*S'il vous plaît*, ladies and gentleman, *á la bouffe*," I said, using the Belgian's favorite slangy phase for *chow down*.

The man, who was probably in his seventies, nimbly pushed the laden cart straight into the dining room, where the table was already set for four. Po Thang, now accustomed to French ways, jumped up into the chair with the doggie setting: a plate and a bowl. No utensils, no wine glass.

"Thank you, sir. We will serve ourselves," I told the man in French. He gave us a formal bow and backed out of the suite.

Our dinner, although not what we probably would have ordered, was heavenly, as was the wine. We were dog-tired. Well, except for the dawg, who was the beneficiary of our fatigue and all-day snacking; not a dab of the savory lamb roast survived.

I was in the kitchenette gathering a couple of overpriced bottles of water to take to bed with me when I heard the secret knock again. Our majordomo, still in his finery, and a female assistant, dressed in a regular maid's uniform, were there to collect dirty dishes, tidy up the suite, turn down our beds and set the breakfast table. However, when he saw me in my jammies, he apologized for disturbing us. He refrained from glancing at his watch, but probably considered going to bed at eight-thirty quite barbaric. As was eating the dinner he'd delivered at seven-thirty.

Waving him inside, I said, "Don't mind us. Go ahead and do what you have to. But we'll attend to our own bed-turning, so if you have chocolates for the pillows, I'll just take those off you."

He smiled, handed me a bag of gold-foiled Lady Godiva chocolates, and hefted a large valise from the floor beside him. "Would you like me to take this to your room, mademoiselle?"

"Uh, that's not mine."

Before he could answer, my phone rang. It was Jenks. "That valise is yours, so have him put it in your room. It's pretty heavy."

Did Jenks have a spy camera planted somewhere? How rude! That's something Jan and I would do!

Jenks, evidently reading my mind, said, "No cameras. I'm just working closely with some in-house staff. Like I said, chill and have fun, trust me on this one. Consider it a mystery trip for a good cause."

"Cause of what? Come on, gimme a hint. Or better yet, let me call you back in a few minutes, from my bed. I promise some dirty talk."

"Dammit, I won't be available, but hold onto that idea for the future. You can do me a big favor though. When you're ready to leave the hotel, please email me photos of all of you. Love you. Bye."

Mystery trip, indeed. Take snapshots before we leave the hotel? What the hell? Actually, I was starting to enjoy all the mysterious drama and, as Jenks asked, told our butler to put the valise on my bed. I followed him, curiosity overriding bone-tiredness in my desire to jump into the feathers. Po Thang, in a lamb-roast coma, was already snoring from dead center in my bed.

He did manage to crack one eye when Jeeves hefted and plopped the mysterious suitcase onto my duvet before leaving.

I was snapping open the catches when Jan sauntered in through an adjoining door. "Heard voices. What's that?"

"Dunno, but let's crack this thing and find out. Jenks knew it was here, but don't know if he sent it. He's being so damned cryptic about this whole thing. It feels like we're on a scavenger hunt of some kind." I popped the top of the leather bag, peered in, lifted the first item, and let go with a belly laugh.

Chapter Seven

SOMEONE WITH A warped or wicked sense of humor was behind the contents of that valise Jan and I opened and cracked up about. Whoever it was, Jan and I loved them already.

Our disguises came with instructions, and just three hours later, we suited up and prepared for a clandestine exodus from the hotel. So much for a good night's sleep.

We piled our luggage in the hallway as instructed, next to that armed guard keeping watch on us. It was collected at precisely two a.m. by the same limo driver who brought us from Paris, and then, one at a time and thirty minutes apart, we were hustled down the freight elevator and whisked into his car. After a ten-minute drive, we were quickly rushed onto a mega-yacht Med-moored in the marina. I went first.

My garb, a full-on belly dancer getup complete with enough veils to cover up my slight potbelly, probably would have been an attention-getter just about anywhere else on God's green earth, but in Nice, exotic dancers being delivered to party yachts in the middle of the night? Not so much. I doubt, however, any of them were forty years old and eternally grateful for scads of concealing scarves.

I thought I closely resembled Fatima, a.k.a. Little Egypt, a famous belly dancer whose likeness—complete with a bullet hole in her navel from a drunken cowboy back in the day—hangs in the Birdcage Theater in Tombstone, Arizona, touted as the "wildest, wickedest night spot between Basin Street and the Barbary Coast." Why it was called The Birdcage, I have no idea, but probably because it housed the "soiled doves" of the day.

Once safely inside my cabin, I ripped off the long black wig and a heavily bejeweled face veil and let a howling Po Thang out of jail. After vigorously rejecting any attempt to dress him in wig and veils back at the hotel, he was relegated to a crate, which was then shoved into a large cardboard box. If our new boss wanted stealth, he picked the wrong dog.

Jan and Rhonda arrived, both looking a danged sight better in their veils than I did. We were, once again, asked to stay out of sight, lest we catch the attention of any curious lookie-loos on shore.

We all went to our cabins, changed into comfies, and reconvened in my cabin, which I surmised was the master, as it was on the main deck and almost larger than my entire boat. As soon as I could, I texted Jenks that requested a photo, taken by a barely straight-faced majordomo, of us vamping it up as, what we dubbed, the Dovies of the Undulating Veils.

We were speculating on where we were headed, when a crewman arrived with a cart laden with all manner of finger food goodies, wine, pastries, dog treats, and coffee.

My drapes were tightly drawn and I was asked to leave them that way until we cleared port. We gathered around a small dining table in a galley equipped with a fridge, microwave, and wine bar, and soon heard the unmistakable sounds of the yacht being prepared for departure.

We'd worked our way through everything but the *Madeleines* and coffee when the engines fired up.

"Okay, Dovies, it is high time we went to work. I don't know where we're going, but we have internet service, and some major snoopery to do."

I killed the interior lights, pulled back the drapes a smidge and sneaked a glimpse of a crew member loosening a dock line. Jan went to her cabin for her laptop, while Rhonda, whose cabin was one deck below, re-secured the drapes and turned all the lights back on. By the time we felt the boat pulling out of the slip, we were already hard at work.

"Okay, so what do we think we know?" I asked.

"We're being shanghaied?" Jan quipped as she opened her laptop.

Rhonda giggled and said, "On a really big boat."

"Yes, it is. When I boarded, my veil obscured my vision, but being the nosy broad I am, I did a fast estimation. The beam is at least twenty-five feet wide, and using that and the time it took to get me and Po Thang into this cabin, I'm guessing at least a hundred feet long."

I unearthed a legal pad, pencils, and measuring tape from my luggage, cleared our dishes from the table, and sat down.

Rhonda, who followed me and brushed remaining the crumbs from the surface, asked, "You travel with this stuff?"

"Tools of the trade. I love flea markets, and am always looking for stuff to someday put in my dream house. I take measurements, snap photos, and do sketches with notes. One of these days I'll show you my scrap book of ideas."

"Not that you can tell by the way she dresses, but Hetta is quite the interior decorator. You should have seen her place in Oakland. Chock full of antiques from all over the world, all now in storage. When she finds something she can't live without, she ships it home for her future mansion."

While Jan was telling Rhonda about the house I'd sold in order to buy my boat, I was already done with an outline of the yacht we were now on, guessing at the layout. When I was escorted to my quarters, we'd passed through a main salon with a galley, dining area, and bar.

Tearing off that sketch, I then did a quick side view, figuring on a flying bridge, a sundeck and probably a toy deck for dinghies, jet skis, and the like.

Rhonda's room being on a lower level, I made that deck cover the entire length of the boat. Knowing how boats are laid out, I figured the crew quarters were probably below my cabin, as well.

I showed my rough sketches to Jan and Rhonda. "Okay, what can you add?"

Jan took a sip of coffee and pointed at my work. "The boat name was obscured—by design I'm pretty sure—under a broad expanse of canvas, but," she picked up a monogrammed throw pillow, "whaddaya bet this is either the boat's initials, or the owner's."

"OXL? Hmmm. I think you're right, but not much to go on there."

Rhonda, not being a boat person hadn't said anything yet, but asked, "Does that Maltese flag they're flying mean anything?"

Jan and I looked up in amazement. Rhonda, evidently mistaking our stunned looks as evidence of disapproval for asking a stupid question, added defensively, "Just askin'."

"Rhonda, you are a gold star genius! How do you know it's a Maltese flag? Is there a falcon on it or something?"

Rhonda's face lit up at my praise. That mother of hers must have been a doozy; I reminded myself to be careful, even in jest, not to put her down like Jan and I do each other. "Actually, that Bogart film was based on a bejeweled hawk made in the sixteen-nineties. The flag of Malta is a bi-color with white in the hoist and red in the fly, with the George Cross in the canton of the white."

Impressed, Jan asked, "Hoist? Fly? Canton? I suppose those are parts of a flag, but how do you know all this?"

"I'm kind of an amateur vexillologist."

"Ha! Hetta's an expert. She vexes almost everyone she meets."

Rhonda snickered. "Vexillology is the study of flags. Since I never got to travel, I compensated by collecting flags of the world and learning their historical significance. The walls of my room back home are covered with them. Pretty pitiful, huh?"

Jan patted Rhonda's arm. "Knowledge is never pitiful. What's a George Cross?"

"King George the Sixth, Queen Elizabeth's father, gave it to Malta in 1942."

"Aren't you just a walkin' encyclopedia?"

Rhonda's face clouded. "It's easy to stuff your brain full of useless knowledge when you don't have a life other than teaching and taking care of an invalid mother."

"I meant it as a compliment, Rhonda. You've gotta get used to accepting them. And trust me, all that brainy stuff will pay off in your new life. Jenks says men don't like dummies."

"And yet...." Jan raised her palm in my direction and smirked. I shot her a digit.

Rhonda smiled. "Book knowledge is useful, but it sure didn't do much for me when I met Rousel. If it hadn't been for you two, there's no telling what would have happened. I'm surprised you still have anything to do with me."

She had a point there, but this was no time to admit it. "Lemme just say this. If I ever play Trivial Pursuit, I want you for a partner. And that Rousel thing? Water under the keel. You'll be just fine now that he's gone and you're finding yourself."

"If this mutual admiration session is over, ladies, how about we figure out who owns this tub," Jan teased. She moved to a chair, pulled her laptop from a side table and her fingers flew over the keys.

"Stop!" I yelled, startling her. "Are you on the ship's internet?"

"Surely you jest. Hell, no, they could hack me. I'm on my own jetpack. While you were making whoopee with Jenks, I had one sent in from the States. It's fast, and secure."

"Dang, all I have is that rented pocket Wi-Fi. Okay, we'll have to use yours."

Rhonda piped up. "I have a jetpack, as well."

"Well, aren't you two just the techie babes. Good."

"Okay," Jan said, "here's the dope. According to this site, Malta is a popular registration destination for owners dodging taxes and remaining anonymous. Let's hope this boat's owner is just a tax dodger."

While Jan did her thing, I went into the head, shut the door and turned off the lights. Pulling up the shade over a porthole, I peeked outside to see we'd pulled away from the quay. The humming port bow thruster turned us slightly and the captain put on a couple of turns as he corrected our position. We glided forward for a few minutes, and I watched harbor entrance lights go by. Then we were out of port and headed out to sea.

After we picked up considerable speed, the boat took a wide turn. I whipped out my phone, brought up a compass and went back to join Jan and Rhonda.

"We're heading south-ish. Jan, can you pull up a map of the area? I'm gonna get our co-ordinates and speed from my phone's GPS. I don't have nautical charts loaded in here, but I can track us on land. How'd you do on finding out the owner's name?"

"Squat."

"What about that crew? The ones we met spoke with a British accent, but I don't think they're Brits," Rhonda said.

"Me neither," Jan added. "To me they look like A-rabs."

Rhonda and I exchanged a glance. Miz Jan can be even less PC than *moi* at times, and Rhonda, being indoctrinated by an education system scared to say *anything* even slightly politically incorrect, seemed nonplussed.

Jan looked up at our uncommon silence. "Oh, fer cryin' out loud. Lighten up you two. I just mean they look kinda like, well, Middle Eastern."

I nodded in agreement. "Ditto. You remember the crew on *Golden Odyssey?*"

"Sure do. And Prince Faoud? You were afraid I was gonna end up in his harem or somethin'. Talk about your stereotyping."

"You were sloshed and I was protecting your honor. Not that you have any, mind you. But that was before we got to know Faoud and found out he's a prince of a prince. And now he and Jenks are roomies in Dubai." I hit my forehead with my palm. "Duh! Whaddya bet this baby belongs to the Prince?"

Rhonda, her head whipping back and forth as she listened to this exchange, held up her hands in a T. "Whoa! Time out. What on earth are you two talking about?"

We told her about being caught in a nasty hurricane in Mexico and making friends with the people on the other boat holed up in Magdalena Bay with us. Turned out the big yacht was owned by a Saudi prince, and we became friends.

"So, we know Princey Poo has a two-hundred-and-ten footer named *Golden Odyssey* and a sportsfisher named *Odyssey's Child*. So let's say the O is *Odyssey*. OXL. *Odyssey Extra Large*? *Odyssey* what?"

"Forty."

Once again we stared at Rhonda and she shrugged. "Roman numerals. Forty. Maybe he got it for his fortieth birthday or something."

Jan was already banging keys. "Bingo! *Odyssey XL*, Maltese registry, 110 feet, Med-based. Available for charter. No owner named. God we are so freakin' brilliant. Is it too early for champagne?"

"It's four in the morning," Rhonda said primly.

"Then we *need* champagne. How do we call room service on this tub?"

"Try that," I said, pointing to a red and gold rococo telephone straight out of a 1940's movie.

Chapter Eight

JENKS CALLED MY cell before we had a chance to use the gaudy house phone to order up that four a.m. champagne. "You all settled in?" he asked.

"Yep, did you get the photo of the Dove sisters I sent you?"

He laughed. "Sure did. Wish I could post it on Facebook."

"You'd better not! So now that we're here on Prince Faoud's boat, you wanna tell us where we're going?"

There was a full thirty-second lull on his end, making me wonder if the call had dropped, but then he said, "It's painfully clear that you and Jan haven't lost your snooping edge. How did you figure it out so fast?"

"Duh, you think you're playing with kids here?"

"Not for an instant. Look, Hetta, I know it's against your nature, but just this once, try not being so...clever. You're not being paid to be Nancy Drew."

"If you'd tell me stuff I wouldn't have to suss it out."

"Yeah, sure, that'll work." Despite his warning, I could hear the amusement in his voice.

"So? You gonna save us a lot of time and just come clean? Like maybe tell me where we're going, and why?"

"Soon enough. Gotta go. Catch some sleep. Love you. Bye."

"No clues, huh?" Jan asked.

"Nah. Jenks is still being annoyingly cryptic. Okay, let's give that gaudy phone a try and order—."

A light tap on the door cut me short, and a purser rolled in a breakfast cart heaped with pastries, cheese, fruit, and champagne. At this rate, we were all going to need more veils.

"I swear they have us bugged," Jan whispered, looking suspiciously around my suite. "I'm gonna have to sweep the cabins...after breakfast and a nap. I'm beat."

"I'm quite sure on a luxury yacht like this one they have domestic help to sweep the floors and that sort of thing," Rhonda said.

Jan and I cracked up. That gal had soooo much to learn.

Despite our earlier snacks, we still put a dent in our breakfast fare and that bottle. Jan and Rhonda dragged themselves to their cabins for some much-needed sleep.

There is nothing more soporific for me than a moving boat, so I was in a near coma when Jan rushed into my bedroom just a little over an hour after I crashed.

"Something's happening," she said. "Wake the hell up. They've cut back the engines."

I crawled from between bajillion Euro sheets, grabbed my phone and cheaters, and pulled up the GPS. What I saw woke me right up. "Cannes! Betcha buck to a peso we're going into Cannes."

"*Magnifique!*" Jan cheered.

A sleepy-eyed Rhonda joined us in time to hear me. "Cannes?"

"Yep. Get ready to shop 'til you drop, kiddo. I left a few stores unturned when Hetta and I were here, and now we can correct that oversight. You think you got some good stuff now? Just you wait."

But Rhonda, instead of being delighted at the prospect of even more new duds, had turned a greenish pale and looked like she was about to barf.

"Are you sea sick?" I asked. I'd seen this shade of green before. On my boat I'd be rushing her outside to upchuck overboard, but we were confined to quarters. I grabbed a waste paper basket and shoved it into her lap.

"Nuh, no. I just got...scared. What if Rousel—"

Jan shook her head. "Returns to the scene *for* the crime, so to speak? Listen to me. The rat is *histoire*. He is incarcerated. Like, forever. Not sure if there is an equivalent to Guantanamo here in France, but if there is I'll bet you anything he's a guest."

"I know. It's just...I don't know who I'm more afraid of. Him, or me. If I could make such a bad decision just a few weeks ago, what's to keep me from repeating myself with some other guy?"

"Hetta and me, that's what."

"Who," the schoolmarm corrected, then managed a weak smile. "Thanks. I'm still furious with myself for being such an idiot."

Jan flapped her wrist. "Naw, just a life lesson you learned a little late. Lowlifes like him are pros, honey. They know how to manipulate women, and nice ones like you are just a little easier. Hetta, who *was* nice once upon a time, is living proof. Look at what happened with Jean Luc. Just thank your lucky stars her subsequent long history with bottom feeders paid off when you needed it. Hey, at least you didn't sleep with him." She gave me a meaningful nod. I shot her a meaningful finger.

"I would have, you know," Rhonda said quietly.

I grabbed the last *pain au chocolat* from a plate and waved it in the air, checking to be sure no one besides Po Thang wanted it. "Last chance. Look, Rhonda, that sex thing was one of the ways he manipulated you. He withheld sex, using "pure" love as an excuse. Sucker's probably impotent. I sincerely hope he's making up for his lost sex life at the whim of a very large and mean fellow inmate about now."

Rhonda tittered. "You have a mean streak, Hetta. I love it."

Jan snatched the pastry from me and took a large bite, then, spitting a few crumbs, said, "Yep, she sure does. I think we should volunteer her for the witness *un*-protection program."

"Speaking of which, what if someone in Cannes recognizes me? Like that friend Rousel was with when he was scouting me out? Or the waiter at the beach café who was surely responsible for letting Rousel know where I'd be going next, since he's the one who recommended the hotel in Gruissan. They make quite a team."

"More like a pack." I gave her a long head-to-toe once-over. "And recognize you? Are you kidding me? Your own mother wouldn't know you if you bumped into her on the street, may she rest in peace. Besides, what are the odds we'll even see either of Rousel's Cannes co-conspirators. I'd be surprised if they weren't keeping Rousel company in prison for being complicit in a conspiracy to commit terrorism. The French take a real dim view on that subject."

The engines slowed more, and I picked up the red phone. When someone answered I asked, "Hey, can we come out yet? Without the veils?"

"Of course. We are scheduled to dock within the hour. Arrival attire is on its way to your suite. Please join me on the bridge when dressed appropriately."

I hung up. "Arrival attire is on the way? What the hell does that—"

There was a brief rap on the door. Jan yelled, "Come on in," and a nattily dressed crew member placed three large boxes on a side table.

After he left, Rhonda took the lid off one with her name on it and laughed. "Look familiar?" she asked, holding up a navy blue jacket, tan khakis, and a crisp white shirt with the boat's logo embroidered on the pocket. The outfit was a duplicate of what the delivery guy wore. Also enclosed was a tan, unstructured bill cap with OXL embroidered in blue.

My box held the same uniform and hat, but Jan pulled out a huge straw chapeaux, a fabulous Hermes silk caftan, and a smaller box, labeled DOG from hers. Dog got a fake-diamond collar, a cravat to match Jan's dress, and a leather leash that fairly screamed hand-tooled designer dawg dud.

Evidently, of the four of us, Rhonda and I were the chopped liver.

In our "appropriate attire," we all joined the captain on the flying bridge just before entering Cannes. He was dressed exactly like the rest of the crew, nary a hint of scrambled egg embroidery on his hat bill to give him status.

I admired the plethora of lights, buttons, and instruments on the mahogany control station which, unlike my boat, was an electronic marvel. I could tell this was not a new boat, but the bridge was state of the art. I watched as he expertly maneuvered the yacht without use of the steering wheel as we glided through the harbor entrance.

Goose-bumps rose on my arms as I recalled watching an old film clip of Grace Kelly telling reporters of the thrill she felt when arriving at Monaco aboard the *Constitution* for her royal wedding to King Rainier III.

Except in our case, Miz Jan was the closest thing to Grace, and I was a deck hand. Have I ever mentioned how crappy I look in any kind of cap?

But never mind, Mediterranean coastal cities can't be beat for a special kind of morning light unlike anywhere else on earth. The only thing close, in my experience, is arriving by boat into Istanbul just as the sun rises behind the minarets and calls to prayer waft out on an offshore breeze.

"Hetta, isn't this just fabulous?" Rhonda trilled, unfazed by being relegated to hired help.

"Yeah, just fab. Gosh, as soon as we get docked, we can grab a mop and swab the decks."

"And Jan can sweep—oof," Rhonda said as I elbowed her.

The captain overheard us and chuckled. "You will not really be required to care for the ship, ladies. It is our custom on the Prince's boat that we all dress alike for security's sake. As you saw when we first met in Mexico." Evidently someone had clued him in that we'd figured out who owned this tub.

I looked closely at him. "Oh, dear, I'm sorry I didn't recognize you. I thought you looked familiar. But you're right, even the prince was dressed as crew."

"So, as you can see, our little subterfuge works. We will execute a complete crew change in Cannes, so we ask everyone to stay in uniform until that happens. It will facilitate keeping any early morning curiosity seekers from distinguishing one of us from the other. Even then, there are locals whose main occupation, it seems, is to spy on yacht inhabitants, but even they don't deem crew as at all newsworthy."

I looked around the decks. There were six of us, counting me and Rhonda, all dressed identically. And then there was Grace.

"So how come Jan is dolled up and stands out like a sore toe?"

"We need someone for everyone to stare at so the rest of us become invisible."

I tried not to be insulted, but it wasn't easy being relegated to wallpaper.

Jan, elegantly draped in the bright pink and orange caftan, blonde hair peeking out from under a fuchsia-colored hat the size of a beach umbrella, and sunglasses like saucers, was doing something akin to a queen wave to the few people out so early on the quay. Po Thang barked and ran from deck to deck, drawing attention to himself, as well. Show offs.

No one, and I mean *no* one, either at the harbor entrance, walking the quay, or working on the boats we passed, gave those of us in uniform a single glance. One obviously American elderly couple I instantly dubbed Gladys and Harry, were loudly arguing over which movie or television star Jan was, and whether they should ask for an autograph given the chance.

Marina workers were standing by to take lines and, once tied up, we all gathered in the dining room for brunch, then the captain bid us goodbye and left Rhonda, me, Jan, and Po Thang alone on the yacht.

"Well, hell, who's gonna do these dishes?" Jan asked, eyeing the cluttered table with dismay. "The captain said we're getting a new crew, but did you notice they left one by one and didn't carry any luggage?"

"He told me they didn't want to draw any attention to themselves, and they're danged good at it."

"Hey, now that we can go ashore if we want to, let's walk that hound of yours. His eyes are crossing."

Po Thang looked at me and whined, but I shook my head. "And leave this boat unattended? We don't even have a key to...anything. Or a dock pass, for that matter. I don't see a quarantine flag, at least, but I'd think we have to clear Customs and Immigration or something."

"Good point. We'll wait."

Po Thang whined again. "Well, hell, can't you hold it?"

He stuck his tongue out at me and re-whined.

"Okay, okay. Lemme change clothes and I'll walk you, but someone," I looked pointedly at Rhonda, "has to stay on board to let us back in, okay?"

"Gladly," Rhonda said. "I'm not ready to go into town yet. I know, I know, Rousel won't be anywhere near, but give me some time to get over my irrational fears. I'll do the dishes or something."

"Hetta, you go and I'll catch up with you at that beach café we like so much. I gotta sweep for bugs before the new crew arrives."

Rhonda's eyes widened. "You really can do that? I thought you were kidding."

"Have you forgotten we bugged your boat on the Canal du Midi when we were stalking that rat you were with?"

"Oh, yeah, you did. Thank goodness. Can I watch?"

"Sure. Okay, Hetta, go ahead and take that dog ashore before he bursts."

"You got it." I pulled a light weight sweater over my uniform and fluffed my hat hair. "Come on, Po. Let us mingle with the rich and infamous."

"See you in an hour. I wanna window-shop for later. I wonder if I get to keep this?" She twirled and at least a thousand bucks worth of silk billowed.

"I'd think so. You gonna wear that for our walk?"

"*Mais oui!* When in Cannes, and all that stuff."

I bowed. "I'll walk three yards behind you with the doggie pooper scooper, your Grace. Don't want to soil your *image.*"

It was still a little early for the *crème de la crème* to be out and about on the beaches of the South of France, what with so many late-night doings available to the rich and randy. After Jan found us, as planned, we had a café au lait and I handed her Po Thang's leash. Only worker bees and a few runners were around to ogle the loverly Jan and her bejeweled and regal furry companion. As promised, I lagged far behind and tried to look like I was out for the exercise, and not attached to them.

After an hour or so of admiring all the stuff we could spend Rhonda's money on, we returned to the marina and called out for her to let us in the gate, but she didn't respond.

"Jeez, she had *one* job to do," I groused.

Jan shrugged. "Maybe she's in the shower. Never mind, I'll get us in." She waved to a guy polishing the gleaming stainless steel rails on a boat that probably never had a speck of dirt on it since it was launched. "Yoo-hoo! Can you let us in? We don't have our card with us."

The man shook his head.

I told him, in French, that we were from the *Odyssey* and needed to get back to our yacht, but forgot our key card. He sighed, put down his rag and plodded to the gate.

"*Merci monsieur*," Jan trilled as he let us through, but he just glowered.

We were about six feet down the dock when I heard him hawk, spit and growl, "*Beurs.*"

I whipped around and yelled, "Hey, asshole, it's a *charter!*"

"How does he know the boat belongs to an Arab?" Jan asked after that rude epithet.

"I got a feeling everyone knows everything about everybody around here. We'd better be more careful."

Rhonda wasn't in her cabin, nor in the galley. The dining area was spic and span, with all dishes put away, so she at least did *that* job.

"Po Thang, go find Rhonda, okay?" Jan ordered.

He sat and tilted his head.

"Who do you think he is? Lassie? Po Thang, tell your Auntie Jan you ain't no search and rescue dawg."

"He's a *retriever*, for crap's sake, so make him retrieve Rhonda."

"Like I can make this dog do *anything?*"

Po Thang suddenly took off like a shot and was out of sight before we could track him. Jeez, I could use another retriever to follow *my* retriever. He started howling and yipping, as though injured, so my motherly instincts—of which I have nearly none—kicked in and I raced to the rescue. As we entered the flying bridge we saw he had some poor schmuck pinned down while he continued to raise all Billy Hell.

"Good dawg," Jan yelled.

"Po Thang! Stop it!" I ordered, which he, of course, ignored. I grabbed his Liberace collar and yanked him back.

The man rolled over and Jan and I both spat different expletives.

Sitting up, Nacho said, "I am deeply hurt. What kind of greeting is this? At least Po Thang covered my body with kisses."

Chapter Nine

NACHO?

Of all the people on earth I could even imagine seeing in France, it was *not* Nacho. In Mexico, we never knew when or where he would show, but Cannes? No way.

He stood and brushed slobber and dog hair from his crew uniform. Po Thang still wiggled and whined, overjoyed to see his old friend, so I let him go to continue his overzealous greeting. He charged Nacho, but the man pointed a finger at him and he instantly sat. This annoyed me even farther. Since when did Po Thang mind anyone?

Jan recovered from her surprise before I did. "Nacho, what the hell are you doing here? And why are you dressed as crew?"

"Because I am crew. I will explain everything soon, but we must wait for the others."

"What others? And where's Rhonda?" I demanded, finally remembering we were looking for her.

"I sent her shopping. Can you believe there is no tequila on this ship?"

"The horror!" I threw my hands up in feigned indignation.

"I see a French vacation has done little to improve your temperament," he said with a roguish grin.

"It certainly has not," Jan agreed. "She's still meaner than snake crap. You should see the way she treats Jean Luc."

"Jean Luc?"

"Her French boyfriend."

"Okay, that's it!" I protested. "I'm going to my room and when you're ready to explain what we've gotten into, call me. And not before." I flounced off, or as close to a flounce as I'm able to execute. When I realized I was flouncing alone, I glared back at my dog, but he was leaning up against Nacho's leg, a dreamy look on his face as he got an ear rub from yet *another* man I'd hoped to never set eyes on again.

Po Thang gave me a, "What's a dawg to do?" look.

Back in my cabin, I called Jenks, but it went to voicemail. Ditto, Prince Faoud. I was pacing and cursing when I heard voices on deck, so I went outside and saw Rhonda returning in the company of what I surmised were two more new crew members. They were all lugging shopping bags. Who knew you could find tequila in Cannes?

I took a hot shower and dressed in a rust-colored chic gauzy thing I'd bought in Cannes a few weeks earlier. Jan said it suited my red hair. I also caught myself putting on more makeup than usual and told my image in the mirror, "This is *not* for Nacho. It's just so I won't look like such a dud next to Rhonda and Jan."

It was nearing cocktail hour so I headed for the bar in the sky lounge, but found it empty. Below me, in the dining area and main salon, my ears detected the lovely clink of ice cubes hitting crystal—always a strong draw for me—and followed the sound. I found Rhonda, Jan, Nacho, Po Thang, and the two new crew members making drinks. One of the men was dressed in the ubiquitous crew outfit, but the other was in chef's whites, complete with the *toque blanche*, the traditional hat. He was putting together a tray of *canapés*.

Both the chef and the other man looked vaguely familiar, but I couldn't quite place them, except for the fact I was almost positive they were Mexican. That would make Jan, Rhonda, and me the only non-Mexicans on board. Well, maybe except for Po Thang, but since I found him on a Mexico roadside, I guess he's technically a Mexican. He has yet to produce an ID to prove otherwise.

Nacho, holding a tumbler of what was surely tequila, gave me a nod and tapped the glass with a small silver fork. Everyone, including the chef, turned toward him and he motioned for us to be seated on one of the leather couches and chairs. I chose an L-shaped settee and Po Thang jumped up next to me. I shoved him off, warning, "You are getting way too big for your britches, you double-dealing dawg."

He gave me a dirty look, slinked over to Nacho, and leaned up against his leg. Nacho gave me a self-satisfied grin. He had changed from his day uniform, and was looking sharp in starched dog-hair-and-slobberless dress whites. His thick black hair, with just a touch of grey here and there, was combed back *à la* Antonio Banderas. Those gleaming white teeth twinkled in contrast to his *café au lait* complexion.

Rhonda, who sat down next to me, sighed and whispered, "Oh, my! Isn't that Nacho just about the best-looking man *ever*?"

"You have absolutely the worst taste in men of anyone I've ever met, you know that?" I growled in response.

Tears welled in her big blue eyes, and I felt rotten immediately; she'd been through a nasty ordeal with a French conman cum terrorist, and I needed to stop messing with her.

Jan stepped in for the save, "Trust me, Rhonda. You can't hold a candle to Hetta when it comes to falling for scuzzbuckets. You're not even a close second."

"Hey, I'm a reformed woman. And sorry, Rhonda, I was only joking." *Well, sort of.* "The thing about Nacho is—"

Evidently my voice had risen above our conspiratorial whispering. "Did I hear my name escape your lovely lips, *mi corazón*?" Nacho purred, wagging his eyebrows at me.

"Yes, I was about to warn Rhonda what an undesirable character you are."

"Me? Undesirable? And here I thought we were close, after all the time we lived together on your yacht in Mexico."

Rhonda looked confused. "You and Nacho? I thought you had a thing with Jenks. Or Jean Luc."

"Who is this Jean Luc?" Nacho asked for the second time of the day.

Jan, by her annoyingly bemused expression, was enjoying herself at my expense. She gave Nacho the same answer she had earlier. "I told you. Jean Luc is Hetta's *French* boyfriend."

"So let me get this straight," Rhonda said. "Jenks is Hetta's *American* boyfriend, Jean Luc is Hetta's *French* boyfriend, and you, Nacho, are Hetta's *Mexican* boyfriend?"

Jan guffawed. "A man in every port. That's our Hetta."

"Okay, that is quite enough!" I huffed and stood to leave. "Jenks is my *only* boyfriend and *that* is *that*."

"And here I thought you only had eyes for me, Loocey," a deep voice boomed from behind me.

I whirled. "Fabio?"

"Yes, it is I, *Capitán* Fabio, *a su servicio*." He gave us a deep bow.

Jan and I rushed to hug him, and he returned our affectionate greeting. We had hired him to captain *Raymond Johnson* from San Francisco to Mexico two years before, and then last summer he later joined us as the research ship's captain for our great Manila galleon treasure hunt. Evidently he had forgiven me for getting him thrown into a Mexican jail during the first voyage from San Francisco aboard *Raymond Johnson*, and then for sinking the *Nao de Chino*, the expedition ship under his command last summer. Not that I ever admitted my guilt, mind you.

Po Thang, who came into our lives after Fabio captained my boat, wasn't real crazy about our lavishing affection on a total stranger, and growled. Fabio, always capable of handling any situation, grabbed a canapé from a silver tray and offered it to my dog, making an instant new friend.

Po Thang is easily bought off.

He learned it from me.

We chit-chatted with Fabio briefly about his wife, Fluff, a blue-eyed blonde knockout who looks much like her nickname, and their son, who was now a teen. Fabio, a licensed boat captain, is also a Navy veteran who graduated from the Mexican Marine Academy. When we'd parted company in Cabo once he got out of jail, his last words to me were, "Should you ever need another *capitán? Por favor*, do not call me."

He later relented when Jan's boyfriend, Chino, needed him to help find a sunken ship in Magdalena Bay. However, when the research vessel went down under suspicious circumstances, he had a strong suspicion it was due to something I did, and he was right. Fabio is evidently a slow learner, for here he was, once again, on a sea-going vessel with me.

Nacho tapped his glass again and was about to make introductions when we heard someone clomping up the boat ramp. There was something extremely familiar about that plodding gait. I looked at Jan, who mouthed, "Martinez?" The door flew open and yep, it was he, in all his picklepussed glory.

Jan and I are big fans of "vintage" TV shows, and one of our favs was "Barney Miller" and especially the character, Detective Fish. Marty Martinez not only resembled Abe Vigoda, the actor who played the curmudgeonly and crotchety senior detective on the show, he even talked like him. The last time I saw *him,* he presented me with a fat bill for his travel expenses to retrieve his pickup, which I sort of stole in Arizona and drove to San Carlos, Mexico.

Given my checkered history with all but two of these men—and that's because they didn't know me yet—one might surmise they had not traveled thousands of miles to bring me early Christmas gifts.

So, just what, and why, were my not-so fan club dudes doing on a yacht in Cannes for crying out loud? And who else was going to show up?

Chapter Ten

"SO, NOW THAT we are all here," Nacho said, answering my unasked question: *And who else will show up?* "I think we owe you lovely ladies an explanation. But first, I would like to introduce Lieutenant Roberto Rogoff, of the Mexican Navy, who is from a well-known family of restaurateurs in La Paz. He is not only a talented chef who studied here in France before joining the military, he speaks French, and is first cousin to the reason we have assembled here in Cannes. While he will act as chef for us, he is part of my investigative team."

I leaned over and whispered in Jan's ear, "I *knew* I'd seen him before. It was in La Paz. This is getting verrry interesting.'

Chef gave us a slight nod and a smile, and Jan whispered in my ear, "He's Mexican? Must'a been a Gringo in the woodshed."

"Shhh. I want to hear Nacho," I hissed quietly.

"And this fine gentleman," Nacho patted the bulked-up shoulder of a dark- complexioned, stern-faced young man towering next to him like a Mayan version of the Incredible Hulk, "is also associated with the Mexican military. We shall call him José Smith, because if I tell you his real name and rank, he will have to kill me. And all the rest of you, as well."

Nervous chuckles filled the room; no one doubted for a minute that the stone-faced, muscled up Joe Smith was fully capable of carrying out Nacho's threat. He gave us a slight dip of his head, acknowledging our presence with dark shark eyes. His thick, jet-black hair was pulled back in a bun; if he was in the military, my guess was he must work undercover, and was maybe the Mexican equivalent of a Navy seal.

Nacho definitely held my attention as the intros continued. "We men all have strong ties to Mexico, even if some of us are...not so Mexican. Lieutenant Martinez is American, but he is of Mexican heritage, despite the fact that he was born and raised in the United States. He still has contacts there due to a long and distinguished career in the Oakland, California, Police Department, from which he is retired. Oakland is where he met Hetta."

Something between a grin and grimace creased Marty's face as he jerked his head in my direction. "She was shooting up the neighborhood."

Despite the need for a fact checker here, I had to laugh. Okay, so I *had* disquieted my neighbors when vaporizing a giant wharf rat in my living room. The big sucker had hitchhiked a ride with my furniture shipment that was delivered that day, after I returned from a project in Japan. Or maybe with the stuff I'd stored in Oakland while I was overseas. Luckily, I had already unpacked my grandmother's .38 caliber Smith and Wesson revolver— she called it her PO-lice special—from a storage crate before the mongo rodent scurried into sight. I was terrified my dog would go after him, so what was a girl to do?

Martinez was the first to arrive after reports of shots fired, and after surveying the bloody mess of furry remains left as a result of me emptying the .38 on the rodent, he lectured me on gun use in the city limits. After I finished laughing—we're talking *OAKLAND* here—the dour dick left me with a warning to keep my nose clean.

Then, sometime later, he ended up at my house again when my home alarm went off in the middle of the night, and I inadvertently forgot to put down my gun before walking outside to thank OPD for answering the call.

Okay, and I *did* blast an inflatable dinghy out from under a guy trying to kill me in San Francisco Bay, but "shooting up the neighborhood" was a stretch.

"She seems to do that a lot," Nacho agreed. "Hopefully France will be safe enough until we can all go home. Can we count on that, Hetta?"

I gave him a non-committal shrug, which meant little since the French authorities were in possession of the only weapon I'd smuggled into France, so me shooting up the country was doubtful.

Nacho's eyes narrowed briefly at what he took as a lame commitment on my part, but evidently decided to let it go. "Also on our team, but working from his office in California, is our Mexican computer guru and cyberspace technician, Rosario Pardo."

"*Our* Rosario? Whooboy, this must be a doozy of a caper," Jan said. Jan and I had busted the little hacker, Rosario, in the Baja when he was trying to run a scam on us, and he had subsequently become a good friend and taught us scads about the fine art of cyber espionage, which comes in handy on occasion. Like today, when Jan used one of his techie devices to sweep the boat for bugs. She found none, but a gal just can't be too careful these days.

Nacho shook his head. "It is not a caper, as you call it, but a mission. A clandestine one, I might add, to seek out and extract a subject. With, if necessary, extreme prejudice. But that part you must leave to us, the professionals." He gave me a stink eye for emphasis.

"Oooh, Tom Clancy talk," I cooed.

"I mean it, Hetta. It is imperative that you do not interfere. Here is the situation. Our chef's young cousin, who recently celebrated her eighteenth birthday here in France, disappeared in Cannes last week. We are going to find and return her safely to Mexico. I will only tell you that she was last seen boarding a large yacht here, in the company of a young man who had invited her to a party. That is all you," he pinpointed me and Jan with those dark eyes of his, "need to know. You women are not to involve yourselves in any way in the investigation. You are merely a front for my team."

"Can you at least tell us her name? And who saw her board the boat?" Jan asked, as though she hadn't heard that 'not getting involved' part.

Nacho looked at her under his eyebrows. "Did I not make myself clear, Jan?" He pronounced it *Yan*. "You are only to be seen, not to act. You are here simply to divert attention from me and my men while we work. Do I make myself any clearer now?"

"As mud," Jan groused. "Okay, can you at least tell us mere *diversions* why this isn't being handled by the French authorities?" She took the words right out of my mouth.

Nacho sighed and looked at our chef, who must have figured it was permissable to answer Jan's question. "Because my family, and especially our grandfather, who is a very influential man in Mexico, does not trust the, as he calls them, *Gabacho*."

"Is that anything like *Gachupine*?" I asked.

Nacho blinked in surprise. "Café, you never cease to amaze me."

I felt that little flutter he stirs up somewhere south of my navel when he purrs his nickname for me.

"And the answer to your question is yes, and no. Both are slurs against white foreigners. *Gabacho* literally refers to the chewed-up leftovers from crushing sugarcane, or white trash. It became a popular derogatory term for the French during the Maximillian invasion of Mexico. *Gachupine* was what the indigenous Indians of Mexico called the invading Spaniards, the Conquistadors. The Aztecs, who had never seen horses, at first thought those astride them were half-man, half-animal, and grew to detest the *gacha*, or four-legged, spear-carrying tyrants."

"You Mexicans are the masters of the racial slur," I quipped. "My favorite is *gringa*, since I am one."

Nacho tipped his head and said, "Might I remind you that you once called me a Spic, *Gringa?*"

"Only after you kidnapped me. And threatened the marina dog. Also, since I thought you were a Mexican drug runner, you didn't deserve any respect. Matter of fact, I still hold some of those thoughts."

"Okay, get these thoughts through that thick, stubborn, Texan skull of yours, Hetta. I. Am. Not. A. *Drogista!*" He had moved into my personal space and was punctuating each word with a poking finger.

I was backing towards the cutlery when Jan stood, pushed herself between us and held out her arms, one palm in my direction and the other at Nacho. "Children, children! Can we get on with this before I have to give you time outs?"

Nacho and I glared at each other for a second, and then we both picked up our drinks and took a slug. "You're right. I was out of line, Nacho. I'm sorry."

Nacho first looked suspicious, then grabbed his heart and feigned shock. "Someone! Please write that down? Hetta said I was right, *and* she apologized! This calls for another drink."

His antics broke the tension and everyone relaxed. We all headed for the bar and refreshed our drinks. I took my Campari Soda back to the settee and settled in, satisfied that I had disarmed Nacho with that fake apology. For the time being, because I needed him, I relegated the subject to a back burner. Or more like in the refrigerator, since revenge is best served cold.

As soon as everyone gathered again, I asked, "Where were we before Jan threatened me and Nacho with dunce caps? Oh, yeah, now I remember. Chef Roberto, you said the man who is paying us is your grandfather? And he's obviously a Mexican who can seriously carry a grudge since it's been over a hundred and fifty years since the French invaded Mexico. By the way, you might not want to tell him that one of my Prussian ancestors worked as a mercenary for Emperor Maximillian I. Of course, he hightailed it across the border into Texas before they hanged the emperor, but with our *jefe's* penchant for keeping score, he just might want his money back."

Martinez cleared his throat loudly and growled, "How about we can the history lessons and squabbling, find the girl, and get us all back home for Christmas?"

Everyone, except for that stone-faced seal-type dude, started talking at once, and Fabio held up his hand for quiet. "I think we can all agree to that," he said. "Except maybe for Hetta on the history thing. For those of you who have not had the privilege of being stuck on a *yate* for long periods with her, her family's *historia* is a constant topic of conversation."

Groans of agreement and head bobbles showed solidarity from my so-called friends. Even my best bud, Jan, looked like a bobblehead and I swear, so did my faithless dog. See what happens when you hang out with those of mongrelized backgrounds? "Hey, at least I know where I come from. Anyhow, this boss of ours, does he have a name?"

"*¡Caramba!*" Nacho said, throwing his hands in the air dramatically. "I *told* Jenks sending you down here was a bad idea! He said he would make sure you stay out of our investigation. Read my lips. You. Do. Not. Need. To. Know. More. *Comprende?* Any leaks about the man's true status in Mexico might...will...make my job much harder."

"Jeez, calm down, *Ignacio*. I get it. We're just window dressing, and you're the big bad dicks."

Even Martinez had to chuckle, but his came out more like someone drowning.

Jan shot me a warning look. "Message received, Nacho. We'd never do anything to endanger that poor girl. Would we, Hetta?"

"Of course not. So, all you want us to do is hang around looking cute and vapid?"

"Not at all. *Your* job, and that of Jan and Rhonda, is to make yourselves quite visible while staying out of *my* way. And out of trouble. *Our* job," he waved his arm at the men in the room, "is to remain *in*visible while executing our mission."

Jan and I shared a glance and Nacho caught it. "I mean it, you two. We had to move so fast on this we didn't have time to get anyone else, and Jenks has assured us you will be more than willing to simply party, shop, eat, drink, and act like tourists."

"You can certainly count on Hetta to eat and drink. Put me down for that shopping part," Jan said, "as long as it's with OPM."

"Yeah, Jan's an expert at spending Other People's Money."

Jan and I squared off, preparing for a spat, but Nacho interrupted. "Please, ladies. Let us stay on topic."

"Well, then, get *to* the topic, *Ignacio*," I growled, using his despised first name again.

Rhonda clapped her hands with glee and cooed, "Oh, this is going to be so much fun!"

Chapter Eleven

"SO, WHAT DO we know? Give me words," Jan said, waving her fingers in a *come here* motion.

Po Thang saw the gesture and tried to crawl into her lap. He got rebuffed for his effort, lest he squash the laptop balanced on a pillow as Jan sat cross-legged on my divan. We were finishing off our pre-dinner drinks and discussing what we remembered from that less than informative earlier briefing.

"I thought Nacho said we weren't to do any sleuthing on our own," Rhonda said, sounding all teacherly.

Jan and I broke into raucous laughter.

"Yeah, when pigs fly," I said.

"Or Hetta tells the truth for one whole day."

"Or hell freezes over."

"Or...."

Jan was trying to come up with yet another cliché when Rhonda giggled and said, "Okay, okay, I get it. So, what are we really gonna do?"

"It's a tried and true word game we play when we go into nosy mode," I explained. "We always start with the basics. It's sort of a brainstorming session we use. We just think of key words and names from what Nacho told us, Jan will string them together and input them into Google. That way we'll try to learn more about what we *don't* know from what we *do* know. I'll start. La Paz, Rogoff, restaurant. The granddad is a prominent Mexican, and his first name is Juan."

Jan looked up. "Oh, yeah, *there's* a clue for you. A Mexican named Juan."

"Hey, it's all we have."

Jan tapped the keys and named the clues as she input them. "Here we go. Rogoff, La Paz, Baja California Sur, restaurant. I gotta put in the Baja thing or we'll get routed to Bolivia." After a pause, she said, "First hit: El Molokan restaurant, touted as the best eatery in the Baja, owned by the Rogoff family. Well, yippee for that. Rogoff ain't no ordinary name in Mexico. I was afraid we'd be dealing with a Garcia or Lopez."

"I can see where searching for Juan Garcia in Mexico might be a bit vague," I joked. "Onward."

She bent back over the laptop and pounded keys. "According to a newspaper article that popped up, El Molokan has been in the same family for four generations, so let's assume our chef is in that forth gen. That would make his great-grandfather's family the founders. Here's something interesting, Chef Roberto Rogoff is an *only* child and was setting up to follow in the family tradition by studying culinary arts in France, then after a brief stint at El Molokan, he upped and joined the military."

I thought that tidbit interesting. "Hmmm. Family fallout of some kind? One do wonder why. And I also find it interesting that he's an only child. Not exactly the norm for a Mexican family. I do believe we are on a roll."

"You stereotyping, Miz Hetta?"

"Naw, it's just that most of our Mexican friends have big families. Then again, I know some who are going to fertility clinics. Hold on a sec." I extracted a tablet from my briefcase and drew a rectangle at the top of a page. In it I printed, Grandfather: Juan Rogoff. Above it I drew another square: G-grandfather?

"Okay, one box sort of down, more to go." Four boxes below I wrote in Chef Roberto's name. And so it went, piece by piece garnered from the internet until Jan found Roberto's uncle. "Bingo! He's married, with...ha! One daughter, Juanita Anna Maria de Cortés Rogoff, who, according to another newspaper article in the La Paz Daily, celebrated her *quinceañera* three years ago. I think we have our vic."

"What's a quincewhatever?" Rhonda asked.

"*Fiesta de quinceañera.* It's a celebration of a girl's fifteenth birthday. It's really a religious ceremony, but is now more of a big party. Juanita is a real doll." She turned the screen, showing us a photo of a real stunner. I had been expecting to see a dark-haired beauty, but was surprised she was a blue-eyed blonde. Either great-grandpaw's Russian genes were mighty strong, or there was more than one gringo taking a dip in *this* family's gene pool.

Jan noted my look of surprise and scrolled the screen. "Take a gander at the mom."

"Wow," Rhonda said. "She looks like a movie star. Who is she?"

"A movie star. Or was, when she was younger. After she married Chef Roberto's uncle, she retired. She's American."

"So if we're on the right track, no wonder they want this kept quiet. We have a tabloid's dream here. Missing girl from a prominent family, a celebrity mother, and a grandfather either high up in the Mexican government, or some kind of mogul. Most times they are both. So, who the heck is our boss? Where does he belong on this chart? He evidently ain't no hash slinger." I tapped my tablet with my pencil.

"Dunno. I don't think he's the girl's maternal granddad, cuz she's an American. So, get out more laptops, gang, and let us find that bugger. I'll stay with the immediate family. Rhonda, you run the mom's career...you know, the celebrity angle. Probably plenty out there."

"What about me?" I asked.

"Just in case I'm off on the wrong track, you do some looking into the victim's mother's family. Who is *her* father's father? I doubt it, but he could be the grandfather who seems to be running this show."

Before getting out my computer, I pulled up my hand-written chart and added a box for the mom's father, and drew a line to her.

Rhonda, excited to be included in our cyber sleuth-fest, took off to fetch her own laptop.

We were all busily snooping when the red phone rang, announcing dinner in a half hour.

"Make sure your computers are shut down and password protected," I said, "then let's doll up for dinner.

Rhonda questioned the necessity of all the security on our computers.

"Because," I said, "this bunch of men seems untrustworthy."

"Sneakier than us?" she asked.

"In their dreams."

Just for fun, we showed up for dinner dressed in our belly dancer outfits, which prompted a round of hoots and smart remarks from the men we knew. The two new players, Roberto Rogoff and Joe Smith, looked like they didn't know what to think.

Nacho seemed delighted. "When I said we wanted you to be conspicuous, I didn't quite have this sort of thing in mind. Then he added with a fake leer, "Not that *I* mind."

In my best German accent I replied, "Vee vere only followink orders." Clicking my finger cymbals in his face, I created a melodic ringing that stopped abruptly with my middle finger an inch from his nose. He jumped back, making everyone hoot again. Po Thang, not liking those *zills* on my fingers, retreated to stand behind Fabio, his newest best friend.

"Don't mess with Texas," I warned Nacho.

"How you gonna eat with all those flimsy things on your face?" the ever-practical Lieutenant Martinez rumbled.

I released my face veil and gave him a low bow that included a rolling arm flourish that dislodged my center veil. "Good point, Master Marty."

Jan grabbed the end of the loose veil and teased, "I dunno, maybe you should leave this one in place. That belly of yours is a mite on the plump side."

"Whoever heard of a belly dancer without a belly?"

The men wisely made no comment or sounds, but Rhonda unsuccessfully stifled a giggle. I forgave her, for she didn't yet know not to mess with Texas.

With apologies, our gourmet chef served tacos, refried beans, and rice for dinner. "I brought the beans and tortillas with me, but tomorrow I will visit the markets in town and stock up with better fare."

"Are you kidding, Chef?" I asked. "This is a real treat for me. We've been eating French cuisine for far too long. Time for comfort food. Maybe I'll make some mac and cheese tomorrow, if I can find cheddar. Chances of finding Velveeta here are probably nil to none."

Jan quipped, "Try the imported gourmet section at that big supermarket. They seem to have everything under the sun."

"I will," I said, as I purposely planted myself next to Joe Smith, the mystery dude from the Mexican Navy who remained nameless lest he have to kill us. I turned to him and asked, "So, what *can* we call you? Somehow Joe Smith just doesn't seem quite right."

He looked at me with shark eyes and the others fell silent, watching our stare down, waiting to see who blinked first. After a full minute that seemed like an hour, he said, "Whatever you like."

"How about Cholo?"

"Hetta!" Nacho warned. "Do not be rude."

I continued to stare at Joe, who suddenly grinned. "Cholo! Yes, it is good. I was one in my youth."

His youth? He still looked like a baby to me. Albeit a very large, and dangerous baby, no doubt. And with those ear studs and shiny black ponytail, he sure as hell didn't resemble any military dude I'd ever seen in Mexico.

Jan, who was evidently as curious as I was about the guy asked, "You were a gangbanger? I can't quite picture you in low rider jeans and a wife beater shirt."

Nacho interceded. "That is quite enough. The less you know about ... Cholo," he sniggered at the name and rolled his eyes, "the better."

Jan, not one to be shut down easily, said, "Ya know, Cholo, with the right clothes and accoutrement, you'd fit right in with the gigolos around here."

Nacho beamed. "*¡Perfecto!* He will be Hetta's, uh, companion."

"What? Whaddya mean, companion?" I yawped. I hate it when I yawp.

"Like I said before, you are to be seen, preferably in the right places, mingling with people who live here and know things. And you speak French, so you can eavesdrop on conversations of others around you. At that, Hetta, you are an expert."

Did he just call me a busybody? Since I couldn't think of a comeback to what was so true, I shrugged. I actually liked the plan, sort of, because it would put me smack dab in the middle of the investigation they wanted me out of, and I could tell them whatever I wanted to, since I was the *French-speaking* busybody. I guess. "So, Cho, you don't speak French?"

"No. Only Spanish and English."

"Then I guess we'll make the perfect team."

It only occurred to me later that everyone seemed to think I was suited to play the part of an older woman being squired by a paid pretty boy escort.

How depressing is that?

Chapter Twelve

AFTER DINNER, JAN, Rhonda, and I went back to work in my cabin, while Nacho took Po Thang for a walk.

In our sweats, computers on our laps, we continued the search for more information on Grandpa and the girl we assumed was the kidnap victim, hoping we were not off on some wild goose chase and tracking the wrong girl. Everything we'd found to date pointed to Juanita, but without any assistance from Team Nacho, we had to follow all avenues.

"Keep in mind that Grandpa might have gone Mexican, since we can't seem to find a Juan Rogoff. Our boss signed his name as Juan on the email he sent me while we were still in Paris, so we have to roll with it."

Both Jan and Rhonda looked at me like I had a little too much wine with dinner. And after.

"You wanna 'splain that?" Jan drawled.

"What if his mother was a Mexican? It's the custom to use *her* last name, not the father's. And, back in the day, some Latinized their first names. Even Carlos Slim was born Carlos Slim Helú, using his mom's last name, even though both parents were of Lebanese descent and still named him Carlos, probably so he would fit in with other kids. Who knows? So, maybe the old man stuck with the Mexican way, losing that foreign sounding moniker in order to fit in. Do we have a clue as to his first name?"

We all went back to work, Googling our little hearts out until Rhonda landed on a story of interest. She was starting to annoy me with all that reference book knowledge of hers, and was, of course, the one to hit pay dirt first. "Hey, I think I've got the granddad!"

"What? How?" I tried not to sound irritated.

"I started inputting keywords, like you guys taught me to."

Jan gave me a snarky smile. She'd picked up on my annoyance and enjoyed seeing me doing my best not to snip at Rhonda. "That's great, Rhonda! You are such a quick learner."

Rhonda wiggled like a praised puppy, prompting me to blurt, "Oh, for crap's sake, what have you got?"

"Hmmm. *Someone* needs wine," Jan suggested.

"I do not. Okay, Rhonda, want to share with us which word did the job?"

"Molokan."

"Molokan?" Jan and I asked at the same time.

"The restaurant?" I asked.

"Nope. Guess what a Molokan is?"

"I figured the restaurant was named after some Aztec god or something."

"Well, it isn't. A long time ago, around the turn of the century, some Russians, called the Pryguny, immigrated to northern Baja."

We nodded, but I twirled my hand impatiently at Rhonda to get on with it.

"And they were called Molokans."

"And this leads us to grandpa how?"

"Well, Roberto's last name is Rogoff, which is of Russian origin, so I checked out Russians living in the Baja and found this article. From there, I re-entered Molokan and came up with Rancho Molokan, which is a huge agro consortium in central Baja."

"Well, for cryin' out loud, we've driven by there a hundred times, Hetta. I've seen the signs."

I recalled a large billboard near Vizcaino, and just thought it was some indigenous name.

"Anyhow," Rhonda went on, "it says here about a hundred families, who fled Russia to avoid the Czar's military draft, first went to Turkey, then on to the Guadalupe Valley in Baja California."

"I've driven through there, as well," I said. "It's wine country. Really pretty. If you cross the border at Tecate, you take a winding road through mountains and valleys, and you end up near Ensenada. Beautiful drive, with all kinds of wineries."

Rhonda nodded. "Yep, they bought thirteen thousand acres and settled in to grow grapes and other produce. Built a community, complete with church and all. Unfortunately for them, they were pacifists, so when they were threatened by Mexican squatters in the 1940's, they just walked away. I looked up the family names of the settlers and found Rogoff. That's Roberto's last name."

"Rogoff. El Molokan. It's just gotta be," I said. "Good work." This time I meant it.

She continued. "There was a diaspora and most of the original Molokans resettled in Southern California, but evidently some Rogoffs stayed here."

Jan, who was following both the conversation and reading the article Rhonda found said, "I'm almost afraid to ask. What is a diaspora?"

"Mostly it is a capitalized noun referencing the dispersion of Jews, but it is also used to describe a group of originally centralized people who disperse to other places."

"Thank you for that, Teach."

She didn't take my smart remark as an insult, but instead beamed at me, making me feel like a heel.

Jan shot me a look I deserved and asked Rhonda, "So, if this guy is *El Jefe*, he's like some kind of agricultural kingpin?"

"I'd say so. Juan Cortés, tomatoes."

"His last name is Tomatoes?'

"Ha! Nope, that's what he grows. Actually, it looks like he owns half of the produce grown in the Baja, but started with tomatoes. And he's politically connected, but just how is a little fuzzy. Google him yourself."

Jan was already on it, and after just minutes she declared. "You were right, Hetta, our boss's mother, Doña Maria Cortés, and her family claim a direct line of pure Castilians right back to Hernan Cortez himself. The spelling got a little tweaked over time. He was probably rolling in his grave when Maria ups and marries a Russian from the *cristianos espirituales saltadores*, or 'Spiritual Christian Jumpers.' Says here they were called that by the Mexicans because their vociferous manner of shouting prayers and throwing themselves on the floor was similar to what my mother called Holy Rollers."

"What's that?" Rhonda asked.

"Pentecostal Church," I answered. "My dad said there was one near their ranch in the Texas hill country. My granddad raised redbone hounds, and when the churchgoers got wound up during their prayer meetings, the dogs, all twenty of them, would set up deafening howls in response. My grandmother said it was about time *someone* in the family got religion."

"Obviously wasn't you."

I had no snappy reposte to Jan's smartassed remark, so we all took the man's name and ran with it. In no time, we had a pretty good idea who we were working for, and why he chose to keep things quiet; he was under investigation by the Mexican government for suspected ties to the Russian Mafia.

"Jeez, why is it," I asked " 'the Russians did it' all of a sudden? I mean, for years every movie's bad guys were Russians, then we had glasnost, and it was someone else. However, in this case, we know we're dealing with

Russians, and I do wonder if grandpa is more afraid of his alleged friends in the Russian Mafia or the amount of publicity that the granddaughter's disappearance would bring on the family if her kidnapping gets out in the press."

"Oh, come on," Rhonda said, "surely you don't think he's more worried about the media than getting Juanita back."

Jan added, "Or maybe the Russians snatched her to keep him quiet about their relationship?"

I shrugged. "Politics and business make for poor relations all the time. But if Juanita has dual citizenship, why hasn't the family stepped up to the plate and sicced the FBI or someone like that on the case?"

"Cuz grandpappy holds the purse strings? Who knows?" Jan said. "Looks to me like the grandfather doesn't trust *anyone,* and if he does have a Russian connection, he sure as hell doesn't want the American feds snooping around. So, he puts his own team together. Could be he's being blackmailed. Maybe the girl is just being held hostage for ransom, and he's afraid to call in the feds from *any* country."

"Murky, me thinks. We have to know more, and I seriously doubt I'll get a damned thing out of my gigolo." I had to giggle at the 'my gigolo' thing, as did Jan and Rhonda. "Anyhow, what was Juanita doing over here, anyhow? She's awfully young to be traveling alone, if you ask me. Wonder if there's a boyfriend involved? We're flying blind, so tomorrow we gotta bug the boat."

Rhonda was at first stunned, and then gleeful, at the idea of spying on our keepers. "Yippee. One thing we really need to know is just who told the family the girl was last seen boarding a large yacht. If there's a witness, why don't they have more info?"

"Good point. Let's make a list," I said, grabbing my tablet.

Rhonda suddenly sat up straight and said, "I just remembered something. I know Nacho said we aren't supposed to get involved, but—"

"Fat chance of that ever happening. Whatcha got?"

"Well, it might be nothing, but Rousel, before he got thrown into a French jail for terrorism, sorta mentioned he'd been to parties—he hinted at naughty ones—on a big yacht in Cannes."

"So?" I said.

"Well, if he was involved in finding vulnerable women, like me, maybe they'd take them to this kind of party to drug them?"

"I don't wish to insult you, Rhonda, but I think we're talking much younger women here."

Rhonda didn't seem to take my statement as a slight. She grinned. "Oh, he had a use for me, but I don't fit the white slavery profile."

Jan eyes widened. "Wow, that's quite a leap. You think Rousel, or men like him, might be complicit in snatching young girls here in Cannes, and luring them into the trade?"

Rhonda shrugged, "Just sayin'."

"Let's run with it. Key words: girls, yachts, Cannes," I said.

We all went to work on our keyboards and after a little time Jan whooped, "Whoa, Nellie." She grabbed her wine glass and took a sip. "Wait'll you hear this." She started reading from an article she'd found. " 'Cannes is a hotbed of thieves, prostitutes, and Eurotrash, some of whom operate from large yachts in the harbor. Young women are lured, drugged, and put into service by the likes of Middle Eastern billionaires. During the Cannes Film Festival, it is not unusual for men to pay forty-thousand dollars a night to "party" on these yachts.' "

"Ha! So, if *our* job is to be part of the local flavor, are we supposed to be thieves, prostitutes, or Eurotrash?" I said, not entirely in jest.

"More like Texas trailer trash," Jan said. "We'll fit right in."

"I resent that remark. My family was partial to doublewides, but I'm too tired to snatch out a plug of your blonde hair, so let's turn in. Tomorrow we strike. How many bugs do we have, Miz Jan?"

"Only three, plus the canine cam. We'll have to put Agent Thang on the job when an opportunity arises. So, Nacho's cabin for sure, and the chef's, since we're pretty sure his cousin is the victim."

"What if they do everything via emails?" Rhonda asked.

"Normally we'd have our favorite little cyber rat, Rosario, hack into Nacho's laptop. But right now, according to Nacho, Rosario is on *his* team, so that's out.

If we ask Rosario to do something like that he might snitch."

"I'll try to plant a video camera somewhere so we can see Nacho's monitor and keyboard. Maybe we can suss out his password. I have to think about it."

Po Thang had put his head on my lap like he always does when I'm trying to work. "Dawg sitter."

"What?" Rhonda asked.

Jan already picked up on my idea. "We rig the critter cam and ask Nacho to dawg sit. If I can aim the camera just right, maybe we can see his keyboard. Let's try it out here tomorrow morning. Right now I'm headed for a nice, soft bed."

"Okay, we meet here after breakfast. Meanwhile, make notes and we'll compare thoughts and come up with a plan."

"This is the most exciting thing I've ever done," Rhonda gushed.

"Oh, just wait for even more excitement. This whole thing is bound to end badly if Hetta has anything to do with it."

After a breakfast of refried beans, tortillas, and *huevos a la Mexicana*, we headed to my cabin to strategize and burp chili peppers.

We fitted Po Thang with his critter cam and experimented with what we could see when he put his head on my leg, which he did as soon as I sat down.

"Good dawg," Jan said, looking at her screen, "but all I see is Hetta's crotch. I'd much rather look at Nacho's crotch."

I pushed Po Thang away for Jan to adjust his harness and camera. Once again, I sat down, but this time Po Thang just sat and stared at me. Jan handed me a bag of expensive French dog treats, and he quickly plunked his head on my lap again.

After several tries, we had what we wanted. The minute I sat, Po Thang plunked, and we had a view of my fingers moving on the keyboard, and the wide angle lens also picked up the screen.

I turned off the computer, walked away, and we prepared for a last training session. Sitting back down, I turned on the computer, Po Thang rested his head on my leg, and when my password prompt popped up, I put mine in. Jan knows my password, so we had Rhonda watch what the camera showed on Jan's computer, to see if she could figure out what I typed in.

"It was seven characters. But I couldn't see which keys you hit. Do it again and this time I'll watch closer. Too bad the camera is so low."

"Let me try something," said Jan. "Po Thang, come here sweetheart." She changed the camera to just in front of his right ear, and this time we had more luck.

Rhonda watched the video five times before she said, "Pothang." My dog trotted to her, and she giggled. "I wasn't calling you, Sweetie. Your mommy's password is pothang."

"Dang, now we'll have to kill you, and just when you were being so useful," Jan said.

Chapter Thirteen

NACHO CALLED A meeting for eleven, giving everyone time to plan their day. Well, for the *men* to plan; he didn't want *us* planning *anything*. Silly boy.

"I've been busy discussing the situation with everyone on the team, and we are ready to make a move," our fearless leader said.

Everyone on the team? He had obviously overlooked my *team. Oh, wait, he doesn't know we have one.*

Nacho continued, not realizing his gaffe. "Jan, you and Rhonda will cruise the beach cafés and bars, making yourselves available for pickup by locals, and gossiping with anyone willing to do so. Make it obvious you are without men."

"Aye, aye, *mon capitán*," Jan said with a sharp salute.

"I am no longer the captain. Fabio now wears that hat, and he will mingle with crews from other boats at the dock, getting an idea of just who is here, who was here, and when. Chef Robert—he pronounced it Row*bear*, like the French do—will mingle with the kitchen crews from other yachts by asking them about where to find the best produce available, and the like."

"Gee, what will Roberto do all day?" I cracked.

Nacho had the good grace to look sheepish with the affectation of Roberto's name, but said, "And that brings us to you, Hetta. You will spend the afternoon shopping for expensive clothes and jewelry for your boyfriend here," nodding toward our giant mystery man, "and getting noticed. We think the new guy will grab the attention of the local lover boys. We are told they keep an eye on any unwanted competition."

I liked the plan. "So, we spend the afternoon smoking out rats. What are *you* gonna do while we're gone?"

"I will stay on the boat, coordinating information as it comes in. I doubt I will often be able to go ashore."

"*Perfecto!* You can dawg sit."

"I would be delighted."

"And so," I chirped, "will Po Thang. I'll drop him and his treats off when we leave."

Lieutenant Martinez cleared his throat. "How about me?"

"Well dang, Marty," I chirped, "I'm fresh out of retired cop treats."

Nacho gave me the look, and said to Marty, "You will shadow Hetta and Cholo, just in case one of the local lotharios decides to get rough with the non-local rivalry."

"Are you kidding me?" I asked, "Have you really looked at Cholo?"

"I meant, I don't want *Cholo* removing someone's head in public, so if trouble starts, Martinez will intervene."

So, I was saddled with a pit bull and an aging gumshoe for the afternoon?

After receiving our 'orders' from Nacho, us women had an hour or so to put our heads together to decide on *our* way of doing things.

"Alrighty," Jan said, "we'll go along with Nacho's idea for today. Of course, in our own way. But it's obvious we have to move fast to get that girl back, so think outside the box."

"You know," I said, "something Nacho said is really bugging me. That girl has been gone an entire *week*? For something like this don't they say after the first forty-eight hours the likelihood of finding the victim alive is greatly diminished?"

Rhonda evidently agreed, judging by her head bob. "Absolutely. I watch all those true crime television shows. Her grandfather waiting this long is sheer lunacy. Unless, of course, he knows who has her."

"Then why would he send in a team to find her? This doesn't make sense."

"Or," Jan says, "he knows she won't be hurt if he goes along with the program. Maybe he's already been contacted?"

"A lot doesn't add up, but we gotta do what we can."

Jan handed me a tiny listening device. "This one is for darling Nacho. Maybe you can plant it under his desk or somewhere when you drop off Agent Dawg before taking your pretty boy off shopping. I just saw Chef Row-bear leave the boat, so I'm headed to his digs to plant one, since he's a family member. That leaves one left. Where should we use it?"

"Nacho said they had a meeting without us this morning, which of course will just not do. I'd dearly love to bug *him* in case he rudely overlooks our precious selves for the next dudefest."

Jan shook her head indignantly. "The nerve. Let's plant one on the SOB. But how and where?"

"I can think of a couple of places to stick it, but they aren't practical. Or sanitary."

After we stopped laughing, Rhonda said, "I noticed he keeps a pen in his pocket...kinda nerdy for a guy like him."

"Yes, he does. Even when he's fishing. Okay, then, you go see him for some reason and get a photo of that ballpoint. Or better yet, steal the pen itself, and we'll see if we can insert a GPS tracker *and* a bug in it."

Rhonda suddenly froze, looking like the proverbial deer in the headlights. I snapped my fingers in front of her face. "Hello? Anyone there?"

She blinked. "I'm scared."

"Perfect, tell Nacho that. Good excuse to see him, play the damsel in danger card, and how you want to help that poor missing girl but are not used to this kind of thing. You can do it."

"I...I'll try."

"That's all we ask. I want him to trust you, cuz he sure as hell doesn't trust *me*."

"I sure do," Rhonda said as she left my cabin on her first mission.

"What a moron," Jan said after she was gone.

"Jan, that is totally harsh. Rhonda is a very nice person. In her own annoying way."

"Yep, she's nice alright, but if she trusts you she's a stone moron."

Rhonda surprised us by quickly returning with Nacho's pen in hand. "How'd ya do it?" Jan asked. "If you had to screw him, that shore was quick."

Rhonda's eyes grew large and her cheeks turned bright red. "No! I mean, I wouldn't know how. Oh, never mind that. I simply asked to borrow his pen for a couple of minutes and that I'd send it back with you and Po Thang."

Jan and I exchanged astonished looks. "That's it? You just asked to borrow it and he handed it right over?"

"Yes."

"I don't like it," I said. "Too easy. He must smell a rat."

"I agree," Jan said. "We'll have to figure out some other way to bug him."

Rhonda was crestfallen. "So, I screwed up?" Realizing what she'd said, she blushed even redder. "Not literally, of course."

"No, no, you did fine, Rhonda. You made us proud. Matter of fact, when I return the un-messed with pen, it'll throw him off."

"I swear, I don't understand how you two think."

"If you figure it out, please let us know," Jan said with a grin. "Cuz we sure as hell don't."

We were herded separately into Jan's cabin to get fixed up, as she called it, after she informed Nacho that there was no way Cholo would pass for a gigolo with "those nails." And, she added, "Hetta needs work as well."

Three hours later my hair was bordering on fuchsia, as were my nails and lips, so I was prepped for late afternoon "tea" at a waterfront hotel, where those of our ilk who had finally managed to climb from their silk sheets hang out. I was decked out in what someone must have deemed "Cannes *après-midi chic*," as was Cholo, whose clean and buffed nails were indeed resplendent.

Surrounded by Christmas season over-the-top décor that only the French seem to pull off without looking gaudy, I think we would have been properly dazzled were we both not ill at ease with our parts in this ruse to smoke out the bad guys.

Taking a handsome young man, my *kept* young man, out on the town was something I never envisioned happening in my life, and the idea that anyone might think I was old and ugly enough to have a paid boy toy didn't sit all that well.

And, my boy toy's Hispanic alpha male pride was obviously taking a blow. He was surly and barely civil toward me, which was hardly going to win him an award as gigolo of the year at the Cannes film festival.

So, in order to break the tension, I ordered champagne.

Chapter Fourteen

BY THE TIME our afternoon "tea" of caviar and champagne was complete, both Cholo and I were more relaxed. I'd made him smile a few times by making snide comments about people at the other tables, like Jan and I do, and that was a bit of an ice breaker. Cholo especially liked me making fun of our glum bodyguard seated four tables away.

Obviously unaccustomed to high teas, Marty Martinez slammed dainty cucumber sandwiches meant for nibbling down his throat, and chased them with copious tiny cups of tea from delicate china not designed for an ex-homicide cop's hands. To make matters even more amusing for us, at least three high-class hookers approached his table, only to be shooed away with a harsh glower. Making sure all bases were covered, the girls evidently sent in a flagrantly gay young man, just in case. Marty turned a dark purple and growled something that sent the man flitting away in alarm.

When I finally deigned to broach the subject of Cholo's military service, his shark's eyes lost any humor, so I surmised *that* subject was a big taboo. I'm clever that way.

Not one to be put off, however, I changed the question as to *why* he was in the Mexican military. He lifted his shoulders. "It is a family tradition that we attend university, and then the military academy. Much of my training was with the United States Navy."

I was surprised he volunteered that much info, which piqued my interest, of course, since Jenks was retired from the Navy. "On ships?"

"Some of the time," he said.

I poured him more champagne. "I love being on the water. I live on a boat."

"Yes, I know. Nacho says you and your friend Jan are a menace to Mexican waters."

I almost snorted champagne out my nose and this made him smile under incredibly long eyelashes, which transformed him into a sort of café au lait George Clooney. I looked closely at him. "Did Jan dye your eyelashes this afternoon?"

He nodded and snorted himself, and our guffaws drew some smiles and a few glares from other tables. The glares were from men seated alone, including Marty Martinez.

"And she shaped and darkened my eyebrows and waxed my face. I have a new respect for women, now that I know what they must endure."

"Well, you look mahvelous, Dahling. By the way, there are three men in the room who either want to date you or kill you. Two of them are behind you, so pretend you're taking a picture of me but snap a selfie. I'll get the other one."

We pretended to vamp and snap, then compared pics on our phones, all the time flirting and tittering. Finally getting back to what set us off in the first place, I said, "That Nacho has some nerve saying Jan and I are menaces."

"Yes, he certainly does. To paraphrase Churchill, Nacho is a mystery wrapped in an enigma."

He startled me with such a scholarly take, but I tried not to show it. "He is that. Do you know him well?"

"Churchill?"

I barked a laugh. This Cholo was growing on me by leaps and bounds. "No silly. Ignacio, a.k.a, Nacho, a.k.a. The Shadow."

He raised his newly tinted and fluffed eyebrows in surprise, but didn't comment on the fact that I knew a great deal about Nacho myself. I detected a hint of eye shadow that lent him that smoky George look. I had to get Jan to do mine like that.

I didn't share that I'd learned of Nacho's alter ego when I lifted his wallet—okay, so I stole his off-road pickup in the Baja and his wallet was in it—and found a California driver's license with his photo, issued to Lamont Cranston. It is only because I am a fan of all things Orson Wells, who did The Shadow's voice in the 1930 radio shows, that I knew The Shadow's real name was Lamont Cranston. Evidently whoever issued that driver's license sure didn't.

"I have known Ignacio quite long enough," Cholo said, with a tinge of sarcasm.

That statement cemented our new friendship, and from that moment on I knew he was a lot more than some Mexican sailor sent in to help a kidnapped—if she was—rich Mexican girl.

And I planned to find how 'a lot more' than a regular sailor he was.

"Are you ready to earn your keep, so to speak?" I teased.

He looked at me with those dreamy smokin' eyes and said quietly, "Hetta, I do not think you would ever have to hire men to accompany you."

"What a nice thing to say." *And*, I thought, *how astute of you to see why playing the desperate older woman part didn't sit so well with me.* "Let's not tell anyone back in Mexico about this little adventure, if that's alright with you. It'll tarnish both our reputations, not that mine couldn't already use some serious polishing."

Taking my hands in his, he gave me a devilish grin and whispered. "Let's go shopping."

Dragging a man into overpriced boutiques was certainly a new experience: Jenks hated shopping, so the only men I ever shopped with were gay.

"It was actually fun, going to all those men's stores. Jenks would rather eat tofu than darken the doors of one of those overpriced joints. It wasn't easy finding stuff in his size, but I did buy Cholo five cashmere sweaters, same sweater, different colors. And a pile of Armani everything, topped off with a gold Rolex. Of course, as told, we had everything charged and delivered to the yacht. I bought a sweater for Jenks, too, but I'll tell him it came from Walmart."

Jan, who knows Jenks so well, smiled.

"So," I asked, "how did you two make out this afternoon?"

"I've never had so much fun in my whole entire life," Rhonda panted. She was as breathless as a kid who just got off a rollercoaster ride.

I refrained from mentioning that was no surprise to me, given what a boring life she was stuck with until just recently.

"Yep, turns out our Rhonda is quite the flirt, after a glass or two of wine. First place we went was to that beach café where she first saw Rousel, and she came down with a case of nerves, but then our drinks arrived, and after that she was a real trouper."

Rhonda beamed and picked up the story. "We quickly found ourselves surrounded by," she made quotation marks with her fingers, "hashtag, hunks. They looked great, but we'd already seen through their fakery, and their bogus lasciviousness of young men on the prowl for women of a certain age."

"And," Jan said, "guess who was the first faker to arrive on the job, obviously alerted by that waiter we suspect makes a goodly amount of moola above his day job pimping out prospective victims to the wolves?"

"Lemme guess. The one who was with Rousel when he scouted Rhonda last fall, and then hit on us just a few weeks later. What was his name?"

"Étienne. Yep, little SOB's still out there trying to make a dishonest living. He recognized me from when we met him earlier this year, but didn't seem to have any recall of Rhonda. Which made it all the better. Gotta give it to him, the guy is persistent. I thought I'd scared him off last time, but nooo."

"I gather he wasn't part of Rousel's little terrorist group, since he's not keeping the bastard company in Club Fed Français."

"Nah, I think he's just a plain old scuzzball. Anyhow, we waved enough bait in front of him that he invited us to—drumroll please—a party on a mega yacht in the harbor this weekend."

"Which one?" There were several yachts too large to enter the marina anchored offshore.

"He didn't say, but he hinted it was owned by some Saudi Prince."

"Does he know we're *staying* on a boat owned by a Saudi Prince?"

"Nah, I said we were visiting a friend."

"You two did good." I grabbed Po Thang's face and said, "How about you, Agent Double-O Dawg? How was *your* day?"

He whined and thumped his tail with pleasure, but then he smelled *pâté de foie gras* on my breath and gave a low growl.

"You'll get some later," I told him as I unbuckled his critter cam harness and handed it to Jan.

She removed the recording device and plugged it into a port on her laptop, hit a few keys and said, "Here we go."

We crowded around the screen and watched dizzying video coverage as Po Thang whirled to watch me leave Nacho's cabin, but as soon as I shut the door behind me he reversed toward Nacho's legs and the hand that held a treat. I was but a dim memory as he chomped on one of the gourmet biscuits I'd given Nacho. My dog's chewing and head shaking made me close my eyes for a moment as my head spun, but then Nacho sat at his computer and Agent Dawg obediently laid his head on the man's knee and stayed still.

"Good dawg!" I said, giving him an ear rub.

"*Wouf.*"

I caught a movement and yelled, "Jan, stop the video and back up! What's Nacho doing?"

She did her thing and cackled. "He's taking apart his pen. You were right. The SOB doesn't trust us."

"How dare him."

She started the video again and, evidently convinced his pen was untampered with, his fingers moved over the keyboard. We rewound and played the scene one tap at a time, and it was obvious he was a touch-typist. And that he had a Spanish keyboard.

"Crap. Stop and Google a Spanish keyboard. I've used them at internet cafés in Mexico, and they're for sure different from mine, but I can't remember exactly how."

Rhonda did the fingerwork on her laptop and said, "The basic letters are the same. Let's start over."

"Okay. Left index finger, top row."

"R."

"Left pinky, middle row."

"A."

"Right index finger, top row."

"Y? Run it back."

And so it went, until I said, "I've got it: raymondjohnson! That's my boat."

"How sweet," Jan drawled. "He wuvs you."

"He loves being a shit disturber."

"See, you're perfect for each other."

Rhonda giggled at our repartee. "Gosh, Hetta, seems like you have an awful lot of admirers. I want to be you when I grow up."

Jan made a rude noise through her lips. "That's easy to do! Just don't grow up, never acquire a set of morals, and annoy the hell out of everyone you meet."

I threw up my hands. "It's a gift."

Chapter Fifteen

AFTER WE'D HACKED Nacho's password using Agent Dawg's critter cam info, I asked Jan, "What now?"

"Back to work. If we're lucky, Agent Dawg got a screen shot of the email address he's using for this caper. My bet is it's not the one he uses for personal stuff."

"Nope, I have that one. Oooh, let's see if he uses the same password for *it*." I grabbed my laptop, typed in Nacho's regular Yahoo handle, and tried using my boat's name for the password. "Oh. My. God. We're in! The idiot reused his password. *Everyone* knows not to do that! There are scoundrels everywhere."

"Quick, close it down, you scoundrel. If he's logged into his email right now, he might somehow be able to see that someone else is. I'm not sure about that, but let's not take any chances. Dang, wish I could call our little hacker back in California, but like I say, he's in the devil's camp."

"Turn on the bug I put under Nacho's desk. Maybe we can hear something, like if he *is* on his computer right now."

Jan put on her earphones and fired up the snoopery device. "Snoring. Send him an email. Ask him a question or somethin'."

I did.

"Bingo!" Jan cheered. "His computer dinged an incoming message. What'd you ask him?"

"If he'll keep le dawg tomorrow while Cholo and I do the town again."

Jan held up her hand for silence. "The ding didn't wake him up. Pull up his emails, fast, just copy and save into your thumb drive. We'll read 'em later. Thank goodness he doesn't close down his computer at night."

"Speaking of closing down, I'm dead tired, and have a gigolo to entertain tomorrow. What's on your agenda, besides snookering that rapscallion Étienne into revealing the name of that so-called party yacht in the harbor, and also figuring out how we're gonna get into Nacho's cabin when he's not there. That bug's battery is going to need replacing before long."

"We have a day or two. Maybe we'll get a break."

"Amen. I'm hoping like hell we can solve this case, liberate the girl, and get everyone where they want to be for Christmas. I think I'd like to go home to Texas on the way back to the boat. How about you, Jan?"

"Baja for me, I guess. Thank goodness, *not* at the whale camp, cuz Chino tears himself away from his beloved whale tagging for a whole week between

Christmas and New Year's for a big family reunion in Mag Bay. It's always lots of fun."

Rhonda sniffled and big fat tears rolled down her cheeks. "I don't have anywhere to go. Can't stand the idea of going back to Mama's house."

"You can come with me, Rhonda," Jan offered. "With that mob Chino's related to, one more body won't even be noticed."

Rhonda perked up. "Oh, I've always wanted to go to Mexico. Thank you! Thank you!"

"If we don't get busy and lucky, we'll still be stuck here. There's one person on Nacho's team we need to get cozy with, and that, Rhonda, will be your job."

"Fabio?" Rhonda asked hopefully.

"Fuggedabout it. He's happily married and I'd trust him with my life. Hell, I have."

"Who then?"

"Chef Roberto. Not only is he the girl's first cousin, he's here to find her and is an insider."

"Right. He's the closest one to the vic," Rhonda agreed.

"The *vic*?" Jan teased.

Rhonda blushed. "I've watched a lot of cop shows."

"So it seems. Hetta's right. He's the one who knows the most about his cousin. Like, what was a seventeen-year-old, now eighteen-year-old, doing in France by herself?"

"Good question, Jan. And for the answer, Rhonda, you'll need to butter up the cook, so to speak."

"Oh, yes, I'll do it. He won't suspect me like he would you two. You guys are way too...notorious."

I laughed. "All too true. Cholo told me, after a glass or two of champagne, that Nacho told him Jan and I are menaces to Mexican waters. Can you imagine?"

Jan harrumphed and yawned. "Well, *there's* the pot calling the kettle black if I ever heard it. Let's pack it in and hit the rack. We have mayhem to wage come the morn."

Before I fell asleep, I heard a light tap on my door. Po Thang barely moved so I said, "Come on in."

Rhonda, dressed in black lace designed for a night of debauchery, slipped into my cabin.

"Forget it, Chica, I'm straight."

Her cheeks flamed vermilion. "Oh, no. I...uh, this was all I had left in my suitcase. Jan made me throw away my onesies."

"Well, thank goodness for that. No wonder Rousel wasn't interested in unbuttoning your flap."

Rhonda looked so stricken, I put my arm around her. "I was just kidding. It's a *good* thing you didn't have anything like this to wear on the boat with him, because he might have been tempted."

She smiled. "Thanks. But as for me getting chummy with Roberto, I don't think I know how to butter up *anyone*."

"You don't have to play the temptress, just be his friend. Tell him you want to learn to cook, that'll get his attention. Now hit the sack and get a good night's sleep, because if my instincts are right, the next few days are going to be a bumpy ride."

I set my alarm for five, because I figured Chef Roberto would be in the galley early, and we had to prepare Rhonda for her first move on him.

We removed Po Thang's critter cam from his collar, put it around Rhonda's neck, and came to the conclusion that the camera on a chain, without the camouflage of a collar, looked like, well, a camera. And when we put the collar on her, she resembled a fledgling dominatrix, hardly the image we wanted to project.

After some discussion, we decided to sacrifice one of Rhonda's new, and very expensive, designer scarves by cutting a piece off one end, then notching a hole in the middle and stitching in a flap with a cut just big enough for the camera lens to peak through. We then fastened a mini-mic in her hair with one of Jan's many jeweled clips, and spritzed our spy with some alluring scent.

"Rhonda, let's test the camera. Put your cell phone on vibrate so, if necessary, we can buzz you, hang up, and call again. Take the call. We won't have to phone unless you paint yourself into a corner and need help with your mission."

"Shall we synchronize our watches?" she asked, with a perfect touch of sarcasm. I recalled a phrase from English Lit: "Growing pride doth fill the swelling breast." Our rookie was swelling rapidly.

"Well said. Nope, we'll skip the watch stuff this time, but I have another idea. Take Agent Dawg with you. He loves galleys; they're full of food. He'll also give you an opportunity to talk to us by saying stuff to him. Whisper in his ear or something."

"And I'll have his company to calm me down."

"Kinda like a service dawg? I'll put it on his resume."

"Just please," Jan said, "make sure he leaves us something for breakfast."

Rhonda left, looking and smelling like a million bucks thanks to Jan's fashion sense. Skinny pants, tight in all the right places, hair and makeup just perfect, a longish turtleneck to cover those areas where Rhonda's new bod still needs a little work, and that scarf to camouflage the camera.

"Ya know, Hetta, that outfit would be good for you, as well. You know, to hide your, uh, fluffy parts."

I shot her my favorite digit.

We watched the incoming video as Rhonda first took Po Thang for a quick walk, making comments to him we could hear as a test, then returned to the yacht and entered the galley area.

"Perfecto. Okay, they're in."

Chef Roberto turned from the countertop where he was carving thin slices from an entire Serrano ham hock, said, "*Bonjour*, Rhonda. And you, as well, *mon petit chien*." He leaned over and gave Po Thang a tiny bit of ham which he ingested with a loud gulp.

Petit Chien sniffed Roberto's hand for more, then lunged for the counter, where he almost succeeded in dragging what looked to be a ten-pound ham leg onto the floor. Roberto grabbed the leg while Rhonda snagged Po Thang's collar and dragged him away.

"Sorry about that, Roberto. I should have left his leash on."

"No harm. We'll just have to keep an eye on him." He cut a slice of twenty-buck-a-pound ham and gave it to my badly behaved dog.

I shook my head at the computer screen and said, "Oh, sure, go ahead and reward bad behavior."

Jan tittered. "It's always worked for us, Chica."

I couldn't argue with that.

Roberto went back to work on the salvaged ham and asked Rhonda, "So, is there something I can do for you this morning? Any special requests for breakfast?"

"Actually, I was hoping to learn something about cooking. I've never really gotten past microwave dinners. Would you mind if I hang around and watch? I can help with grunt work."

"I would be delighted. You shall be my *sous-chef* today."

"Oh goody. What's a *sous-chef?*"

"Literally, it means 'under the chef.' "

"Well, my goodness," Rhonda cooed. "That sounds like fun."

Roberto laughed. "What it really means is you chop stuff up and scrub pots and pans."

"I can do that."

The chef reached into a locker and pulled out an apron. "Here, you'll need this."

"Yes, I suppose I will. Can you help me put it on?"

Jan and I exchanged appreciative looks and gave Rhonda a thumb's up, even though she couldn't see us. "Whoa, she *is* a quick learner," Jan whispered. "I hope she's not going to go overboard. Don't want to scare him off."

Roberto looped the apron neck strap around Rhonda's neck, lifting her hair in the process and hopefully getting a whiff of Ralph Lauren Seduction. I held my breath, hoping the mic wouldn't dislodge, then breathed relief when he disappeared from view, probably to tie the back.

"How's that?" we heard him ask.

"Gosh, if I knew how good putting on an apron could feel, I would have signed up for Culinary Arts."

We heard an ever-so-slight intake of breath, hoped it was Roberto's, and then the camera went blank.

"Crap, one of them adjusted the cowl and our turtleneck fabric collapsed over the lens." I grabbed the phone, buzzed Rhonda once, hung up and then called back like we'd discussed.

She answered immediately. "Hi, Hetta, watcha need?"

Jan rolled her eyes at the ceiling in a you *have* to be kidding me gesture, and mouthed, "Some spy."

"Fix the turtleneck, the lens is covered."

"Yes, he's being a *very* good boy."

Did she mean Po Thang or Roberto?

"We'll see you at breakfast. I'm learning to cook, how exciting is that?" She evidently tugged on the turtleneck and we saw Roberto's back as he stirred something on the stove. My stomach rumbled.

"Good, everything is working now. Rhonda, don't come on too strong. You want *him* to come after *you*."

"Gotcha."

I hung up and Jan sighed. "So much for stealth calls. Hello Hetta? Classic."

"Yeah, but that apron thing? Her instincts are right."

We settled in to watch, but all they did was cook and talk about food.

"At this rate it'll be Christmas before she gets any info. Oh, well, let's go eat."

We shut everything down and secured our laptops before leaving the cabin. You just can't trust anyone these days.

Rhonda, with her apron still on, was putting out coffee and tea when we arrived. I pulled her aside and whispered, "You need to talk about more than food."

"I'm buttering him up, just like you said."

"But—" the butter*ee* carried food to a side table, and I clammed up.

"Good morning, ladies. That dog of yours tried to steal an entire *jamón*, but Rhonda saved it. She's volunteered to be my *sous-chef*, and I am delighted. She is a very fast learner."

My thoughts, exactly.

"I have an excellent teacher," Rhonda said, admiration in her voice. "I'll earn my keep by washing dishes."

"Fine by me," Jan said, "but remember we have to go out later this morning to troll for gigolos and other goldbrickers."

"Can't wait. This trip just keeps getting better and better," Rhonda gushed and gave the chef an adoring smile.

Hmmm. Maybe info wasn't all she wanted to squeeze out of Roberto, so to speak. I got a chance to talk with her for a moment after breakfast and whispered, "Rhonda, somehow find out how it is a seventeen-year-old was allowed to travel to France on her own. I was seventeen once; I know how letting *me* loose like that would have turned out."

"I'm on it."

"Good, just watch yourself. Do not get emotionally involved with Roberto. Not yet anyhow. Once this is over, go for it if you want to."

"He is very sweet, but I don't think he's interested in me."

"Well, you know what Mae West said?"

"What?"

"Love conquers all except poverty and toothache."

Chapter Sixteen

JAN AND I returned to our cabins to spiff up for our separate dirt-digging forays into the upper and under crusts of Cannes. I was piling on makeup when Rhonda and Po Thang rushed in.

"Hey there, Agents Dawg and Rhonda."

Po Thang, with a goofy galoot grin only Goldens have, galloped at me, put on the brakes when he suddenly recalled his hard-earned manners, and skidded in for his kiss and hug. He smelled like Spanish prosciutto. "What did you and Aunty Rhonda find out for us today, boy? Besides how to con the chef out of exorbitantly priced ham? Jan and I got bored watching that little domestic scene, but we have everything on video if anything important happened."

"Well, then, you missed it," Rhonda announced proudly.

"What?" I blurted loud enough that Jan, who must have been on her way to my cabin, heard me.

"Yeah, what?"

Rhonda made sure the door was shut and whispered, "Juanita had a travel companion, evidently a cousin who is an old maid. Kinda like me."

"You hardly qualify as that," I said kindly, thinking little white lies aren't always so bad, not like the whoppers I'm capable of, at least. Plus, if Rhonda's an old maid, what did that make *me*?

Jan must have had similar thoughts. "We are not spinsters," she declared. "Spinsters are elderly, and that is not us. Although there are some in Texas who secretly think of us as 'not suitable for marriage' age. "

"Well, Hetta may not be married, but she's certainly a *worldly* unmarried female."

"More like world weary," Jan just had to say.

"Hey, you ever heard the term, 'tired blonde?'" I asked, referring to a clever turn of phrase that'd stuck with me from a novel I'd read, but couldn't recall which one.

Rhonda held out her hands for a time-out. "Hey, do you two want to know what I learned, or just sit around insulting each other?"

Jan, of course, had to have the last word in our little face-off. "What I was about to say is that in Mexico, any unmarried female over thirty is considered yesterday's tortilla. Okay, tell us all."

"And," I added, refusing Jan that last word. "Did you get a name? And where is she now?"

"I have her first name, and that she's holed up in the hotel room she shared with Juanita. She's distraught and worried that the family will hold her accountable. And that she was finally given her one big chance to be something besides the family old maid, and she didn't want to blow it."

I was impressed with what Rhonda had obtained in such a short time. "Roberto told you all this after breakfast?"

"Uh, not exactly."

"How, exactly?"

"Well, he went out to the farmer's market to buy stuff for dinner while I cleaned up the galley, and he left without his phone. So, when it rang a few times and then went to voicemail, I sort of listened in."

"Good girl. He didn't password protect his phone?" Jan asked. "What a ninny."

"Maybe," Rhonda said, somewhat defensively, "he doesn't have anything to hide?"

"Bring his phone up here and we can clean out his bank account," I suggested. "Just kidding." Sort of.

Rhonda blew her bangs off her forehead in a perfect mimic of Jan when she's frustrated. "Do you two want to hear what I have to say, or not?"

"Go. We'll shut up."

"It was a message from a woman, who said she missed her cousin—"

Forgetting I'd just said we wouldn't interrupt, I interrupted. "Wait a minute, you don't speak Spanish. How do you know what she said?"

"Because she was speaking English, that's why."

"English? If she's a Mexican talking to another Mexican, how is it she's speaking English?"

"I have no idea, but she spoke English most of the time. However, I picked up on a somewhat non-Hispanic accent."

Jan did her own time out. "We've jumped to a conclusion here. Who says she's Mexican at all?"

"I need an aspirin," I said, and headed for the bathroom. After downing a couple of gelcaps, I returned as Rhonda was explaining how she figured the woman might even have had a Russian accent. Turns out our gal Friday not only collects flags, she and her other nerdy friends make it a habit to learn more about the country's holidays, and the like. "She throws in a few words of Spanish, but then she used the term *novyy staryg god* at least once. Maybe twice."

"Well, hell, that explains everything," I said, rubbing my temples.

Jan stepped in, saving me from having to strangle Rhonda to get answers. "Rhonda, what does that mean? And in what language?"

"Sort of Happy Old New Year, in Russian."

"I wish those pills would kick in. Back up and tell us the entire message, okay?"

"I'll try to tell you exactly what I got from the message." Rhonda closed her eyes and scrunched up her face, trying to recall what she heard. "She said her name was *Dueña*, she missed her cousin terribly, she was lonely by herself at the hotel, and hoped Roberto would quickly accomplish his mission so they'd all be back in Mexico in time for the family *novyy staryg god*—New Year's celebration—on January fourteenth. Oh, and that the family would someday forgive her for the disappearance of her young cousin."

"When did the New Year get moved to January fourteenth?"

"Long ago. January fourteen is the old traditional Russian new year, ironically *called* Old New Year. It's a family thing, and at least one of the great-grandparents *was* a Russian immigrant, so the tradition must have been passed down through the generations."

Jan took it all in, then said, "Her *name* isn't Dueña. *Dueña* is a Spanish word for a kind of chaperone. Actually it really means an owner, but in Baja, it's used to describe someone, usually an elderly female, who is given the job of accompanying young women to parties and even on walks. We really, really need to talk to this broad. If Juanita disappeared on her watch, she's *the* key witness, and most likely knows details that these male chauvinist shipmates of ours are not willing to share with us. You didn't, by any chance, get her phone number, did you?"

"Sorry. I was worried Roberto would return and find me fiddling with his phone, plus I wanted to tell you guys about that call. Do you want me to go back to the galley and take a look at the incoming phone number?"

"Yes!" Jan and I said at the same time.

"Check my sound wire. I don't think I'll need Agent Critter or his cam this round. Besides, he keeps trying to filch everything off the counters, even spoons and spatulas. I can do without that distraction. If Roberto is back from the market by now, I'll figure something out."

"I think it's time we bugged the galley. I'll rig it up and you can stick it somewhere. Because the place is so busy, our battery won't last any time at all, so I won't activate it until after you leave, since you're wired."

After Rhonda's wire was properly tested and she had instructions on planting the bug, we sent her on her way with an encouraging shoulder pat.

I grabbed a bottle of water as Jan sat down at the computer. "So, to summarize, what do we have here? A seventeen-year-old Mexican-American girl from an influential family is allowed to go to France for her eighteenth birthday? Even with a *dueña*, does this strike you as unusual?"

"Yes, but the chaperone is a cousin, after all."

"Still, would your mom, or my parents, have gone along with something like that?"

"No way in hell. And from what we've learned in Mexico, girls in that economic status don't go for ice cream without bodyguards these days."

Jan shrugged. "Maybe this *dueña* is some kind of old maid ninja warrior?"

"Hey, enough with the old maid stuff, okay? Who knows, this gal might be built like a Cossack. However, as a bodyguard, she's not a very good one, since her charge has vanished and is presumed kidnapped. Anyhow, the victim's Russian-Mexican grandfather hires a bunch of Mexican cops and military types to get her back?"

"Or perhaps the young lady disappeared on her own? Gave her *dueña* the slip and took a powder?"

"There's a thought. Maybe Juanita wangled the trip over here to meet up with someone, maybe some guy she met on the internet or something. It happens all the time."

Jan opened her mouth to comment, but we heard a beep. "Shhh. Rhonda just went live." She hit RECORD just as we heard Rhonda say, "*Hola*, Roberto. How'd the shopping go? Get anything great for tonight?"

"Better than great. *Fantastique!* Look!"

We heard a rustling sound and Rhonda ooh-ing and ahh-ing over Roberto's fantastic foraging finds of the day—although shopping for delicacies in French food markets can hardly qualify as scrounging.

"Jeez, what did he find, a puppy or somethin'?" Jan drawled.

"Shh."

"What is this?" Rhonda asked.

"*Agneau de pré-salé*. Tonight we shall dine on the leg of a lamb that was fed on marsh grass and is, therefore, pre-salted."

Rhonda gulped, no doubt trying to wipe the picture of a furry baby lamb with chubby little legs happily munching on grass, and then said leg ending up in butcher paper. "Uh, great, I guess. I'm kinda sticking to veggies these days."

"It will be your loss."

"Well, maybe I'll take a small bite, just for you."

Jan and I did a synchronized *gag me*.

"In that case, *mi dulce*, I will be very careful in the preparation so it will be *perfecto*."

"I'm sure it will," Rhonda simpered. I wondered if she even knew he'd just called her *my sweetie*. Okay, so we couldn't see her, but it sure *sounded* like a simper. This was getting downright sickening, but the gal was doing her job, especially when she threw in this offhanded remark: "Oh, by the way, you had a phone call. Something about your cousin."

There was dead air long enough for me to think the wire went wonky, but then Roberto asked, "Which cousin? I have so many."

"I don't know. You left your cell phone here and when it rang I hesitated to answer, but I thought maybe it was you calling from somewhere, trying to locate your phone. Which I have to do all the time. Anyhow, by the time I picked up, there was a message, so I listened, still thinking it was you. It was a woman who said something about missing her cousin. For some reason, I got the impression whoever it was is here in Cannes. You'd better listen for yourself."

"Yes. I will."

"I'll get your phone for you," Rhonda said.

"Uh, no, that's…"

But we heard Rhonda on the move. "Here it is."

"Thank you," he said. He didn't listen to the message immediately, but Rhonda waited him out. We heard her walking away. Finally, he must have figured she'd already listened in once, and was far enough away so as not to overhear, and we heard a beep when he hit the playback key.

The speaker was on, probably thanks to Rhonda, and we got to hear and record most of the message before Roberto recovered and squelched the sound, or just stopped the playback.

Jan and I shared a high five.

"I'll bet his bowels are in an uproar about now," Jan whispered, even though no one could hear us. "You know danged well Nacho has warned him how sneaky we are, and Rhonda, after all, lives with the enemy."

"Everything alright, Roberto?" we heard Rhonda ask. "You look upset."

So, we were right about that bowel thing.

"No. No, not really. Rhonda, please, you cannot tell anyone I told you this, but that message was from Juanita's *dueña*. Her chaperone. She is a cousin to both Juanita and me, and feels terribly guilty and upset for the disappearance of our cousin. She refuses to leave the hotel in hopes Juanita will return. She is alone in their suite and I feel badly for her."

"My lips are sealed."

I smiled. Technically, Rhonda didn't have to break her promise; we heard these bits of information directly from *Roberto's* lips.

"Oh, the poor woman," Rhonda said with great sincerity in her voice. "Well, it's none of my business, of course, but don't you think she might be less lonely and distressed if she was here on the boat with the rest of us? I mean, what with it being almost Christmas and all?"

Jan pumped her fist in the air. "Way to go, Rhonda! We may have to give that gal a raise."

After a pause, Roberto said, "Well, uh, perhaps. She is reluctant to leave the hotel, thinking Juanita might return, but perhaps you are right. However, you must promise not to tell Hetta and Jan that you know about her. At least until I can speak with Nacho."

"Cross my heart and hope to die. I won't speak a word of what you just told me to anyone."

"Dang, she's getting good at this. Sounds like something you'd do, Hetta. She's telling the truth while lying through her newly bleached teeth."

Roberto started talking before I could protest. "Well, then, I will find a way to discuss her coming to the boat with the team."

Little did he know he was talking to the *real* team.

Chapter Seventeen

WHEN RHONDA RETURNED to my cabin after her mission to record that mysterious message left on Roberto's cell phone, we played back her handiwork. We listened carefully, then Jan gave Rhonda a fist-bump, and I patted her on the back. "Success! Well and very cleverly done, Miz Rhonda!"

Our praise brought tears to her eyes. "I don't think you two have any idea what it means to me to be told I've done a respectable job. My mother never once did that, no matter how hard I tried to please her. If I made A's in school—we still used letter grades back then—she wanted to know why they weren't A-pluses. When I was Salutatorian, why wasn't I Valedictorian? I just couldn't win with her."

Jan handed her a gold-monogrammed tissue from a golden-monogramed box. "She must have been very disappointed in herself to be so jealous of you."

Rhonda's eyes widened at Jan's statement, which I thought very insightful, then she dabbed away her tears, looked at the damp tissue and giggled. "Who the hell monograms Kleenex, for crying out loud? In gold?"

"A guy who is considered a disgrace by his own family," Jan said. "So, he literally gilds the lily!"

"There you go, success is the best revenge," I said. "Look at you now, Rhonda. You look good, feel good, you're on a luxury yacht in the South of France, and in the company of such cool folks as Jan, Po Thang, and myself."

"And all that nerdy stuff you and your friends did for entertainment?" Jan added. "It's stashed under that slick new hairdo and paying off in spades."

"You two rock," Rhonda said, giving us both a hug.

Po Thang whined and she grabbed him. "Sorry. You *three* rock."

"Now, enough of all this schmaltzy stuff, let's return to major snoopery." Jan put the speaker on and played back Rhonda's recorded conversation with Roberto, and the partial message on his phone from the mystery woman.

"'¡Hola¡ Roberto. It's *Dueña*. You haven't called this morning, so I suppose you are very busy. I am anxious to know of your progress. I love and miss my special cousin so badly, and pray Juanita will be returned in time for our *novy*—.'" That's evidently when Roberto managed to kill the speaker.

"Boy," I said, "did we get lucky, or what? Timing. Right place. Right time. And a new player in this mystery we didn't even know existed. Nacho sure as hell wasn't gonna tell us about her, you can bet your sweet arse on that."

Jan nodded. "Got that right. Our Nacho, control freak that he is, sure ain't gonna play nice and make us privy to anything he doesn't want to. We called it mushroom management when I was working for a large accounting firm."

Rhonda snorted. "I know that one. Keep us in the dark and feed us *merde*, right?"

"Right. I do believe, team, the gauntlet has been thrown. Shall we pay the poor woman stuck in that hotel a visit?"

"Great idea, Hetta. Only one problem: we don't know *which* hotel, and if we did, we don't have a name. And I imagine Roberto has shared with us all he's going to. Nacho bringing her into what he considers the enemy camp...namely us...fat freakin' chance."

I flicked my wrist. "Details, details.

We'd had a super productive morning, but now it was time to get back to playing the roles Nacho assigned us. After all, we had to let him think he was in charge, right? He called an after-lunch meeting before we went off to mingle with the *beau monde* and lowlifes in Cannes.

"You all know what to do now," he said, "so maybe today we will uncover some helpful information. Yesterday was fairly non-productive, but it was only day one," Nacho said, trying to sound upbeat, but he looked grim. "I had hoped for some progress, but we are stuck at square one." He sighed deeply. "We had expected our employer would receive a ransom demand by now, but it is not so. He is prepared to pay whatever they ask, but first they must ask."

Jan waved her hand in the air and Nacho gave her a reluctant nod to speak. "Are you sure she was kidnapped? What if she's, like, taken off with a boyfriend or somethin'? It happens, ya know."

Roberto shook his head. "Juanita would never worry our grandfather like this. She would have at least let him know she is safe. She adores him, and knows he has a bad heart."

Nacho shot the chef a look of warning. Roberto had mentioned his cousin by name, and that was the first time anyone on Nacho's team had done so. Or so he thought.

"So *Juanita*," I emphasized her name and gave Nacho a satisfied smile, "didn't have a boyfriend you know of? By the way, I've been meaning to ask, how *Juanita*," I rubbed it in, "ended up in France at such a young age without her parents?" I directed my question at Nacho, but my peripheral vision caught Roberto's eyes widen slightly. He cut a look at Rhonda, who gave a slight, innocent-looking shrug and an almost imperceptive head shake.

Nacho hadn't been in a particularly good mood at the beginning of the meeting, and having the victim's name suddenly revealed to us lowly women didn't help. "And why is this your business?"

"It's not really. Just doesn't make sense a grandfather, especially a Mexican grandfather who dotes on his granddaughter, *Juanita*, would allow her to travel alone at her age."

Nacho huffed, then sighed in resignation. The cat was out of the bag. He looked to Roberto for permission to speak freely. Interesting.

Roberto nodded, probably since he was the one who loosed the *gato* in the first place.

"You are correct," Nacho admitted. "If you must know, Juanita was not alone in France. She was with a trusted companion, a family member, who is devastated with the girl's disappearance, and does not need strangers annoying her in her grief. Do I make myself clear, Hetta?"

"Me? Annoy someone?"

After we finished dressing for our afternoon reconnaissance missions, we gathered in Jan's cabin for final touches and, in my case, makeup correction. "Well, crap," Jan said as she added too much blush to my cheeks, "I had hoped for a clue from Nacho about the girl's *dueña's* whereabouts, but no luck there."

"Actually, he did say something before that might be of use. Remember at our first briefing, he told us the girl was last seen boarding a yacht? By whom, and from where, one might ask, my dear Watson."

"Genius. The *dueña*? Maybe from her hotel window?"

"It's a stretch, but somewhere to start. Dang, we have so little to go on. I'll drag Cholo to waterfront hotels today, but only those with a view of the yacht harbor. My gigolo and I will hit those with promise, try to figure out which suites have the views. Did I just say *my gigolo and I?* How far and fast the mighty can fall."

"The only thing mighty about you, Hetta, is your ass. These afternoon teas certainly aren't doing much to help. Especially after that lunch you just destroyed."

"It's the pressure. Leave me alone."

"Your funeral. Okay, Rhonda and I will try to ferret out which yachts hosted parties last week."

"We also need to zero in on the exact date she disappeared, which we still don't know. I'll brace Cholo, and Rhonda, pay Roberto another quick visit before you and Jan leave. Then you two mine the beach cafés for more info. The way I hear it, this place is a hotbed of yacht parties, so we need to know which yacht and day to narrow our search. And, dontcha just wonder, though, how Juanita would have gotten an invite?"

Rhonda reminded us that Rousel, the would-be gigolo slash terrorist, told her about finding women to party on yachts. And his fellow gigolo, Étienne, was still around and would be their target of the day, since he'd hinted at yacht parties in the works.

Yachts and gigolos; good grief, what happened to baguettes and brie as French favorites?

My gigolo groused at being dragged into the fifth hotel in as many hours. In each one, I steered us into either the bar or tea room, then excused myself for the ladies' room. Lieutenant Martinez, our watchdog/bodyguard, was also looking more dour than usual, but since he couldn't approach us, he grumpily slurped yet another tiny cup of coffee while I made for the front desk.

As I had at each hotel, I approached the concierge and asked about waterfront view rooms available, even though I knew they were probably all booked. He apologized as to lack of availability, but I said it was for next year, so he was quick to give me the info I needed for suites with views of the boat harbor, and the suite numbers for when I booked.

Stuffing brochures and suite plans into my large carryall with the others I'd collected, I went back to join Cholo. He stood as I approached, and even though annoyed, bussed my cheek and pulled out my chair. Just as I sat down, I heard someone say, "Hetta? Hetta Coffey? *Est-ce vous, ma chère?*"

Well, crap.

Nacho was livid.

"You were recognized? How is that possible?"

"My fiery hair and spectacular looks?"

"*Not* amusing. Who is this person?"

"Uh, she's the cousin of a friend of mine who owns a home here in Cannes."

"What friend?"

"Jean Luc."

Rhonda, watching this confrontation like a puppy happily chasing a laser beam, chirped, "Jean Luc d'Ormesson. You, know, Hetta's *French* boyfriend. He's very rich, and handsome and—"

I cut her off. "He is *not* my boyfriend. He's an...old friend. And by the way, running into Nicole just might work to our advantage."

Nacho lost some of his frown. "How is this?"

"Nicole knows everyone in town. She lives here and manages the family properties, as well as dabbling in high-end real estate. She also knows who is in Cannes, and why. She can be an invaluable resource. We're having dinner with her tonight."

"We?" Nacho bellowed.

"Yes, me and Cholo. She also asked Jan, but I said she was busy."

"Hey! I'm not busy," Jan huffed.

"I know that, but I figured I could get more out of her if it was just me doing the digging. Cholo will be my silent partner, but taking mental notes. If I can keep the conversation in English, anyhow."

"I forbid it," Nacho huffed, stabbing an index finger into the air.

"Cholo, break that finger."

Cholo stood and advanced on Nacho. Nacho, taken off guard, stepped back, then realized Cholo was just messing with him. They both laughed, breaking up the standoff.

Martinez, who joined the laughter, albeit almost choking to do so, cleared his pipes and said, "Hetta, you got Cholo trained a hell of a lot better than that mutt of yours."

Cholo cut those obsidian eyes at me, as though awaiting the nod to deal with Martinez's insult, but I waved him off. "Respect your elders, Cholo, you'll live longer."

Jan reached into a cabinet and pulled out a can of air freshener. Spraying the room, she mock-gagged. "Ugh, *way* too much testosterone floating around in here."

Nacho fanned his hand in front of his nose. "It's Hetta. She has more *huevos* than anyone."

I wasn't sure whether to be flattered or pissed. "Just keeping the pecking in order," I countered, practically daring him to dredge up the word, "hen."

Nacho is smarter than that. He poured himself a tequila and asked, "What, exactly, do you hope to learn from this Nicole."

"Not sure yet, I'll have to wing it."

"Let's sit down, have a drink, and put together a list of questions for Hetta to get answered, if possible."

We made that list, even though my agenda clearly trumped his in importance, but hey, I say let a man have his dreams.

While I was getting dressed for dinner at Nicole's, Jan asked, "So, what's your take on Nicole's thoughts about you and Cholo's, er, relationship?"

"She was extremely discreet, as if she ran into me all the time in the company of an obvious boy toy. I couldn't get a read. These people down here are so effete I doubt my doings would even raise an eyebrow."

"True that."

"I have a feeling that Cholo and I are her amusement *du jour*. My guess is she's gathering the local dilettantes and plans to use us as the main attraction. Kinda like Romans throwing Christians to the lions."

"But you're going anyway?"

I shrugged. "Throwing myself into the arena for the cause, as it were. They love nothing more than talking about themselves, and who's who in town, so getting info should be a piece of cake."

"Just how did you introduce Cholo when Nicole ambushed you at your table?"

"As my bodyguard. She could barely resist a burst of hearty laughter at the idea that my body would need guarding, but she somehow managed to contain her mirth in those hollow cheeks of hers."

"She's probably still wondering how it is her cousin, Jean Luc the Hunk, is so enamored with you. Hmmm, I wonder if she's more interested in Cholo than she is in you. He *is* pretty exotic looking compared to most of the metrosexual men around here. After all, if you recall, when we met Nicole at Jean Luc's house, she wasn't exactly spellbound by our self-proclaimed irresistible charms, if you know what I mean."

"I do recall. However, like I told you then, her ilk can consider us useful for amusement purposes during the slow season."

"Or, as you so charmingly put it, they find us *très amusantes,* kinda like stray puppies, until we pee on their Aubusson rugs."

"I will do my best to refrain from doing so. At least for tonight. We need their local knowledge, *then* maybe I'll finagle an invite for the master pee-er, Agent Dawg."

Po Thang quickened at his name, and looked for all the world as though relishing a possible legally sanctioned pee on a carpet, an action which would, on *my* boat, result in his being rendered unto shark bait.

"Whacha gonna wear to this little soirée?"

"I'll pass that decision to you. Too bad I can't squirm into one of your chichi outfits."

"Betcha Rhonda's got something you can wear. Let's raid her closet."

"Fat chance there. She's really slimmed down."

"Not so much as you might think. She's taller than you, and looks slimmer because, well, she has a small waist."

"Thank you for that."

"What I mean is, you wear about the same size...."

"Unless there is a waist involved?"

"You have much better hair."

I'd arranged to meet Cholo in the lounge during cocktail hour, figuring a good stiff drink would be in order before going off to mingle with the local masters of self-superiority.

Cholo took one look at me and smiled, not something he does frequently. Nacho, always the charmer, wolf-whistled.

I had to admit, when Jan wasn't trying to make me look like an over-dressed and painted up South of France harridan, she had a knack for creating some serious glam. Decked out in one of those dresses with peek-a-boo shoulders that are the rage now, I was swankily swathed in a couple of layers of rust-colored gossamer silk that set off my hair, and that gauzy look covered all manner of sins.

"Ready to do battle, Cholo? You sure look it."

He blushed. I think. At any rate, his dark skin turned a little darker around the cheek area. He was wearing one of the outfits I'd bought him on our shopping spree, and had been quickly tailored to his size. I doubt he'd ever worn white silk in his life, but it evidently suited him, for Rhonda was practically drooling.

Martinez entered the sky lounge and gave us a once over. "Not bad. Not bad at all."

For Marty Martinez, that was the infinite compliment.

Nicole's *pied-à-terre* in Cannes—her main abode was in Paris, of course—took up the entire top floor of a four-story building that was probably built nearly a hundred years ago. If she considered this her 'little foot on the ground'—second home—I could only imagine her digs in Paris.

I suspected that most of the Belle Epoque décor was original, and I instantly spotted an Alphonse Mucha poster, *Bières de la Meuse*. I'd had a copy of it myself, but I'd bet my bottom euro this was no reproduction. I had a serious moment of poster envy.

Nicole noticed my fascination with the Mucha and said, "Lovely, *non?*"

Cholo, who was staring at the red-haired, flower festooned woman on the poster, said, "Yes, she is. She looks like you, Hetta."

Nicole smirked. "You think so? Of course, it is a beer sign, so...."

I wanted to whop her, but we were on a mission, and clobbering the hostess in the first few moments doesn't lend itself to schmoozing her later.

Cholo was at first at a loss for words, then his fists clenched in anger. He'd probably never been exposed to the supercilious nastiness that only the French seem to excel at, so I saved her life. "Why, thank you, Cholo dear. I've always admired the Mucha period, and the women he depicted before they all discovered anorexia."

I was feeling pretty self-satisfied with my clever retort until I spotted what was surely an original Matisse oil hanging over an ornate hand-carved marble fireplace. A covetous hatred for this chick was building, and I considered blowing the whole evening by letting Cholo off his leash.

As I was trying not to drool over her artwork, I caught her staring at my diamond bracelet. The one her cousin, Jean Luc, recently gave me in Paris. The one he'd meant to bestow upon me twenty years before as a consolation prize for being dumped like steaming dog doo-doo on French cobblestones.

"*Mon Dieu!*" Nicole breathed, "is that Cartier? I have been looking for one like it for years."

I wanted to say, "You should have raided your cousin's closet," but instead said, "They *are* so hard to come by, *n'est-ce pas?* Thank goodness I already had the earrings and brooch. Having the complete *parure* is so satisfying."

Her eyes narrowed slightly when I used the proper word for a jewelry set, then she gave me a touché nod.

As we were introduced around the room, Cholo feigned indifference to the beautiful people and surroundings, maintaining a slight sneer worthy of a Frenchman, but he said to me, under his breath, "Wow."

"Indeed," I whispered back, as I refrained, just barely, from secreting a Lalique vase into Rhonda's Christian Dior handbag.

No wonder they count the silver when mingling with the hoi polloi like us.

Chapter Eighteen

NICOLE SEPARATED CHOLO and me at the dining table, probably in hopes one of her nosy friends would sniff out what kind of relationship we had. Unfortunately, she seated my perceived boy toy next to a Spanish duke, which made it imperative that Cholo stick to English, lest *El Duque* figure out by his accent that he was a Mexican. It turned out not to be a problem, as everyone at the table was speaking English.

For my part, I was given the dubious seat of honor on Nicole's right. To *my* right was a woman with hair so scarlet it made mine look downright washed out. She was draped with peacock feathers, yards of velvet redder than her teased-up hair, and diamonds galore. To *her* right was her escort, a dapper younger man who fawned over her.

If Nicole had arranged this placement as a dig at me—as though putting the older women together—she failed miserably, for the woman and I hit it right off and spent the entire meal chatting with each other. Actually, she did most of the talking, which would normally annoy me, but her stories were good, and I was fascinated with this French version of Auntie Mame. She was introduced to me as the Baronensse de Montesquieu, but was quick to tell me to call her Monique, and that she married the title, which her dearly departed husband bought using the last of his inheritance. After blowing his money buying into *la noblesse*, he quickly married her for her money before his expensive wardrobe became threadbare.

I want to be her when I grow up.

It was during the dessert course that I hit pay dirt. Monique not only lived in one of the hotels I'd investigated as a possible hidey-hole for *la dueña,* she *owned* the hotel.

"What a life you lead. Gee, I wonder if you could help me find a friend. I know she's here in Cannes, but I forgot which hotel she's staying in. Maybe it's yours? I haven't heard from her in over a week and am getting worried. Of course, the front desk wouldn't give me any information. Your security is tight."

"Well, my dear, our guest list is, shall we say, top drawer. At least in their own minds. We must protect them or we'll lose our reputation. If you give me your friend's name, I will make a discreet inquiry."

"That's part of the problem. My friend told me she's using an alias at the request of her employer, and didn't share her assumed sobriquet with me."

Monique's frown made it clear I was treading on thin ice. This woman didn't know me from Adam, and I was trying to glean information held sacred by her establishment. I gave it one last shot. "She is chaperoning a young woman of some social standing in her own country, and all I know is my friend and the girl have a suite with a view of the harbor. My friend was supposed to meet me at the yacht, but we've been here three days and so far she has failed to do so. It is concerning."

"Well, uh, you must realize…"

"Hetta! How delightful to see you again so soon," a voice that once upon a time literally charmed the pants off me boomed throughout the dining room, putting a halt to all the chit chat.

Nicole jumped to her feet. "Jean Luc. I didn't know you were in town!"

Like hell she didn't. The bitch just couldn't wait to throw me and Cholo into what she hoped was an embarrassing situation.

At the speed of sound, a servant materialized with a chair, which he was in the process of scooting to Nicole's other side when intercepted in mid-scoot by Jean Luc, who shoved it between me and my hostess.

Nicole who looked for a moment as though she'd bitten into a lemon, quickly regained her sangfroid as she turned toward her cousin and asked, "Would you like something to eat, Coco?"

Coco looked pained at the use of his cousin's endearing term for him, and countered. "Just wine, thank you. I dined *en route* when I feared you were actually cooking."

That got a laugh from the guests, and our hostess's face reddened, but she air-kissed him just the same. "You are such a bad boy. Perhaps that is why the women all love you."

"Of course we do," Monique said, leaning across me to pinch Jean Luc's handsome cheek. "He is my favorite nephew."

"*Tante* Monique!" Jean Luc jumped to his feet again and passed behind me, trailing his hand across my bare shoulder as he did so. "Had I known you would be here, I would have arrived early enough for dinner. Nicole wouldn't dare attempt to cook for a woman with such refined taste."

"Refined enough to know a scoundrel when I see one in action."

"You wound me," Jean Luc crooned, then picked up my hand and kissed it. "Hetta, I am so pleased to see you are wearing the bracelet I gave you."

Nicole looked like she was about to blow a gasket.

Monique only raised an eyebrow, when Jean Luc added, "And, Tante, I see you've met the only other woman I ever truly loved."

"Certainly a well-kept secret on your part," Monique quipped, reaching over to pinch his cheek again. "One I shall cherish and guard until I need a favor."

Jean Luc laughed. "Blackmail? From a woman of your refinement? Sorry, my dear, it will not work. Until very recently I hadn't seen Hetta for over twenty years. *Before* I married."

That was a stretch. Five whole days *before he got married.*

Jean Luc returned to his seat on my left, and a cadre of waiters setting an array of crystal glasses and dessert dishes in front of him caused a distraction, which I used to get back on mission. His untimely arrival threatened to derail my success with his aunt. When I swiveled to face her, I was met with an under-the-eyebrow, amused look.

"So, where were we?" I asked, a little lamely.

"I was on the verge of telling you to get lost. Do you have any idea how ridiculous that story of your misplaced friend sounds?"

"Yes."

And the evening went downhill from there.

It seemed my quest to learn the whereabouts of the mystery chaperone was a bust until, upon parting, Monique whispered in my ear, "Please, join me for coffee tomorrow morning. Say ten o'clock? My driver will collect you at your yacht."

I didn't bother asking how she knew *which* yacht.

Back at the boat, Jan was waiting for us in the sky lounge. "So, how did you do? Tell all, I'm dying to know."

Cholo just shook his head and went to the bar. I followed, Jan right on my heels.

As Cholo poured himself a tequila, and a wine for me, he held the bottle toward Jan. She raised her glass for a top-off. "Judging by your need of a tequila, Cholo, might I surmise your evening wasn't all that great?"

"Oh, to the contrary. I think I'm engaged."

"Huh?"

"You hadda be there," I said.

"Would have loved to be a fly on the wall." She went back to the settee and patted it. "Sit and tell all."

Just then Po Thang bounded into the room, Rhonda hot on his heels. "I knew you were home," Rhonda said, slightly out of breath. "Po Thang went nuts, so I let him out of my room and followed him."

I hugged my dog, he sniffed around my mouth and nosed my hand, looking for some of whatever lingered on my breath. "Sorry, Dude Dawg, the French don't do doggy bags."

Miffed, he curled up and promptly fell asleep.

Jan, whose patience had run out, demanded, "Well?"

"I'm beat," I said, cutting my eyes toward the bulkhead I knew separated Fabio's captain's quarters from the sky lounge. "Let's take our drinks to my cabin and I'll fill you in while I get into jammies and wipe all this crap off my face."

As we bid Cholo goodnight, he just nodded and sat down in a big comfy chair, tequila in hand. This gigolo business was starting to grate on him, especially when that Spanish count considered him fair game for a little tryst.

After we all washed our faces, brushed our teeth and slopped on the stuff that's supposed to keep us younger looking despite our lifestyles, we gathered for my debriefing. I summarized the evening while giving Po Thang a beauty brushing of his own, and told them I was having coffee with Jean Luc's aunt in hopes of getting more info on the elusive chaperone.

"How do you know you even have the right hotel?" Jan asked. "The chaperone could be in any of those overpriced palaces."

"I don't, but this old lady has a right smart finger on the pulse of Cannes, and now that she knows I'm friends with her favorite nephew, I think she'll help us out. Meanwhile, however, Agent Rhonda needs to be on kitchen duty tomorrow, very early in the morning. We need a name, or at least the hotel's name, preferably before my coffee meeting."

Rhonda gave me a salute and a smile. "Aye! Aye! Ma'am, I'll do my best."

"And you, Miz Jan, might consider a move on Cholo. I'm still not sure he's on Team Hetta, even though he seems to be leaning in my direction. He was hired by Nacho, but I sense there is no love lost there. We need to find out what he knows, and I can't think of anyone more qualified to pick his pockets, so to speak."

"How deep into those pockets?"

"Use your discretion."

Rhonda's mouth was hanging open. "You don't mean...I mean...oh, never mind." We caught a glimpse of crimson ears under her black hairdo as she whirled and left the room.

Jan and I shared a high five. "Lord, give us strength," I said, taking a big slug of Evian.

"She'll get used to us one of these days. I'll borrow Cholo in the morning and ask him to accompany me while I walk Po Thang. I'll make up some story about why I want him along."

"Of course you will."

It was after midnight when I finally hit the feathers. Okay, it wasn't really a feather bed—which, by the way, would have been extremely unpractical in a saltwater environment—but some very expensive foam. Anyhow, my head just hit the pillow when Nacho called to announce a six a.m. meeting in the War Room, which was his new name for the Sky Lounge. This was my seventh day in a row without a decent night's sleep, and to say I was less than civilized when he called so late and announced such an early meeting would be putting it politely.

Let it suffice to say he felt my wrath.

So, still in our jammies and sweat shirts, Jan and I dragged in at six to find Chef Roberto already had coffee made and croissants at the ready, evidently with the help of Rhonda. She commented she'd been on the job since before dawn, and the dark circles under her eyes were proof.

Even Po Thang, usually chipper at the promise of any kind of food, dragged in behind us, gave the entire entourage a dirty look and curled up to get his self-allotted beauty rest.

Once we all had a hit of caffeine, a grim-faced Nacho announced, "We have received a ransom demand."

Chapter Nineteen

TAKING IN HIS less-than-elated demeanor when Nacho told us there was a ransom demand, I asked, "Isn't that a good thing? I mean, the old man has the money, we deliver it to whoever wants it, and we get the girl. Case closed."

"It would seem so. I suppose, in a way, you are correct," he said with an uncharacteristic cadence. I gave his new eye bags a closer look; I wasn't the only one losing sleep. "El Jefe is willing to pay anything to get his granddaughter back, and now he is pushing us to meet any demands as soon as possible."

"Why is that a problem?" Jan wanted to know.

Finally revived by my second cup of French roast, I now noticed the others on Team Nacho were all as exhausted-looking as I felt, including Chef Roberto, who was as pasty-looking as his daily dough. Nacho had called me at midnight; had their team been up all night? There was an edginess in the room that spoke of more tension than losing a few hours of sleep warranted.

I stood and faced off with Nacho. "What Jan said. Why am I getting the distinct feeling there is more? Obviously, we are not in the loop and dammit we need to be."

To my surprise, Nacho agreed and pulled a couple of pieces of folded paper from his pocket and handed them over. Jan and Rhonda rushed over to peer over my shoulder as I unfolded them. The color prints, obviously produced on a better printer than my little portable, left nothing to the imagination.

The photo was of a large gold hoop earring placed on a white china plate. The fastener was encrusted in what looked like dried blood. My stomach did a looper. "Oh, no."

With great trepidation, I unfolded the other printout, and it took a second for my brain to tell my eyes I was looking at a close-up of a torn and bloody earlobe, surrounded by matted blonde hair and what looked to be a bruised and bloody cheek.

Jan sucked in her breath. "*Merde*."

Rhonda bolted for the bathroom.

All the photos were date stamped two days before.

Roberto, who was even paler than he'd been earlier, said, "My grandfather gave those earrings to Juanita as a special early birthday present. They were very expensive, and if you look closely at this one, you can see her name is inscribed on it."

I pulled glasses from my pocket and moved the photo closer to my face. "Juanita" was written in ornate cursive on the huge hoop.

"Why," Roberto asked, "would someone do such a thing? Surely, they know the ransom will be paid. It is only three million dollars, after all."

"My thoughts, exactly," Nacho said. "I made some calls to experts in this field, not divulging any information about our case, of course, and learned that this type of thing indicates a more sinister motive along with the money. Perhaps revenge? As we know, *El Jefe* has many enemies."

"We do?" This was the first I'd heard that juicy tidbit. We weren't even certain the grandfather we *thought* we had identified as El Jefe were one and the same, but now we at least knew our boss had foes.

Nacho frowned. "I told you from the beginning, you are here for window dressing. You," he looked pointedly at both me and Jan, "are on a need-to-know basis."

"Yeah, well," Jan said, as she subconsciously rubbed an earlobe of her own, "dontcha just think we need to know *more*, since you're dangling us out there as bait for these dirty rat bastards? And without a safety line?"

"You are told what you need to know," Nacho said, somewhat sanctimoniously.

I stood up, yelled, "That's it. We quit!" and marched out of the room, Jan and Po Thang loyally following behind. Rhonda, back from tossing her croissants, stayed put at Roberto's side.

As soon as it was safe to talk, Jan said, "Did you notice their slip-up?"

"How could I not? Three million dollars? That's chickenfeed."

"And, it seems our Rhonda isn't willing to take one for the team. Might I ask what that 'we quit' thing was all about? I just followed your lead. Why, I'll never know."

I shrugged. "I dunno myself, it just sounded good. Let them figure it out. I liberated us to do what we want to do, which is our own thing."

"What about Rhonda?"

"Who cares? Let's wait and see where she stands. Maybe she's showing false loyalty for Team Nacho to get more info. I hope so, at least." I yawned. "I, for one, need a quick nap before I have to get dressed for my coffee date with *Tante* Monique."

"You still want me to go after Cholo?"

"Absolutely. More important now than ever. Work your magic. He's a man, and you know how to manipulate them."

"Let's just say I sure as hell have more luck using my wiles than you do with gunpowder. Shooting at them rarely works, ya know."

"I never shot...oh, never mind. Let's concentrate on getting Juanita back before these bozos get her killed."

My snooze never happened, because just as I was dozing off, I remembered those papers in my pocket and went looking for Jan.

She was, as I expected, on her computer. "I thought you had to rest up before a tough day at a coffee klatch."

"I wanted to give you these photos to enhance. Maybe pick up a clue or two. And, we need to have a look at that ransom note."

"You think you're playing with amateurs here?" She hit PRINT and there it was, fresh off Nacho's computer.

This is Juanita's earring. If we don't get three million in non-sequential twenty-dollar bills within forty-eight hours, then the rest of the ear will arrive. In other words, she will arrive in little bits.

"Sadistic bastards! No wonder Roberto looked like he was about to pass out. This is scary."

"Yes," Jan said, "and familiar."

"What do you mean?"

"Remember that book we read a few years back, about John Paul Getty III's kidnapping? They cut off the kid's ear? Take a look at this."

She clicked on a bookmark and brought up an article about that famous kidnapping and scrolled down. The first ransom note read: **This is Paul's ear. If we don't get some money within 10 days, then the other ear will arrive. In other words, he will arrive in little bits.**

"Almost word for word," I said. "Jeez, that was 1973 and they asked for seventeen million dollars, what's with this paltry three million? Haven't the kidnappers heard of inflation?"

She hooted. "Good point. However, if grandpa is the tomato king we think he is, whoever grabbed his granddaughter made a smart move if you ask me. The old man probably considers three mil chump change, and keeps more than that in his safe. El Jefe will pony up faster than a speeding chihuahua, and we'll be home for Christmas."

"I hope so. Jan, I think you might want to hold off on the Cholo thing and stand by the computer in case something changes. I gotta go have coffee with Jean Luc's Aunt Monique."

"Can't you cancel? I mean, why do we care who the chaperone is now?"

"We don't really. I just like the old broad and besides, you never know when we might be back in Cannes and need a friend. Or a great place to hide."

"Excellent point. I'll be here."

"And," I growled in my best Schwarzenegger, "I'll be back."

I was ready to roll when the limo arrived at ten; evidently la Baronnesse de Montesquieu didn't think me capable of walking four blocks to her hotel. I was delivered, via private elevator, to the penthouse she calls home and, as expected, was blown away at the sumptuous décor and spectacular views. I could see *Odyssey* clearly from her balcony.

Her idea of morning coffee was my idea of a serious brunch. Jan was right, I thought, as I shoved down a dollop of pâté, I had to cut back. One of these days.

I'd worried that Monique had invited Jean Luc to join us, but it was just us two. Well, just us two, and a cadre of servants who kept coffee, water, and champagne flowing while cooking crêpes and omelets at the table. I held it down to two glasses of bubbles, as my energy level was running on empty with my continuing loss of sleep. Any more bubbly and I'd probably do a face plant into one of her lustrous, white on white, tastefully decorated plates.

I leaned over and gave the gleaming china a close up look.

"It's the family crest that came with my husband's bought title. We have the original china set, in color,"

Embarrassed I'd been caught in mid-ogle, I said, "Sorry. I'm being rude."

"Nothing of the sort. He would be so pleased you noticed. He wanted to paint every dish in the hotel with the crest, and in full color. I balked, and we agreed on this more demure white on white, under-the-glaze pattern. Much less ostentatious, don't you think?"

Even though I concurred with her choice, I was in no way going to agree with her that her husband had no taste. I dodged the question by complimenting the design while spooning caviar from it onto a toast triangle.

In French fashion, we chatted about everything except the elephant in the room: my request for information on my so-called friend. As the plates were being cleared, my phone vibrated and I sneaked a peek. It was from Jan. "Monique, would you mind if I read this? It might be important."

"Please do. I'll go powder my nose."

Monique left a trail of exotic *parfum* in her wake, and I read the text. **Rhonda scored. Chaperone's name is Sascha. She's his third cousin.**

When Monique returned, she said, "I've made inquiries, and I think your friend might, indeed, be staying here. The young lady she is with, however, has not been seen in several days, and your acquaintance never leaves the suite. I am, however, still not at liberty to tell you anything more. I wish I could, but you must understand our need for maximum discretion."

"Yes, I certainly do. I appreciate your helpfulness, but the truth is, I have been in touch with her. I just wanted to have coffee with you this morning, and I'm delighted I did. *Merci.*"

Did that sound sincere enough? I sort of meant all of it anyway, except the 'in touch' part.

She looked surprised and gave me a sly smile. "So, you weren't just kowtowing to an old lady in order to pump me for information?"

I laughed. "Guilty as charged, but not only are you not that old, I hope I've made a new friend. I would love to return your hospitality before we leave France. Also, if I ever need to discreetly disappear I now know exactly where to stay while in Cannes."

It was her turn to chuckle. As we talked a little more, an idea formed in my meddling mind, and I invited her to the yacht for cocktails the next evening. She declined, saying she suffered from *mal de mer*, even at the dock, but not one to be stymied by a polite *non*, I said I'd call very soon with another location. Then, as I prepared to leave, and much to my surprise, she instructed her butler to escort me to the Swan Suite.

Oh, boy, was I on a roll, or what?

When I recounted the morning to Jan, she asked, "So, then you met Sascha?"

"Nope. She'd cleared out. Gone."

"As in flew the coop?"

"Yep. Even Monique's stone-faced butler was taken by surprise. Either that, or he suddenly had to hold back a fart."

"Well, crap. I wonder why now? The chaperone sits tight for over a week, then bolts? My guess is it had something to do with that ransom demand."

"Grandpa might have called her and told her to split before someone grabs her as well and doubles the ransom."

"Anything new on Nacho's computer?"

"Nope, nor has he received any phone calls."

"How do you know? We don't have him bugged, only his cabin."

"Agent Thang is keeping him company."

"Aha! And Rhonda? Where is she?"

"Where else? Puppy dogging after Roberto. At least we know she's on our team, but she shore has the hots for the chef."

"I think Rhonda just has the hots, period. I have this sudden and urgent need for a snack."

"After that breakfast? Never mind, you always have a sudden and urgent need for a snack."

I could have protested, but she was unfortunately right. I should stay out of the galley if I ever wanted to lose that extra ten—Jan says twenty—pounds I carry around, but snooping is hunger-making work, so I led the way.

Rhonda and Roberto were not alone, and Rhonda did not look happy about it.

"Hetta! Jan! I want you to meet my cousin, Sascha. She's Juanita's traveling companion, and now that we know we will have our young cousin back soon, she has joined us here on the yacht until we all return to Mexico."

I couldn't help staring. All the *dueñas* I'd seen in Mexico were dumpy little old gray-haired ladies dressed in black. Sascha was definitely none of those things.

Chapter Twenty

DUEÑA SASCHA WAS neither old, nor gray, nor dumpy.

She *was* dressed in black, but the tight skirt and cashmere cardigan set did little to conceal her curves, and her heavy rimmed glasses barely disguised huge doe eyes, which were slightly puffy and red-rimmed. High cheek bones and blonde hair denoted her Russian DNA. She held a linen hankie to her nose and sniffled on occasion.

"I am so happy to finally meet you, Hetta," Sascha said. She had that slight lilt to her voice, which I recognized from our hacked recording of her phone message to her cousin. "Roberto speaks very highly of you. And your friends."

Her handshake was firm, but finishing-school ladylike. Jeez, if she was an old maid, what the hell did that make me?

Not sure what to say, I blurted, "Uh, thanks. Glad to finally meet you, as well." And, never one not to use an occasion to shake things up, I added. "I stopped by your suite this morning, but you had already left."

Both Roberto and Sascha looked startled, but said nothing.

"Any word on the drop?" I asked Roberto. "Is the money here yet?"

"On its way, on my grandfather's plane. By the way, he says you are welcome to join us on the return flight to Mexico."

"Air France already has us covered, but we'll see. When is the plane due here?"

"They land at Nice Cote d'Azure within the hour."

It was a short twenty-kilometer run from Cannes to the international airport. I wondered how they were going to get three million bucks past French Customs, but for a man like El Jefe, with years of experience dealing with the ingrained corruption of Mexican officialdom, it should be a piece of cake.

"Will there be a doctor onboard to see Juanita?" Rhonda asked.

Sascha's eyes widened and her lips trembled. "Doctor? Why would Juanita need a doctor?"

Rhonda was appalled by her blunder, especially since Roberto threw an unkind look in her direction. He took his cousin's hand. "It is nothing."

Nothing a good plastic surgeon can't fix.

Remembering the image of that bloody earring, the brown crust so vivid against white porcelain, along with the shot of Juanita's ruined earlobe, gave my tummy a jerk. "Uh, I think what Rhonda meant is that Juanita has been held captive for several days now, so it is a good idea to examine her. Right, Rhonda?"

"Yes, that's it! You know, they always give hostage victims a physical when they are found, in case they are traumatized or something."

Jeez, keep digging that hole for yourself, Rhonda. See if you can traumatize everyone.

"Who wants a drink?" I offered. "I think we can all use one. This waiting is downright nerve-racking. Rhonda, could you track down Nacho and Po Thang and see if my mutt needs a quick walk?" I added, giving her a chance to skedaddle before she put the other designer shoe in her mouth.

"Sure thing." Rhonda took off like the hounds of hell were on her heels.

Roberto looked relieved. "Thanks, Hetta."

I wasn't sure whether he was thanking me for getting rid of Rhonda and her mouth, or for the glass of wine I handed him. Just as I took a sip of my own drink, Cholo joined us.

I introduced Sascha to him, and he said, "I see Hetta found you."

Jan and I exchanged a surprised glance. Cholo *knew* I was looking for Sascha?

When in doubt, punt. "Uh, no, not exactly. I was looking for Juanita's chaperone here in Cannes, but Sascha actually was here on the boat when I returned."

Cholo, who, unlike Rhonda can take a hint, said, "Great. Anyway, welcome aboard." He turned to Roberto. "Any word on the next step?"

Roberto explained about the money, and the plane. He also repeated the offer of a ride home to Mexico. Cholo accepted.

Jan excused herself, saying, "Whatever ride we all choose, looks like we might as well go pack. This thing is going to come down fast and I, for one, have had it with Nacho and Cannes. Did Rhonda tell you what we found out this morning?"

"No. What?" Rhonda hadn't returned from the dog walk, and I had a feeling she was going to make herself scarce to avoid embarrassing herself again.

"Not that it matters anymore, but we did find out which boat hosted a party on the night Juanita disappeared. It's still here. On the dock."

"Really? Which one?" I asked.

"At the end. I walked down there and had a chat with some of the crew. The boat is a beauty, registered in the Caymans, and guess what? All the guests that night were gay guys. No women. So, no Juanita. But, by the way, our local gossip guys say the owner *is* a Russian."

"Russians, Russians, Russians. I'm tired of Russians," I joked.

Roberto laughed. "Hey, those are our people."

"Yes, we know," I said. "Your great-grandfather was a Molokan, right?"

"How do you know this?"

"Google, how else."

"Google, Google, Google. I'm tired of Google."

Nacho walked in while we were sharing a much-needed group laugh. "Is this something I should know about?" he asked, then he spotted our newcomer. "Ah, Sascha, how nice to see you again, and welcome aboard. You must be so relieved that this entire nightmare is soon coming to an end."

Sascha's eyes teared up again and she dabbed them with that ever-present hankie. I was beginning to wonder if she suffered from allergies. Bad Hetta.

Po Thang loped in, sans Rhonda.

"Oh, what a beautiful dog," Sascha cooed. She dropped to her knees and my dog buried his snout in her abundant cashmere-clad cleavage. Nacho looked a bit envious.

"Were you looking for anyone in particular, Nacho?" I asked, a little curtly. I was pissed he was so chummy with la *dueña* and had never even told us she existed. What else hadn't he shared?

"As a matter of fact, I was looking for you, Café."

"Little old me? What could you possibly want to lie to me about *now*?"

Po Thang, picking up on my strident tone, wiggled away from Sascha's embrace, leaned against me and whined. He does not like his humans being cross with each other.

Nacho harrumphed and shook his head. "I never lie to you."

"Technically, I guess not. You simply leave out small bits of important information. Like Sascha here. And El Jefe's real name. But never mind, I found out all that with not one iota of assistance from your secretive ass."

"Of course you did. But at least you were kept occupied and out of my way for a short time. If you are annoyed, I apologize, but I have come to you for your help."

"Then you shall be sorely disappointed."

"I think not."

"Well, I think—" My curiosity trumped my desire to bicker. "What kind of help?"

"We should speak privately."

"Oh, goody. This sounds like my bank account is about to get a boost."

The wind, which had piped up almost every afternoon, died out, and it was bordering on hot. I'd grabbed Jan's oversized straw hat and Po Thang's leash before the three of us strolled along La Croisette under ideal conditions. It is days like this that draw French tourists to the area, away from the frigid temps in Paris.

"Have you spoken with Jenks today?" Nacho asked.

"No. You?"

"As a matter of fact, just did."

Perfect! Later, when we returned to the yacht, I'd be able to listen to Nacho's end of that conversation. I dearly love bugs.

"And how is Jenks on this fine day?"

"Unhappy."

"Oh? With me? Or you?"

"Me. When we started this mission, I promised him I would not involve you in anything dangerous, but now...."

"Now what?"

He stopped and looked me in the eye. "Now the kidnappers wish you to deliver the ransom money in exchange for the girl."

Jan paced and threw questions at me faster than I could answer them after I returned to my cabin and told her what Nacho said. "There was nothing on Nacho's computer about this! And they want you to what? And why you? When? Where?"

"Deliver the money. I don't know why me. Soon. I don't know where. Anyhow, I guess it's a done deal."

"No. You can't do this. I forbid it. Can you imagine what Jenks'll say?"

"I think he knows. I'll call him. By the way, Nacho said he talked to Jenks, so it must have been after Rhonda took Po Thang for that walk, dammit. Maybe he called while Nacho was in his cabin. I'd like to hear what was said. Is our bug still working?"

"I hope so. I haven't checked in a while. Maybe Jenks was the one who told him about this outrageous demand for you to deliver the money."

"Let's see what we have."

She went for her laptop, hit some keys and said, "Musta been a phone call. Nothing on his email account. Standby, I'll see if I can find something from the audio."

It took a few minutes, but she handed me the earbuds. Once they were in place, Jan hit a key and I heard Nacho discussing the situation with Jenks. Nacho was right; from what I could hear on his end, Jenks was a very unhappy camper, but they both agreed, that if I was willing to do the exchange, they couldn't risk endangering a young girl's life by refusing I be the delivery girl.

Well, this was one mell of a hess, as my dad would say. On the one hand, I was relieved I wouldn't have to lie to Jenks about what I was going to do, but on another level, I was kind of hoping he'd flat refuse to let Nacho throw me into the lion's den. Cowardice runs right smart in these veins and I had begun obsessing over what could go wrong.

Or how I could simply abscond with the three mil and move to Argentina.

Chapter Twenty-one

THE ENTIRE CREW gathered in the sky lounge for cocktails at five, where Roberto had laid out a cold buffet for dinner after our meeting.

Emotions were a mixed bag. I was caroming between elated and terrified. Jan was furious with me for agreeing to do the deed, and sat across the room shooting eye-daggers at Nacho like it was his fault the kidnappers asked for me to be their transfer agent.

I'm sure the atmosphere was somewhat like a locker room before the Super Bowl: elation mixed with abject fear of failure.

Conversation was muted, no one wanting to speculate on how the game would turn out, but everyone faked optimism. Except Jan. She had a serious pout going. Po Thang, sensing her unhappiness, sat with his head in her lap.

At a little before six, Nacho turned on the large television. The blue screen filled the room with an eerie glow to match the outdoor light, as the sun had dropped over the horizon and a wintery twilight still lingered.

"As I told you earlier, we will be hearing from El Jefe via a satellite feed soon."

"You mean we'll be hearing from the tomato baron," Jan spat.

Nacho's shoulders fell. "Yes. The time has come to be honest with each other."

"Well, *there's* a change."

"Jan, please. You are not helping."

"And neither did you. If you hadn't been such a secretive jerk, we could have found that girl before you had to send one of us into danger."

"We don't know that," I told my best friend. "It is what it is. Even Jenks had to admit we have no choice but to meet their demands."

That quieted Jan down, but she chugged her drink and went for another just as the screen came alive.

An elderly, but still very handsome man, his face a mask of anxiety, was sitting behind a large desk, family photos galore lined up on shelves behind him. I recognized Juan Tomato, as we called him, from our internet searches.

"Are you there?" he asked.

"Yes, Grandfather, we are all here," Roberto answered. Evidently this was not a Facetime call, for we could see him, but he not us.

"Ah. Good, good. As you know, my plane has landed in France and the money is now available."

I noticed he didn't say exactly *where* the airplane and moola were. Hmmm, maybe he didn't trust someone in the room, or was afraid the kidnappers might somehow hack his call. Maybe even from inside Mexico?

"So now we wait?" I asked, wondering if I could pull off that Argentina run while there was a lull in the play.

"That must be Hetta Coffey talking."

"Yes, sir."

"I have heard wonderful things about you."

Okay, so maybe I wouldn't abscond with the money. Yet. "Uh, thanks. I'm ready to go when they are. We'll get Juanita back."

"They are ready. We have received our final instructions, which Nacho will have at the close of this conversation. In a little over twenty-four hours, I pray my darling Juanita will be on her way home. I do wish to..." he choked up, "...I wish to extend my gratitude, and *vaya con Dios.*"

The screen went blank, and Nacho raced for his cabin.

"Gosh, that was short and sweet," Jan growled. "Did we miss the 'thank you, Hetta' for going it alone, to meet up with the kind of bastards who would mutilate a young woman and then threaten to deliver her in pieces?"

I shot her a warning frown. No one was supposed to know we'd actually read the ransom note. Luckily, Nacho wasn't there to hear Jan's statement, and a quick look around the room for reactions told me all I needed to know: Roberto, Sascha, and Team Hetta were the only ones left out of that loop.

Roberto and Sascha exchanged a horrified glance, then Roberto tried to cover his shock with an apology. "I am sorry, Hetta. My grandfather is not used to thanking anyone for anything. He grew up hard, made his fortune without help from others, and…"

I patted his hand. "Look, you don't have to apologize for him. It's obvious he's stressed out."

"Self-centered old troll." Everyone looked at Jan after yet another harsh statement. "Well? Am I wrong?"

"In truth, I suppose not, entirely," Roberto admitted. "He has used his money to get his way over the years, and now he is at the mercy of something he cannot control. He could very well be described as self-centered, as you say, but where Juanita is concerned, he is devoted to her, and she to him."

"Got him wrapped around her little finger, as we say back home," I said. "At least he has one soft spot. Anyway, Nacho will be back in a minute with the details of the exchange so we can get this rodeo on the road *and* be home for Christmas. So, here's to Grandpa and his dough."

Everyone toasted except Jan. Her glass was empty and her pout had hardened into a mask of mad.

I sat down next to her, but she turned away. "Why are you so pissed off at me?" I asked. "It's not like I *asked* to be the one to deliver the money."

"Just leave me alone. For years you've behaved like some kind of juvenile delinquent on a joy ride, and I went along for that ride. This, this…stupid act of putting yourself in danger? It's way over the top and you know it.

If you finally send Jenks packing, you only have yourself to blame. You didn't even try to include me as backup, and that's it, I'm done. *We're* done. I'm not sticking around for this kind of grandstanding."

Anger roiled in my chest. Standing up and leaning into her face, I yelled, "Fine by me. I've had it with you, too. And believe you me, I will definitely leave you alone. Matter of fact, why don't you just leave?"

She got to her feet, towered over me and hollered back, "I'll just do that!" and stomped out of the room.

Everyone was dumbfounded into silence, including me. I melted down onto the settee, and we were all sitting like statues, still staring at where Jan had exited, when Nacho returned with our instructions.

Our collective attention was drawn to him as we waited to hear the next move. "Hetta, you are to deliver the money tomorrow evening, and in exchange, Juanita will be handed over to you."

"Fine," I said. It came out a little warbly, which was about all I could manage. I was still smarting from Jan's fury. She and I had had our disagreements over the years, kinda like sisters sometimes do, but she had never, ever, walked out on me, or threatened to end our friendship. I was numb with impending grief over such a loss. And her warning that I might lose Jenks, to boot, cut even deeper.

"Hetta? Are you alright?" Nacho asked.

"Yes. Sure. It's just that…I want to talk to Jenks about this. I need to be absolutely sure he is onboard with what I'm about to do."

Nacho pulled me away from the others and whispered. "He is, I promise. You cannot talk with anyone outside this yacht. We are being monitored. Everything we say during the next twenty-four hours will be heard."

"How?"

"I do not know, but I believe them. They say if we contact anyone outside of this vessel, they will drop Juanita into the sea with an anchor around her neck."

My entire body went numb. A few years before, that happened to some cruisers I'd actually met, and the idea of being thrown overboard, tied to an anchor, and sinking to a terrifying death was, for me, a nightmare that actually caused me to lose sleep.

"But if they do that, whoever they are, they won't get the money. And an innocent girl will die. For what?"

Nacho shook his head. "I wish I knew. One thing for certain, though. Someone hates the old man enough to drown his granddaughter."

"How do you know that?"

"Because if we do not deliver the money as promised, they will not only kill the girl in this grisly manner, they will video it and send the footage to El Jefe. That is their threat."

"Bastards!" I spat, too loudly, causing everyone within hearing distance to talk at once.

Martinez, who had little to say during this entire mess, called for silence. "Look, folks, we are only a day away from having this girl back, so we need to calm down. And, I might add," he looked at me, "calling the kidnappers names when they might be listening ain't the best idea."

"Yes," Nacho said, "please remember that."

Several of us mumbled choice names for the kidnappers under our breath, but Martinez had a point and I, for one, planned to use the possibility we might be heard to full advantage. "Marty's right. Let's all settle down and get this done. Nacho, what do they want me to do? Where and when?"

"You are to leave here at three tomorrow afternoon, rendezvous after dark at a given location, give them the money, and they'll turn over the girl."

"Sounds good to me. What are we going to do for the next few hours? Twiddle our thumbs in silence?" I was already trying to figure out how to contact Jenks, but the phone was out. Text? Could it be intercepted? Were they that sophisticated?

"No, Fabio is going to give you driving lessons."

"Huh?"

"You are to take *Odyssey Forty* to sea, alone, for the meet."

"Whoa! I can drive *my* boat, but this thing?" I waved my arm toward *OXL*'s flying bridge. The controls rivaled those of a Boeing 747. "You weren't on board when we arrived here in Cannes. It took the entire crew of ten to park this baby, and that didn't even include dock personnel handling some of the lines. I can't just start this bucket up and take off."

"The kidnappers are aware of that. They will allow crew to stay aboard until we reach open water, then we are to return to shore, and you will cruise to a set latitude and longitude and simply wait for them."

"That I can handle," I said with more confidence than I felt. "Uh, what's the weather report for the next twenty-four?"

"Just like today. Perfect conditions," Fabio answered. "And with your sea knowledge and boatmanship skills, teaching you what you require to know about operating *Odyssey Forty* will be easy. You will soon see that driving this ship is not so different from your own *yate*. You are an excellent boat handler."

I was pleased with his assessment. "And then you'll come out and bring us back into port?"

"Yes. Once Juanita is safely aboard, you only have to wait at least an hour before leaving the pickup area, then call us in for the return trip into port."

"Great. Sounds like a piece of *gâteau*."

"I am certain it will be. And, Hetta, this time, would you be so kind as not to sink a boat I am responsible for?"

Jeez, did he have to add that?

Some people are *so* touchy.

Chapter Twenty-two

I RUSHED TO Jan's cabin after the meeting ended, anxious to make up. I wanted to assure her all would be well, apologize for pissing her off, and fill her in on the details for the drop. Her cabin was empty and her suitcases gone. No computer, no nothing. Dang, that gal is fast when she's on a tear.

Racing onto the deck, I tried to catch sight of her, but no luck. I was out of breath and in tears when I returned to the sky lounge. Everyone was still there, quietly discussing our situation. "Jan's gone! She's left the ship. And I can't even contact her. It's unbelievable she's so upset. Good grief, we've been through much worse, and she's never flat walked out on me like this."

Nacho looked like he'd been sucker-punched. "*¡Madre de Dios!* What if the kidnappers think Jan heard their terms before she left? What will happen now?"

Martinez held up his hands in an everyone-just-calm-down motion. "Nothing. If they can hear us, they know she left before Nacho told us what comes next. And if they can't? They won't even know she's gone."

He was right. I wiped away tears and said so, adding, "I guess Jan finally reached her limit, and I can't really blame her. We've always been a team, through thick and thin, and me leaving her out like this? She just snapped. I'll find her when all is said and done, but right now we have to concentrate on me being able to maneuver this vessel once the rest of the crew leaves for shore."

Fabio smiled. "It will not be a problem. Let us go to the bridge and I will give you a brief rundown now, then tomorrow our lessons start in earnest. We captains make the job seem much more difficult than it really is to protect our high-paying salaries. And, most important of all, it is not my boat."

Everyone laughed at his joke, but I knew he was serious. When he was helping me and Jan take my boat to Mexico from San Francisco, whenever I suggested something that wasn't considered in the realm of boating safety, his pat answer was, "No *problemo*. It is *you* boat."

Fabio and I went to the bridge and spent two hours going over the controls. Overloaded with information and operational details to remember, I retired to my quarters. Still wired, I put on my jammies and started a WHAT IF list.

As in, what if the kidnappers decided a paltry three million bucks was aiming too low, and decided to hold *Odyssey Forty*, me, the money, *and* Juanita, to raise the stakes? Unfortunately, I knew the answer to *that* WHAT IF: you're plumb screwed, Hetta Coffey.

After Jan and I made the plagiaristic connection to the Getty ransom note, we'd checked out other famous demand letters, and one stood out from the JonBenet Ramsey case. The alleged kidnapper demanded one hundred eighteen thousand dollars for return of the little beauty princess, and the odd amount raised many an investigator's suspicions. The fact that it was the exact amount of the little girl's father's Christmas bonus fairly screamed insider info.

Was it possible Juanita's grandfather was known to keep that amount of ready cash in a safe?

Needless to say, I didn't sleep well. I kept waking up and checking my email for an answer from Jenks to the one I sent, despite the warning not to. He needed to know Jan had flown the coop, and I wanted to know if he was aware I was about to take the prince's yacht to sea, all by myself.

I finally gave up trying to sleep at five a.m. and was rewarded with a waiting email from an unknown source, which I opened anyway. This was not the time to worry about hackers, and besides, the email was made to look like something from Booking.com or some other travel site.

Subject: *Rate your recent experience in Cannes.* Please visit our Facebook page and give us your thoughts.

There was a link, which I followed, joined, and immediately received a personal message: **Hi, beautiful!**

Normally this kind of thing would alert me to a troll, and I would immediately report the poster to the FB spam police, but again, this was no time for caution. Certain the Facebook page was a direct link to Jenks, I pm'd him back, filling him in on the entire plan as I knew it, and telling him I loved him.

I got an immediate reply: **I love you back, and just know I am so proud of you. Go get 'em, Red.**

My reply was met with a notice that Facebook page no longer existed, and sure enough, when I searched for it, it was gone, but I was elated. Just knowing Jenks had my back boosted my confidence by a thousand percent, and I girded my ample loins to meet the enemy.

To steal and paraphrase Commodore Perry's famous message: **I will meet the enemy and make them ours.**

Or something like that.

In anticipation of the evening's rescue mission, everyone packed up to abandon ship. Rhonda, as soon as she had her cabin cleared, took care of mine and Po Thang's stuff, as well.

Nacho told me he'd called and booked a suite in Tante Monique's hotel for the crew, using my name as a reference. Surprisingly enough, that landed him a view of the harbor, and a balcony where they planned to set up a telescope he'd lifted from the observation tower on *Odyssey Forty*.

"Wait a minute. I thought you said we couldn't use the phone," I said, when he told me where the crew would be hanging out while I bobbed around offshore.

"Not for anything they could use against us. If I was overheard booking a hotel room, no harm. We must go somewhere, as standing around on the docks would be sure to draw attention." He had a good point. The crew was allowed to stay aboard Odyssey until she left the harbor entrance, a plan designed, I'm sure, not to raise questions about them all leaving like rats in full view of spectators.

"Yeah, I guess you're right."

"Are you all set?"

I lied and said I was. After all, Fabio and I were done with boat operating lessons, and we'd entered waypoints into the GPS system for my voyage away from, and back to, the harbor entrance, as well as the coordinates for the rendezvous. Which, to my dismay were not just offshore, as I expected, but fifteen miles out, in international water. This was worrisome, but there was nothing I could do about it. I felt calmer than I probably should have.

The money, when it arrived, was packaged very much like what we jokingly refer to back in Mexico as square grouper: plastic-wrapped packages of cocaine and marijuana that float on the tide after being dropped by mother ships and airplanes into the Sea of Cortez. I had seen many like them on crossings, and always gave them a wide berth.

Seeing three million all wrapped up and ready to go awakened the avariciousness that lurks in my soul. I found a large paper chart of the area, plotting distances. Gee, I could just take the ship and the money, spend several hours at full speed heading north or south, jump into a dinghy, and head for shore. Call a cab, and disappear. With that much money I could—

"Don't even think about it, Hetta," Nacho warned, breaking into my reverie.

Jeez, that man knows me all too well.

The day dragged by, all of us on edge as we awaited our three o'clock departure. Fabio had filed a float plan with the marina, telling them we were going out to party for the night and would be back in the next day. Evidently this wasn't all that unusual in Cannes, and I'm sure there was a wink, wink, exchange between him and the authorities.

I wondered if that was exactly how Juanita disappeared in the first place, but we were way past investigating that particular scenario. It was now or never. Given a choice, I would have voted for never.

Grandpa's plane was on standby at the airport, limos were lined up at the hotel, and Nacho wanted everyone in the air as soon as possible. I had opted out on the flight, deciding to take Air France's offer in hopes of first locating Jan, and maybe even spending a few days with Jenks when this whole mess was over.

Rhonda decided to stay, as well. We were convinced that whoever took Juanita was somehow connected to Russia, and were not worried about staying in France for a few days. No one had an axe to grind with two middle-aged American broads, right?

Before we left the dock, Rhonda took Po Thang to the hotel. The last thing I wanted was to have him ride in a dingy, albeit a very large one, back to shore with the crew.

"Rhonda, you know what to do," I whispered. "Take all our stuff to the hotel, rent us a good-sized car, and go here." I gave her Jean Luc's address in Cannes, and his cell phone number. "Call Jean Luc as soon as you get to the hotel, and if he's already gone back to Paris, ask him for the combination to the gate. Just stay there until I get back. If he asks questions, tell him I'll fill him in as soon as I can."

"Isn't he going to want to know where you are?"

"Probably, but stall him. We don't want any more people involved in this caper, which should be a done deal by dawn, okay?"

"I'm worried about you all by yourself out there, what if—"

"Trust me, kiddo. I'll be fine. I have a secret weapon."

"Really? What?"

"Duh, it's a *secret*."

She giggled in spite of her worry.

I didn't tell her that my secret weapon was abject stupidity.

Chapter Twenty-three

PO THANG HAD plastered himself to my side all day, becoming increasingly agitated with the flurry of preparations for my evening of derring-do.

Strangers came and went, picking up bags left by crew on the dock. The whole scene was a little weird; still fearing we had listeners and watchers, no one spoke a word to the people who took our luggage and carried it to various vehicles.

My dog knew something was up, and evidently suspected he was going to be left out of it. No amount of treats or soothing talk calmed him down. He was as jumpy as the rest of the crew.

Rhonda had gathered our stuff and piled it on the dock, but when it came time for her to take Po Thang ashore, he balked and stubbornly refused to budge. Rolling onto his back, he went into his dead dog, dead weight mode, and short of asking a couple of crewmembers to pick him up and carry him off, I took over from Rhonda.

I tried more special treats, kind words, gruff tones, anything I'd found effective in the past, but he adamantly resisted to cooperate.

Finally losing patience, I managed to strap on his full harness by rolling him back and forth until I had him firmly buckled in. Enlisting Cholo in the battle, we used brute force to literally drag him along the deck, and push and pull him onto the swim platform, and finally onto the quay. The minute we got him onto land, I tied him to a light pole and collapsed next to his still prone body. This got him to stand, but only the fact that he was strapped into his full harness kept him from bolting. Thrashing and setting up an unearthly howl reminiscent of his wolf ancestors, he caught the attention of everyone within hearing distance.

Thankfully, Rhonda'd decided to have the rental van delivered to the dock instead of the hotel. Passersby gave me dirty looks as I tried to quiet Po Thang, and probably would have accused me of dog abuse had I not gotten two crew members to wrangle him into a crate and shove him into the back of the van.

Po Thang's plaintive wailing could be heard for blocks as they drove away. Next stop: Jean Luc's house until I joined them. I didn't envy Rhonda's night if she couldn't settle him down.

I'd instructed Rhonda not to go directly to Jean Luc's, but to head out of town and make sure she wasn't followed. Since we didn't dare communicate via my cell phone, I had to trust she'd be careful before doubling back.

Before she left, she told me she'd used the rental van driver's phone to contact Jean Luc's cell phone. He was in Paris, but gave her the main gate combo, told her where to find a key to the service entrance, and how to turn off the alarm. I had fond memories of that house's servant's entrance; it leads to an incredible wine cellar Jan and I raided frequently when we were staying in the pool house.

Back on *Odyssey* I pushed away thoughts of happier days not so long ago when raiding Jean Luc's wine cellar, and tried to prepare myself mentally for what promised to be a very long and stressful. And without the aid of Valium.

I wasn't really concerned with the operation of the boat, because all I had to do was drive it in a confined circle until the bad guys showed up with the girl. The money was already loaded into an inflatable, as instructed, which I would lower over the side once Juanita was safely on board. What niggled at me was what if something went wrong? What if, as I feared, they decided to off both of us? Dead people don't make great witnesses.

Reading and watching mystery stories and police procedurals for many years wasn't helping my already vivid imagination with worst case scenarios, and that threat sent earlier of dropping Juanita into the sea with an anchor tied to her didn't help.

"Are you ready to be a hero, Loocey?" Fabio asked, as he smoothly maneuvered us past the harbor entrance and out to sea.

"Lucy never got into anything this dangerous. Stupid, yes. Zany, yes. Life-threatening? Nope. I'm terrified."

"You've handled worse situations."

"I guess. But I was in control. Who knows what these lowlifes have up their sleeves?" I was past caring if they heard me by now.

Fabio whispered, "You don't have to do this, you know. I will take them the money."

"Thank you, Fabio. I know you would, but that is a recipe for disaster. If I don't show up they'd kill her for sure, and probably you as well. If I do what they say...."

"They might kill her anyway. And you."

"Gee, sounds like a win-win situation to me."

Fabio brayed a laugh, and I joined him. "Oh, gawd, I needed that laugh. I miss Jan so much."

"She'll get over it. She just doesn't like you having all the fun."

Nacho joined us and heard Fabio. "Some fun. We're almost there, and," he looked at his watch, "right on schedule. I wish all these boats were not out here. What the hell is going on?"

"Looks like a late afternoon regatta to me. And a few cocktail cruises, that's my guess. On such a perfect weather day, everyone's taking advantage."

As if to back me up, the breeze carried the sound of laughter and music from a boat headed into port. The sun had just set, so I expected everyone except us to be harbor-bound before it got really dark. The city lights in Cannes were already on, and we were making twenty knots, so we were closing in on the waypoint where I lost my crew.

Nacho grabbed my arm with one hand and motioned me to follow him with the other. "Bathroom," he mouthed.

"No, I'm fine."

He rolled his eyes and hauled me into the sky lounge loo. Once he closed the door, he pulled a cell phone from his pocket, hit a key and handed it to me. "It's for you."

He left, giving me a 'make it short' sign.

"Hello?"

"Hetta, how are you holding up?" Jenks asked.

Tears sprang into my eyes. "I fine," I said, my voice quavering in spite of me trying to control it.

"I wish we could talk longer, but I just wanted to make sure you remember everything I told you."

"Got it. Matter of fact, it's written on my thigh."

Silence. Then a low laugh. "Wish I could be a fly on the wall if you need to read it. Love you, we'll talk again soon. Keep the phone."

He disconnected and I let the tears flow, then splashed water on my face and was patting it dry when the engines slowed.

I looked at myself in the mirror, growled, "Show time" and went to take the helm.

Chapter Twenty-four

WHEN FABIO BROUGHT the *Odyssey Forty* to full stop at a designated waypoint, I took the helm.

He stayed with me while other crewmembers lowered a large inflatable into the calm water and moved it to the swim platform. Under his watchful eyes, I held the ship in place, keeping just enough way on so we weren't broadside to a slight swell. Yes, the weather had been very mild for a couple of days, but we were well outside the protected harbor, in the Mediterranean Sea, and there was nothing but four hundred nautical miles of open water between us and Algeria, so a little lumpiness was inevitable.

"Very well done, Café," Nacho said, then, in an uncharacteristic move, reached over and hugged me. If I ever had an inkling I might not survive this handoff, that cinched it.

Before I could make some snide remark, he quickly left the bridge.

Fabio, a trained captain, remained stoic as he gave me last minute instructions, then saluted and said, "You are now *capitán* of this ship. Fairwinds, *y vaya con Dios.*"

"Isn't there a female version of captain in Spanish?" I asked, trying to lighten the gloomy atmosphere.

His teeth gleamed in the glow of the bridge lights. "Sorry, just habit, *Capitana* Coffey."

"That's better. Now, go. *Hasta la vista*, Baby."

"Yes, we *will* see each other again, very soon."

"Yes, we will. Thank you for everything, and if...."

"There is no *if*." With that, he left me alone.

Once the entire crew was safely in the shore boat, they pushed away from Odyssey and streaked toward shore. I watched them on radar for a minute or two, then dialed in my destination latitude and longitude, and the ship steered a course toward my destiny.

During the hour it took to reach the designated exchange point, I plotted a large grid, put in more waypoints as I'd learned to do when searching for treasure in Magdalena Bay last summer, and sat back to let Otto—that's what I call the autopilot—do the work.

A beep let me know I was at the rendezvous point, so I switched over the system to run in large circles around it. Running a grid is a stultifying task, but at least when you're scanning a screen for nifty stuff like shipwrecks, bottom anomalies, or even just watching fish like we did last summer, it beats the hell out of cruising in circles at night without underwater lights or cameras. OXL had them, but I had been told not to use *any* lights, so I was running dark.

At least I didn't have to worry about getting run over by a freighter; an automated system would alert me if I had company within two miles. I sat back in the leather captain's chair to wait. And wait. And wait.

For lack of anything else to do, I stared at the blank radar screen until my eyes watered. Digging eyedrops from my pocket, I used a drop or two in each eye, then closed them for relief. Exhausted from both lack of sleep and stress, I nodded off and jerked awake when my head hit my chest.

My Kindle lay nearby, so I decided to let the boat do all the work while I entertained myself. My book in progress was a sea adventure, and I quickly realized that might not be the best choice, what with it involving bad guys with intent to do harm, chasing the protagonist all over the water. I found a bodice-ripper and lost myself in the doings of a virginal heroine and a dastardly pirate. Or so I thought.

An alarm jolted me out of a deep sleep, and for a few seconds I had no idea where I was. Unfortunately, I quickly remembered.

Checking first the clock, then the radar, it dawned on me I had dozed off for almost an hour, and a small boat had entered the two-mile radar zone and was running straight for me.

I took control of the helm, steered for the rendezvous coordinates, and reset the autopilot. Ten minutes later I was right on the money, so I switched to manual control and brought the engines to idle. Until the exchange was made, I would use the bow and stern thrusters to keep the stern into the swell. Not that a boat the size of *Odyssey* is affected by such small waves, but my company was coming from shore, and I wanted to get a visual on them as soon as possible.

Standing up, I hit a few switches and changed control of the ship to the starboard docking platform, although I was reluctant to leave the safety of the enclosed bridge. Before I was able to make out the oncoming boat, they lit up the bridge with a bright spotlight and I knew when I stepped outside, I'd be a virtual deer in the headlights.

However, I did go out, averting my eyes from the intense light until they suddenly killed the spot. By the time my vision adjusted to the darkness again, they were out of sight, and then I heard and felt them bump against the swim platform. I could also hear their outboards idling, and the muffled burble of my own engines, but other than that, the scene was eerily silent.

A disembodied, amplified, voice boomed, making me jump. I was reminded of swat teams using a bullhorn when some idiot barricaded himself into a building. "Lower the money," they demanded.

That was *not* the plan. I stepped back inside and pushed my own PA system's slider to maximum. With speakers all over the boat, I knew I was about to give them an earful in return. "Not until I see Juanita safely on my deck." My counter demand could probably be heard in Cannes, fifteen miles away. "That was the agreement."

I heard them talking amongst themselves, but couldn't understand what they were saying, or in what language. One thing was certain, though; these people were no boating experts. First, they hit the swim platform too hard, and now they didn't realize their voices carried so well as they compensated for the combined boats' motor noises. And, the numbskulls were downwind, meaning they were also getting a goodly whiff of diesel fumes. Anyone who knew what they were doing would have instructed me to do a one-eighty, bow to the swell.

Odyssey, as instructed, remained dark, inside and out. I was sorely tempted to scare the bejesus out of the jerks by lighting them up with a few of the yacht's 1000w spots, but I had to worry about Juanita, and what would happen to her if I did.

True, I controlled the money, but they still had the hostage. I hoped.

The next voice I heard was female. "Are you Hetta Coffey?" She sounded young, and scared.

"Who wants to know?"

"It's me, Juanita. They say they will let me sit on the swim platform, then when you lower the money and let it float away from your boat, they'll check it's all there and only then will they cut the anchor line tied to my waist. Please, please, do what they say."

"Don't worry, I will. However, I want to see you. Whoever you are in the dinghy, shine a flashlight on Juanita, untie her hands if they are bound, and put a life jacket on her. Once I see she's safely on the platform, I'll lower the money, but not before. You get that?"

No one answered for a moment, then a gruff male voice said, "Agreed."

From what I could hear, but not see, it took a little doing to follow my demands. I imagined them trying to transfer a heavily weighted and bound girl from an inflatable onto the slightly moving platform. I just hoped they didn't accidentally drop her in the drink in the process.

After what seemed forever, but was probably no more than five minutes, they turned their spot on Juanita and I could clearly see her for the first time. She was drenched, probably the result of the ride out from the beach in a ten-foot dinghy. The minute I saw she was onboard, I concentrated on trying to make out who was in the skiff in the back-glow of the spot. I made out two figures dressed in black, faces covered with those balaclavas popular with ISIS. It was a chilling sight, as were the large automatic weapons they brandished. One might wonder why they hadn't just picked me off when they had me in their spot.

I couldn't tell if the kidnappers were men or women. Not that it mattered, as all they represented at the moment were ominous black beings that I wanted to get paid off and away from, *tout de suite*.

Shifting my attention to Juanita, I saw she was trembling, She sat, head bowed, cross-legged on the platform. A thick length of rope encircled her waist and snaked a few feet to a good-sized anchor resting on the platform with her. I estimated the anchor to be about at least a forty pounder, close to the same weight of the stern hook I use on *Raymond Johnson* when I want to anchor fore and aft. I'd been forced to let it go a few times due to a wind shift in the middle of the night, and when I went to retrieve it the next morning, it took all my strength to get the anchor back onto my deck. That hunk of metal tied to Juanita would take her to the bottom in no time flat.

As I'd demanded, her hands were free, and they'd secured a life preserver under her arms, but I doubted it was buoyant enough to overcome the pull of that anchor. That thought gave my gut a turn, but I somehow managed to clear my throat and work the scared tone out of my voice.

"Thank you," I said, "I see you listened to me, and so I want to fully cooperate with you to get this exchange over with as soon and safely as possible." What I really wanted to say was, *Eff you, you cowardly pieces of donkey dung, for terrorizing an innocent young woman.*

Just to keep myself talking, and therefore in control of the situation, I asked, "Juanita, are you injured?"

She raised her head and looked in my direction. Lifting her hand to her ear, she reminded me of that photo of her ripped earlobe. To her credit, she said, "No."

"I can't hear her," I said into the mic, even though I had read her lips.

They held the bullhorn to her mouth and she said, "No, I'm not hurt. Just, please, do what they say."

"Don't worry, honey, I will. All I want is to get you to safety." *And rip these bastards' balls off and stuff them down their throats.* "I'm going to lower the money on the port side. I'll have to turn on a deck light over there so I can guide the dinghy down. Is that alright?"

I didn't get a reply, but saw the two nod at each other, so I flipped a switch and lit up the port side control platform. Another button powered up the winch and I hoisted the lifeboat filled with cash, gave it a nudge with my foot to make sure it cleared the hull, and began slowly lowering it.

Feeling extremely vulnerable, what with being lit up and clearly within shooting range of the perps' large automatics, I mentally lambasted myself for not stashing a Valium in my pocket.

My hand movements could be clearly seen from the kidnappers vantage point, so I reached up with one arm to create a distraction, hoping the SOB's watched my left hand while my right hit a set of buttons. Blessing Prince Faoud for his paranoia, and Jenks for giving me the information I needed, I activated a set of hidden infra-red cameras that no one, not even Fabio, knew existed. I didn't think the bad guys could see the six-screen array from their dinghy point, but to me the screens looked the size of Jumbotrons in sports arenas. I whispered to myself, just to make me feel better, "Pucker up for the fans back home, you SOBs."

Evidently, they couldn't see the screens, for one of them stepped onto the dive platform with Juanita, while the other drove their dinghy slowly along the port side of *Odyssey* to grab their filthy lucre.

My anxiety was bumping the ozone layer, and for a split-second I considered making a run for the sky lounge bar and grabbing that bottle of Nacho's tequila, but decided against it. Hell, knowing him, he'd probably sent it ashore with his luggage anyhow. And I needed what little wits about me I had left. Things were going just a little bit too smoothly, and my inner cynic was sending flares into my nerves.

Slowing the downward progress of the money boat, I gently maneuvered it until it was only four feet above the water. As I hoped he would, the driver moved in close, almost under it, so when I remotely removed the clip, the skiff plummeted into the water, missing his dinghy by inches. Amateurs!

He—it was a male—was standing in his dinghy, reaching upward when I let the money boat go. He yelped, and nearly fell into the water as both his dinghy and the one I'd dropped rocked wildly. Grabbing a gunwale on the skiff, he barely managed to keep it from capsizing.

On the aft camera screen, I watched the other bad guy rush to the port side end of the swim platform, lean out, and peer down the side of *Odyssey*, trying to see what the commotion was all about. Perfect.

In a flash, Jan materialized in a third camera's range, climbing out from under the canvas cover of a ski-doo. With amazing speed, she rushed the rail, leaned over right above Juanita, lassoed her with practiced skill, and did the same with the anchor. Quickly cinching in the slack, she wrapped it around a cleat, threw her arms skyward with two thumbs up, and then grabbed tightly onto a rail herself.

Sometimes it pays to have a best friend who is a once-upon-a-time rodeo queen with scads of goat roping trophies in her mom's den back in Texas. I planned to add another, *if* we survived this caper.

The swim platform bad guy suddenly spied Jan and was raising his weapon toward her when I jammed the engines into forward and both throttles to full speed ahead, launching him into the drink.

Yeah, I wanted to keep Juanita *and* the three mil, but I figured if we left the money behind we might have half a chance of getting out of harm's way while the perps were rounding up the cash. Or drowning.

I was hoping for the latter, but Jan reported, when we slowed down enough for her to cut Juanita lose from the anchor and get them both to the bridge, that she saw the kidnappers swimming toward their unharmed dink, which was surrounded by floating bales of cash. Damn.

Chapter Twenty-five

ONCE JAN AND Juanita joined me on the bridge, we steamed straight for Cannes at *Odyssey's* top speed. I called Nacho on the cellphone he'd given me, told him we had an ETA of fifteen minutes so they could meet us offshore. I figured we were home free when the radar alarm went off. A small boat was rapidly closing on our tail.

"Jan, check that out, will you?"

Using night vision binoculars, she took a long look, blew her bangs off her forehead and said, "Oh, yeah, it's them, alright."

I looked at them on the radar screen, hit a button and got a readout. "Collision course. ETA five minutes. Well, crap."

"Why in hell are they chasing us?"

"They want to give us our money back? Come on, Jan, we already know they're capable of kidnapping, terrorism, and mayhem. What's a little murder added on?"

"Murder?"

"Yep, dead women don't tell tales. They don't want any witnesses."

Juanita's eyes widened and she started to shake. Here she'd thought she was safe, and now she wasn't. I pushed her down onto the deck and told her to stay put. Since we were on autopilot, I knelt down as well, but these guys were closing on us fast, and that little saltwater bath I gave them wasn't going to affect their automatic weapons.

"So you figure they have a firing range of, say, a third of a mile or so?" I asked Jan.

"Not sure, but that's probably about right. Which is way too close in my book."

"Yabbut, there's not much we can do about them until they pull even closer. I hate the idea of returning the prince's boat full of bullet holes, but I guess that's what we'll have to do. Take cover, Chicas, it's gonna be a wild ride."

Jan nodded. "So, we go with Plan B?"

"Yep. Some eejits just do not know when to quit while they're ahead."

Jan grabbed a large canvas bag I'd placed next to the steering station, hefted it over her shoulder, and strode purposefully toward the aft sundeck.

Juanita, lying flat out on the deck asked, "What's in the bag, and where is she going?"

"To deliver the unexpected. That's what you gotta do when thugs just won't learn that you don't mess with

Texas. Why do *you* think they're still on our tails? Did you overhear anything that would give us a clue?"

"No. They said once they had the money, they'd let me go."

"Gee, they lied. What a surprise. Did you ever see their faces?"

She shook her head. "They always wore those masks."

"Balaclavas. Hell, you can buy them at Walmart back home. Matter of fact, that's where Jan and I got ours. Pardon me, I have to make a phone call."

When Nacho answered I said, "Houston, we have a problem."

We lay on the deck and rode out the next five minutes in silence, my eyes glued to the outdoor camera screen and the radar painting our tormentor's progress. When they got within range, it was a given they'd open fire, and there wasn't a damned thing I could do about it. However, randomly firing at a large yacht was basically useless unless they got lucky and hit something that exploded. Luckily for us, the prince was a security freak, and his yacht was pretty much bulletproofed. Princes simply cannot be too careful these days, you know.

We couldn't outrun that dinghy, and although help was on the way, the bad guys had the guns. On the bright side, these two had already proven themselves to be amateurs, and my money was on us.

I called Nacho again, he said they were just leaving the marina and I told him he'd better hold off nearby unless he was heavily armed.

We just had to be patient, something neither Jan nor I are very good at.

At the moment I thought we had the advantage, I yelled, "Hang on everybody, and Jan, keep your head down!"

Jan sprang into action, scrambling to the bow in a low crouch while dragging the heavy bag behind her. She positioned herself between two large tanning beds, pulled out a nasty-looking weapon from the bag, and gave me a thumbs-up.

I stood and took control of the boat, making a sudden turn that was probably more suited to a ski boat than a huge yacht, and from the crashes we heard, I imagined all manner of debris flying around down below. However, the wide aft end of *Odyssey* was too large a target, and besides, why let these guys have their way with us?

Steering us straight for the on-coming dinghy, which was just barely out of firing range, we had to plow through our own wake, making for even more mayhem below. As soon as we escaped the tumultuous water we displaced, and the boat steadied out, Jan kneeled, took aim, and pulled the trigger on her handheld grenade launcher.

The grenade exploded in the air, just short of the pursuing boat, but we certainly got their attention.

Rattled, they turned tail and now *we* were chasing *them*.

Jan continued to fire grenades at them until I called a cease fire, as we'd bought enough time for Nacho and the gang to catch up with us, and besides, the dinghy full of money was now well out of our range…and we, theirs.

I made a U-turn, more carefully this time, and met up with Nacho and our crew.

Juanita, open-mouthed with shock, asked, "Where on earth did you get those…whatever they were?"

"Grenades. This yacht belongs to a gentleman of means who is also extremely paranoid. My kinda guy, but I gotta speak to him about beefing up his arsenal a bit."

"Yeah," Jan said as she joined us topsides. "If we'd a had a missile launcher I'd could've blown them and the money to Kingdom Come. Too bad they got away, and with the loot, to boot."

The explosions offshore couldn't have gone unnoticed, but I guess everyone back in Cannes thought it was just a fireworks display of some kind, because after we got Nacho, Fabio, and Cholo on board, we cruised into the marina with little fanfare.

After Fabio took over the helm, I headed to the sky lounge, which looked as though a grenade might have gone off *there*. I did, however, locate an intact bottle of tequila and plopped down on a sofa for a quaff or three.

Jan, drenched with salt water from her bumpy ride on the bow, took Juanita downstairs for a hot shower and some clean clothes.

Martinez, who isn't real keen on riding in dinghies, waited for us on the dock with a doctor who was brought in to check Juanita out. The doc sanitized and re-bandaged her ear and declared her fit to travel. She, Fabio, Cholo, Martinez, and Nacho shared a waiting limo for the twenty-minute ride to the airport. Chef Roberto and la *dueña* had gone to the plane as soon as it landed to supervise the offloading of the money, and then wait for Juanita and the rest of the crew to arrive so they could take off for Mexico immediately.

Jan and I took a cab to Jean Luc's house, where Rhonda and Po Thang were waiting. Po Thang was ecstatic to see us, but Rhonda was confused. She started to ask how it was Jan was with me, but I held up my hand in a stop sign and said, "Later. Let us raid the wine cellar, and make our plans for flying back to the States."

Jenks called while we were uncorking a five-hundred-dollar bottle of wine, said Nacho had clued him in on how well things went, congratulated me on a job well done, and asked me to meet him in Lille the next day.

Yes!

Back in the living area, I made a toast to our success, then said, "I'd say we did a damned good job, huh, gang?"

"Everything came out just fine," Jan agreed. "Except for *Odyssey*. I certainly don't envy the prince's crew when they board her and find the mess Hetta left."

"What happened?" Rhonda asked.

"Hetta happened. She drove that boat like a crazy woman. God only knows what it'll cost to clean it up. Everything's broken."

"Not everything. I did find a bottle of tequila that survived, but I gave it to Nacho. Of course, there was about three inches missing, but it's the thought that counts."

Jan grinned. "You deserved a drink. We got the girl and you saved our skins, so the mission was a success."

"No, I just drove the boat. You were the one who scared those bastards off. Here's to Jan: Wonder Woman."

"I did what I could. If that danged yacht had been properly equipped with a couple of SAMs instead of that measly grenade launcher, you wouldn't have had to pull those wild wazoo-puckering stunts, *n'est-ce pas?*

Chapter Twenty-six

AS IT TURNED out, Rhonda had actually witnessed our little offshore fireworks show from Jean Luc's balcony, and videoed it on her phone.

"Grenades? With a launcher? Wow, I sure wish I'd been with you. Where on earth did you get them?"

"From the grenade safe, where else?" Jan told her. "Dang thang was in a special locker under Hetta's bed all the time. Who knew?"

Rhonda shook her head as if to clear it. "You'll have to explain it all to me. It's been a very long night. I couldn't sleep, so I just sat upstairs, looking out to sea, even though I couldn't see anything. And then, BOOM! fireworks. So, I grabbed my phone and took a video."

"I had the combination to the arsenal locker written on the inside of my thigh, so I gave it to Jan as soon as the rest of the crew left the boat. Jenks gave me the combo, just in case, thank goodness."

"Very impressive. Jan, you know how to use weapons like that launcher thingy? I thought, like in the movies, you pulled the pin with your teeth and threw them."

"While I was hiding below, I studied the instructions in the bag Jenks told us about. Anyhow, the launcher was already attached to an M4 carbine, so all I had to do was load and shoot. There were a dozen forty millimeter grenades in the bag, and more below, but I figured if a dozen didn't do the job, we were toast anyhow. One thing for sure, it beats the hell out of Hetta's potato gun."

"Neat. Uh, what's an M4? And potato gun?"

This led to Jan reciting into a long discourse on various automatic weapons, 40mm grenades, and finally, the potato gun I keep on board *Raymond Johnson*. "Jenks once used that potato gun to launch Molotov cocktails at a panga full of dudes hell bent on killing us."

Listening to this bit of history made me downright nostalgic.

"Gosh, you guys live such an exciting life," Rhonda said.

"Hetta does. The rest of us just go along, kickin' and screamin'."

"Oh, come on, Jan, you've been in on the money part, as well. But I have to admit, since we arrived in Mexico, our excitement factor has amped up. So many bad guys, so little time."

"Sounds like it. And here in France, as well. It's a shame you had to let the kidnappers get away with the money, especially since they tried to double-cross you."

"You got that right," I told her. "But we sure as hell weren't going after them once they took off. I still wonder about that three-million-dollar ransom demand. It's weird. But, oh well, we have to decide—"

My phone rang. It was Jenks again. "Hey, what's up?" I said, walking outside to get away from prying ears.

"What did you do to Faoud's boat?"

"Uh, we sorta had a little dust up out there, but thanks to you, we prevailed."

"You used the uh...I guess we should talk about this later, in person. Nacho told me everything went down as planned. Then the prince called and said it looks like a bomb went off inside *Odyssey*."

"Please give him my sincere apologies and tell him to send the bill to Juanita's grandfather. We sort of had to take evasive action. I'll tell you all about it tomorrow. Anyhow, all's well that ends well. And, Jenks, Jan says for you to tell Prince Faoud that his boat could really, really, use a surface-to-air missile or two."

There was a brief silence, followed by that wonderful deep laugh I love so much. "I can't wait to hear the rest of this story. So, see you in Lille tomorrow?"

"Is there a cow in Texas?"

We drove the rental van to Paris the next day. I dropped Jan, Rhonda, and Po Thang at Jean Luc's apartment building, then I continued on to Lille. The three of them were scheduled to fly on an Air France charter to Mexico the following morning.

We stayed in the L'Hermitage Gantois in Lille, which is now owned by Marriott and had been greatly updated since I'd visited there before. Kinda funky, but hey, how much can you do with a 15th century building?

While Jenks attended meetings during the day, and since the hotel was in the middle of everything, I went to museums and shopped. I was feeling flush, what with the money from the Baxter Brothers courier job to France I'd just completed, and then El Jefe's generosity, so I bought as many goodies as I could cram into suitcases to take home for gifts. I wasn't given my own charter like Jan, Rhonda, and my dog, but I *did* fly first class, thanks to Air France, which beat the hell out of the C-130 I'd arrived on.

Jenks and I were in Lille for two days, then he had to return to Dubai, and I headed for Texas, where my parents would pick me up in Austin on Christmas day. Loaded down with Godiva Chocolates, pâté, and the like—Jan had taken most of my loot with her to the Baja, and if I was lucky, she, Po Thang, and Rhonda wouldn't chomp through all of it before I got back to Mexico—I said my tearful goodbyes (okay, so I managed not to cry until I got on the plane) to Jenks. Who knew when I'd see him again?

Those tears were a reminder that, as a forty-year-old woman, I'd had very few New Year's Eve's dates, but since meeting Jenks, that had improved greatly. I don't know what it is about that particular evening, but I think every woman in the world wants *SOME*one for company to ring in the promise of a new year. I certainly did.

I cannot count the New Year's Eves when, if I did venture out alone, I'd see all these couples and it made me sad. Somewhere along the line, I had decided to throw New Year's Day late brunches, with eggnog, champagne, eggs Benedict and the like, for all my friends, so the night before, I was kept busy cooking and cleaning. Jan always showed up to help the next morning, but she also had a date the night before.

Mom and Dad invited me to a local New Year's Eve dance at a local beer hall, but I decided I'd rather be back on my boat in Mexico. Sometimes being lonesome in the company of others is worse than actually being alone.

Being single is living a life of liberation, but can also really, really, suck.

Suffering from an abundance of roasted turkey—fresh shot, my fav—along with copious amounts of Shiner Bock and brisket on white bread sandwiches, I finally made it back to La Paz airport. I took a taxi to the marina and was actually looking forward to time alone on the boat. I'd been with other people almost constantly for a couple of months, and that is not my norm.

Pushing the dock cart in front of me, I was greeting other dock dwellers—newbies and old friends—while making a mental list of stuff I had to do, when I was assaulted by a large furry critter.

I dropped to my knees and rubbed my nose in his soft ruff, which smelled of Chanel No. 5, reminding me of his arrival at the Canal du Midi a few weeks before. "Po Thang! I thought you were at the fish camp!"

He was dancing around me, then stopped to sniff packages in the dock cart, a diversion that shorted out his little doggie brain so he plumb forgot he was glad to see me.

"Merry Christmas!" Jan yelled from in front of a decorated artificial tree on my boat's bow. "What did you buy me?"

A norther had raised its windy head during the late afternoon, so by cocktail hour, we celebrated our reunion on the aft deck of *Raymond Johnson*. I choose my slips according to the seasons, if possible, so as to be bow-to the prevailing winter wind. Not only does this make docking easier, it also gives me a snug place to sit most afternoons.

I can fully enclose that deck by shutting doors and zipping up canvas with see-through Eisenglass panels, but on this evening all we had to do was close off the hatch leading to the flying bridge and shut the ones to the walk-around deck. The nice thing about La Paz is that it doesn't get the strong winds and really chilly temps of the northern Sea, so we were comfy cozy as we ate Jan's canapés and sipped our drinks while—a little smugly I have to admit—watching white caps build out in the bay and boats getting smacked around while kiting on their hooks.

The La Paz Waltz makes for some fairly uncomfortable times in the anchorage, what with a brisk wind holding your boat broadside to a ripping current during incoming and outgoing tides, or vice versa. While I love being anchored out, I avoid doing so in La Paz.

"I'm gonna buy a boat," Rhonda declared. "Know any for sale?"

"Every boat in this marina and out there," I waved my hand toward the anchorage, "is for sale. Just a matter of price."

"Even this one?"

"Sure. Write me a check for two-hundred and fifty grand and she's all yours."

Jan almost snorted wine through her nose. She and I both knew my boat would sell for two-hundred, tops, on a really good day. Like April 1, for example.

"Gee, that sounds pretty cheap," Rhonda said. She looked as though she was about to make a dash for her checkbook, but then she said, "But, I don't know anything about boats."

"Oh, trust me, that's no problem. Hetta knew *nada* from nothin' when she bought this one."

"Really? How did you learn?"

"I'm really smart."

"Liar, liar, pants on fire," Jan brayed. "She got immensely lucky. She met Jenks not long after getting this boat. Up until then she was about as nautically challenged as you can get."

"Hey, I learned to dock it."

"Yeah, at every bar's dock on the Oakland Estuary. I gotta admit, it was fun. But it was Jenks who turned Hetta into the sea wench she is today."

"True, so true."

Rhonda was soaking all this in. "And then you brought the boat down here."

"Fabio got us and the boat as far as Mag Bay, where you and I just spent Christmas with Chino's relatives, Rhonda. Then Jenks flew in and took us to Cabo, where I jumped ship to be with Chino. Hetta and Jenks made the trip to La Paz, and the rest, as they say, is history."

"So, I could buy a boat and hire someone like Fabio until I learned, right?"

"Sure you can. Let me get your checkbook for you," I volunteered.

She was gazing at one of Carlos Slim's yachts docked on the end tie behind us. "What does one of those cost? I see a lot of crew coming and going over there. They've been washing the boat all day."

"That yacht gets washed every single day. Whaddya think, Jan? What's a boat like that run?"

Ever the CPA, Jan said, "Around eight, nine million. But the upkeep? I dunno, at least a million a year."

"See, Rhonda? My boat is looking better by the minute."

"Wish we could have snagged that ransom money," Jan mused. "We could 'a had a bigger boat."

"Speaking of that caper, have you seen or heard from any of the other players since we all left France?"

"Nary a peep nor a sighting."

"Then I deem it high time we snooped. I suggest we go out to dinner. At El Molokan."

"But," Rhonda asked, "how's that gonna help? No one is supposed to know we were involved in rescuing Juanita."

"Call it a gut feeling."

"Yeah, trust Hetta's gut…it's sure big enough."

"Po Thang, kill!"

Chapter Twenty-seven

LEAVING PO THANG on the boat while we went off for dinner didn't set well with him. He'd gotten used to going just about anywhere we did in France, and now we were back to the reality of living in Mexico, where he was treated like a dog.

Because of the building blow, we crammed into my little red Ford Ranger pickup for the run to El Molokan. Normally we'd walk it, but not only was that wind chilly, I was weary after a flight from Texas to San Diego, then hopping another from Tijuana to La Paz.

When we entered El Molokan, the man I recognized as the owner did a double-take, then rushed over to seat us, thanking us all the way to the table. So much for anonymity. I don't think there is even a word for it in Mexico.

I whispered to Jan as we took our chairs, "See, my gut was right. Thank God there are no secrets in this country. I'm going for max info."

"Okay by me. I'll follow your lead."

"Me too," said Rhonda. "Uh, what are you going to do, exactly."

"Watch and learn, *amiga*."

When the owner returned with his wife in tow, I asked them to join us and they didn't hesitate. Since it was so early, there were only two other occupied tables, and the waitstaff was handling them.

"So, *señor*, I trust all is well with your family now that the, uh, incident has ended happily."

Grinning from ear to ear, he bobbed his head eagerly.

Jan jumped right in. "And how is Juanita? Fully recovered, I hope."

"She is very well," Roberto's mother said. She then whispered, "The ear? You cannot see there was any...injury."

"Oh," Rhonda said, "that's wonderful. And how is Chef Roberto?"

Our hosts' faces fell in unison, and we all leaned in to find out why.

La señora spoke first, "He is leaving the military. We want him to come here, of course, and take over the kitchen, but it is his desire to open his own French restaurant in Puerto Vallarta. We would love to be able to help him, of course, for it is a large undertaking and he is a chef, not a businessman. But, he will be so far away."

Trying to be more upbeat, I said, "He is an excellent chef and, after all, how many French restaurants can there be in PV?"

"Maybe ten, but only two that he considers competition. He has an investor who thinks Roberto will be a success."

"If he has a money guy, then they probably have someone with business experience, and they're willing to give Roberto a chance. Sounds great to me," Jan said.

"Perhaps. We do hope so, for his sake."

"Is he working here tonight? I would love to see him," Rhonda asked, unmasked hope in her voice.

"He has the evening off. He has been working here every night since he returned and wanted to meet with his potential investors tonight. Please, come back tomorrow, and he will be here."

"Oh, I will," Rhonda said with a smile. "He taught me so much about cooking while we were in France. How about *la dueña*—Sascha—have you seen her?"

"No, she is in Mexico City. Roberto tells me she is still very upset about Juanita's...troubles, even though Juan doesn't hold her responsible."

Hearing that El Jefe didn't blame Sascha for Juanita's kidnapping was a relief; after all, what could she have done, short of nailing the girl's foot to the floor? I never had a chance to talk to her about how the whole thing actually came down, but I was eighteen once, and it's a miracle I'm even still alive!

Changing the subject, I complimented Roberto's mother on the seasonal decorations in the restaurant and outside. She filled me in on events I might be interested in during the next few days and invited me to join them at El Molokan for New Year's Eve. Her kind invitation made my eyes sting, as I had wondered if I was going to be stuck on the boat with only a large furry critter, a bottle of champagne, and a pity party for that evening.

Stuffed like a Christmas stocking on free food and wine, compliments of El Molokan, I waddled down the dock, climbed wearily onto the boat, and gave a pouty Po Thang a hug and a hunk of prime rib. His mood improved by leaps and bounds and, since the wind had died down for the night, managed to bully-whine me into taking him for a much-needed, for both of us, walk.

The *malecon,* a waterfront walk that stretches from Marina de la Paz for a little over five kilometers along the bay, was spectacularly decked out with Christmas lights, and so were the stores, restaurants, and clubs on the other side of the street. Now that the Mexicans had come out for the night, every eatery and bar was filling up with holiday revelers. Christmas in La Paz starts in early December and runs through January 6—*El Día De Los Reyes* (Three King's Day)—so it was like I was given three Christmases this year: one each in France, Texas, and Mexico.

I'd forced Po Thang to wear a Santa hat I'd bought for him in Lille, and he wasn't all that happy with it until he must have somehow realized how much attention it was getting him. We were photographed everywhere we went, and children that I thought were up way past their bedtime gathered around to pet him. More than one of them lost an ice cream cone or piece of candy in the blink of an eye, and while they giggled with delight, I reminded myself to muzzle him next time, lest I have to live with noxious dog farts for another night.

Walking off all that food and wine was invigorating, so I turned inland, toward the town's main plaza, which I knew would be lit up and surrounded by the ubiquitous *tiangus*, or tarp-covered stalls, that took over the area every year. Selling food, jewelry, clothing, and everything else under the sun—I wondered what lucky person was destined to receive the gift of retreaded tires this year—they somehow didn't seem to know that Christmas was over, but then again, much of the gift-giving in Mexico takes place on Three King's Day, while December 24th and 25th are reserved for religious ceremonies and family get-togethers.

We had turned back toward the water when I caught sight of a familiar face: Chef Roberto. I started to raise my hand and holler out when I froze in my tracks. At the moment I spotted him, he turned his back to me and leaned into a wall, bending down slightly to plant a smooch on his companion.

Stunned, I whirled and urged Po Thang into a jog before he spotted his kitchen buddy and barked a greeting. I think we were halfway back to the boat before I finally slowed and took a breath.

Jan was already snoring in the guest cabin when I returned, so I urged Po Thang to wake her up while I stayed out of slugging distance.

"What the...? Oh, hell, Po Thang! Jeez what have you been eatin' for God's sake? Yuck, go brush your teeth!" Jan yelled, but I could hear laughter in her voice.

Po Thang emerged, a grin on his mug, with Jan following close behind. "Hetta, dammit, I was asleep. You—" she stopped grousing when she saw my face. "What's wrong?"

I looked around. "Where's Rhonda?"

"No idea, why?"

"I gotta tell you something I don't want her to hear. Wine!"

Jan, who knows me so well, didn't even question that one word command. She headed for the fridge, pulled out a white, uncorked it, and headed up the stairs leading to the aft deck.

Once we both had a glass in hand, we settled under the lap blankets I keep on the lounges. "Okay, Chica, this must be good because you look like you saw a ghost, or ate a canary. Hard to tell in this light."

"I just got a big surprise, that's all. You are not going to effin' believe it."

"Try me. After all these years with you, I'm used to your bombshells."

"Yeah, well brace yourself for a big one."

"You gonna tell me, or am I going to have to strangle it out of you?"

"I saw someone we know in town."

"And this is surprising?"

"Actually it was *two* someones."

Jan stood and reached clawed hands for my throat.

"All *right*, already. Chef Roberto, was one of them."

"And?"

"Our king of cuisine had *la dueña* pinned against a wall, with his tongue halfway down her throat."

Jan, who had just taken a sip from her glass, almost choked. "You're shittin' me!"

"You owe the cuss jar five bucks, but I'll even the score. I. Shit. You. Not!"

Chapter Twenty-eight

FOLLOWING JAN'S STUNNED outburst upon hearing that Chef Roberto and Sascha were kissing cousins, I grabbed a notebook and pen, scribbled out two IOUs for five bucks and threw them into a cuss jar.

"Wow. Holy...sugar. I can't afford to say what I really want to," Jan said.

Jan and I had decided we had to clean up our potty language a couple of years back, so we both kept cuss jars scattered around our abodes. Our scatology account was well over two grand by now, and just grew by ten bucks.

"Good thing I don't have to add moola for all the words I said to myself on the way back to the boat. I mean, they're *cousins*, for cryin' out loud?"

"You're the genealogy nut, Hetta. You figure out how."

I went to my office area and grabbed the hand-drawn family tree charts I'd sketched out while we were still in France. At that early stage of the game, we were still trying to figure out who El Jefe was by backtracking up the family line from the kidnap victim. Cousin Sascha wasn't even a known entity then, so her side of the family wasn't important.

"Here we go. We have a lot more info now. Here's Roberto," I tapped a box, "and Juanita. They're first cousins. So if we back up to Juan Tomato, the grandfather, and go from there…" I drew a line parallel to grandpa's box, wrote his brother's name in, added some boxes below him and, "Bingo! Sascha!"

Jan counted the boxes and mocked wiping sweat from her bow. "Whew! Third cousins. Perfectly legit, if a little creepy, for them to fool around. But since when? I sure as hell didn't get a clue while they were on *Odyssey*, and you know I can usually sniff out hanky panky at forty paces."

"Soooo, this foolin' around is either something new, or they are consummate, you should excuse the double entendre, actors."

Jan hooted at my clever play on words, which set me off in turn. We were still giggling when Po Thang woke from his after-walk-and-junk-food snooze, charged down the steps into the main salon, and out onto the port deck, whiney-barking all the way.

"Betcha that's Rhonda," Jan whispered. "We can't tell her what you saw. She'll be heartbroken. She has it pretty bad for Roberto."

"Agreed."

Rhonda followed Po Thang to the aft deck and plopped down into a chair.

Jan made a show of checking a non-existent watch on her bare wrist. "And just where have you been, missy?" she asked. She sounded just like my mother used to when I tried to sneak in after curfew.

Rhonda pointed toward the large yacht slips. "Walking the docks. Looking for a dreamboat."

"That sounds somewhat illegal, if you get my drift. You're really serious about this boat thing, are you?" I asked.

"Sure am. I loved living on that little boat on the Canal du Midi with you guys, and then the prince's yacht? Well, that was beyond fantastic. I figure something right at fifty feet will do the job."

"I'll help you find it," Jan volunteered, jazzed at the opportunity to spend some OPM. "We'll start here in La Paz tomorrow, but I'd wager we'll have to go to the mainland, or even the States, to find what you want."

"So, Rhonda, how much of your inheritance are you willing to let Jan blow on this yacht of yours?"

"I'm thinking somewhere between three hundred and four hundred thousand. Do you think that's enough? That's about what I'll get for mom's house when I sell it."

"Depends. I can tell you from experience, the first year will cost you a bundle in updates, repairs and the like, though. Unless you buy a new one, and even then it can get you over four hundred grand."

"I can go five. Where do we start?"

"Where else?" Jan said. "The internet."

"And, I suggest you look for a 45-footer, cuz anything larger and you start paying through the nose for docks, and you're probably going to need a captain."

Jan yawned and stretched. "We'll commence the great yacht search first thing tomorrow. I, for one, am hitting it right now."

We all left the back deck, but after Rhonda went into the cabin she was sharing with Jan, I whispered, "Not a word about you-know-who."

"Yeah, yeah. I know who. But yachts aren't the only thing we're gonna look into tomorrow. Enquiring minds want to know the scoop on those kissin' cousins."

"Amen."

I woke up at two o'clock when some loudly cheerful party animals stumbled down the dock. I would have been annoyed if I hadn't done the same thing so many times. Ah, to be young again.

Unable to go back to sleep, I surfed the internet for fortyish-foot yachts for sale and was pleasantly surprised to see prices had gone down, until I realized mine had probably lost value, as well. Checking out sister ships for *Raymond Johnson*, I saw they were selling for about what I paid for her, and decided that wasn't bad, even what with all the dough I'd poured into her over the years. Boats do not appreciate, and you're lucky if they don't take a dive, so to speak.

I found Rhonda's boat within ten minutes. Okay, so it probably wasn't what she had in mind, but it was what I would buy if I could: a brand new forty-foot power cat.

It was in Thailand.

A vacay in Phuket on Rhonda's tab sounded just dandy.

I, too, can spend OPM.

We all arrived in the galley at the same time the next morning, and headed for the Keurig. Jenks had given it to me for my birthday, with a six-month supply of Busteo Café pods. Six months' worth, that is, if I could keep people off my damned boat.

"Hey, Rhonda, I found you the perfect boat. It's in Thailand."

"Really? That's great! How soon can we get it here?"

Jan groaned. "Oh, lawdy, Rhonda! Please, please, do not go into a yacht broker without one of us with you."

"Give me *some* credit, Jan. I was kidding. I'm not *that* naïve. Matter of fact, I woke up real early and sneaked out to the sundeck and did some cyber-shopping on my own. I found one in Marina del Rey that is just about perfect. Matter of fact, it looks a lot like *Raymond Johnson*, only bigger, newer, and much more luxurious," she said prissily.

"Yeah? Well," I broke into song, "I saw Roberto kissing Sascha cuz, underneath the mistletoe last night." For good measure, I added, even more prissily, "And it damned well wasn't on the cheek."

Rhonda's face fell and headed for her cabin.

Jan shook her head. "Childish, Hetta. So childish. Just because Rhonda is shopping for a bigger and better boat than yours, you go and say something like that? You ought to be ashamed of yourself."

I was. Sort of. "Competitive instinct?"

"When she stops bawling and unlocks that door, you should apologize."

"She should have waited to brag about that boat until after I had my coffee."

"Hey! Just what in the holy hell is bugging you? You aren't usually *this* mean."

"New Year's Eve."

"Oh, hell, not that again? I thought you'd finally gotten over obsessing about that crap since you met Jenks. Evidently not."

"You *always* have a date."

"Which I sometimes broke to be with you, I might remind you."

She was right. This fixation of mine on New Year's Eve was stupid. I mean, lots of people are alone that night. *Lots.* Especially women with forty cats.

"You're thinking about that cat thing again, aren't you? That is such a cliché. Besides, you're allergic to cats. Tell you what, I'll pry Rhonda out of our room, you make nice and say you're sorry, and we'll make plans to ring in the New Year together, and in grand fashion, okay?"

"Don't you want to spend that evening with Chino?"

"Gee, why would I want to do that when I can be with you and your forty cats?"

Chapter Twenty-nine

"RHONDA, I'M SORRY. I shouldn't have told you what I saw. I know you have a crush on Roberto. It was very unkind of me."

I was talking through the door to the guest cabin, since Jan hadn't had any luck getting Rhonda to come out.

"Y-y-you really saw them? Are you sure you didn't just misconstrue the circumstances?"

I rolled my eyes at Jan and mouthed, "This woman will be the death of me." *Or me the death of her, more than likely.* I knocked my head with my fist, turned my eyes up for divine guidance and said, "You know, you could be right, Rhonda," I cajoled. But then the devil took over, along with a goodly amount of sarcasm. "I just might have *imagined* that passionate French kiss and boob massage. The lighting *was* a little dim."

Despite herself, Jan let go with a loud guffaw.

The door suddenly opened and a red-eyed Rhonda leaned out. "But they're *cousins!* This is just so wrong."

"Yep. They bring a whole new meaning to that old phrase, vice is nice but incest is best."

Rhonda garnered a crooked smile before she remembered her misery. "I am such a fool. I thought he really liked me."

"He's the fool. You have lots of money, and she's a failed nanny who managed to get her cousin kidnapped. Okay, so she's drop-dead gorgeous, but still a loser."

Jan fixed me with a frown of disapproval. "Hetta, couldn't you just shut up when you're ahead for once in your life? Rhonda, go throw water in your face and let's go shopping while Hetta sits in yon corner for a time out."

As soon as they left, I called Jenks, needing a friendly voice and contact with someone, besides Po Thang, who didn't think I was the wicked witch of the west. Even Po Thang was shooting me dirty looks, but that was probably because I wouldn't let him tag along with Jan and Rhonda.

"Hey, Red. How's the boat?"

"Fine."

"Uh, you don't sound so fine."

"Jan gave me a time out."

"You've been a bad girl?" His voice went down a couple of octaves, which set up a tingle in my nether parts.

"Very bad. You should be here. I'd show you just how bad I can be."

"Don't I wish. Too much work. I know it's only been a week since we were in Lille, but it seems longer."

"Yes, it sure does. I have gossip."

"Tell me. These guys here in Dubai never have anything good."

I laughed and told him about going to El Molokan the night before, then my walk when I saw Roberto and Sascha in a lip-lock.

"Whoa! That sounds so...wrong. Roberto told his parents he wanted the night off for a meeting with a possible backer for his Puerto Vallarta restaurant, and you catch him playing kissy face with his cousin, who is supposed to be in Mexico City? Love is strange."

"That's what they all say about you and me."

"I *like* us."

That brought both a song to my heart and a tear to my eye.

Jenks always knows just the right thing to say.

After my upbeat chat with Jenks, I forgave myself for being mean to Rhonda—after all, she really needs a pair of big girl panties, *n'est-ce pas*? But to placate what should have been a guilty conscience, I did a little internet research on that yacht of hers so that when she and Jan returned, I could redeem myself.

I perused YachtingWorld, the ultimate internet site for nautical dreamers the world over, and came up with a couple of possibilities, but my mind kept wandering back to the smokin'-hot alley scene from the night before. Just when *did* that romance spark? Those two certainly didn't give anyone an inkling they had a sexual relationship when we were on *Odyssey Forty*.

Of course, we were focused on a common goal: get Juanita back safely, and out of France. Mission accomplished. It still irked me that we actually paid the ransom, but, oh well, not my money. Darn it.

I switched gears and Googled El Jefe, a.k.a. Juan Tomato, to see if there was even a hint of news that his granddaughter had been kidnapped and rescued, but found nada. Same result from a peek at Juanita's Facebook page; just a few photos of her in front of French tourist attractions. No, *OMG! I was kidnapped!* kind of stuff.

As a rule, when I finish a project or a caper, I feel...vindicated? Not sure that's the right term, but I really hate the word "closure." It has a psycho-babble ring to it. Hearing one say they need closure makes me want to lock them in an airless vault and slam the door. Now, *that's* closure.

Before I worked myself into another crappy mood, I told Po Thang to get his leash. "Let us go find food, dawg. And perhaps a Bloody Mary?"

Maybe it was my guilty imagination at work, but I swear he looked at the clock when I mentioned booze so early in the day.

"Ya know what Benjamin Franklin said? 'Wine is constant proof that God loves us and loves to see us happy.' And I want to be happy, so there."

Drawn like a fly to a bull turd, I headed straight for El Molokan, even though they didn't open for lunch for another hour.

I didn't know what I was going to do there, besides eat lunch, but I had an inexplicable urge to see Roberto. Not that I planned to confront him. After all, if he and Sascha were getting it on, far be it from me to judge; I was just miffed that I could have been hornswoggled so easily back in Cannes.

Walking to the rear of the restaurant via a driveway, I found a door wide open and heard the clatter of kitchen work underway. I tied Po Thang to a post and stuck my head inside. "Yoo-hoo! Roberto, are you here? It's Hetta."

Wiping flour-caked hands onto a dish towel, Roberto rushed out to meet me. "Hetta! My mother and father told me you were back in town. Come in! Come in! We can talk while I work." He glanced at his watch and sighed. "No matter how early I start, there never seems to be time enough before our first guests arrive."

"I won't stay but a minute. I know you're busy. I actually planned to be one of those guests, but I have Po Thang with me, so I guess I didn't think it through. Too much time in France?"

"Perhaps on the patio. If," he grinned from ear to ear, "you can keep that 'foreign canine with questionable table manners' under control," he said, quoting *Le Parisien.*

"Pure slander," I protested. "He was innocent."

"Why do I doubt that, when he stole so much from my galley on *Odyssey*?" As he talked, Roberto whisked shaved ground dark Mexican chocolate—70% cacao according to the Ibarra package nearby—into a divine-smelling *mole* sauce already simmering over a double boiler. I could already detect garlic, oregano, cumin, cinnamon, and chili powder steeping in a nearby pot of chicken broth. There was no doubt what I was having for lunch: whatever he planned to put the sauce on.

Much like Po Thang, food has a way of making me forget original intent; after one whiff of that mole I didn't give a hoot who Roberto was screwing, or for how long.

But, evidently there were others who did. Po Thang and I were seated in the patio area before the doors opened for business, and the first ones to arrive were Jan and Rhonda.

What a couple of quidnuncs!

That's Latin for busybodies.

"Well, lookee here," Jan said to Rhonda when they were ushered onto the patio. "Who told you your time out was over, Hetta?"

I was hanging on to Po Thang's leash so he didn't upset any tables, but that tail of his was going bonkers, threatening to throw glasses and cutlery asunder.

"Get over here and plant your nosy rears," I told my friends, "so he'll settle down."

Jan pointed her finger at him. "Sit!"

And he did.

"We've been doing a little re-training while you were messin' around in France and Texas. He was getting out of hand."

"Now there's an understatement," I said, as Rhonda and Jan pulled up chairs. My lunch had just arrived, and Rhonda stared at my plate. "What *is* that? It smells divine, but looks like a pile of, well, crap."

"Chocolate chicken."

Her eyes grew large. "Chocolate chicken? Ewww, gross."

Just as she said it, Roberto came out of the kitchen, bringing Po Thang a plate of tidbits much more suitable to his constitution than a dish laden with garlic and hot peppers. Not to mention chocolate.

"*Bonjour, mes amis!* All together again! And, Rhonda, perhaps *mole* dishes are not the most eye-appealing in the world. There is a legend that it came about when some nuns were serving a bishop and used everything they had at the time to come up with this sauce."

"Looks to me like what happened to the bishop after he ate it," Rhonda growled.

Roberto's face fell. It was so out of character for Rhonda to be rude; that was usually left to me.

Jan stood, hugged Roberto, and said, "Well I, for one, can't wait to try your *mole*. What ingredients do you use?" While they discussed his recipe, I ate my fiery chicken dish before it got cold.

Po Thang had already inhaled his saucer of plain diced chicken breast and was eyeing my plate while inching forward, hoping we wouldn't notice. Jan gave him the evil eye, pointed that finger of doom at him and he backed off. Turning back to Roberto, she said, "I know you're busy right now, but let's get together, maybe on Hetta's boat, when you have time off? Are you working tonight?"

"Unfortunately, yes. My parents need my help this time of year. How about breakfast? I can come tomorrow."

"Great," I said. "Jan'll cook. You know of anyone else in town from our little French adventure?" I hoped I looked and sounded innocent.

"No. See you tomorrow. Say, nine? I know where your boat is."

He took off to prepare for an onslaught of orders as townsfolk in holiday spirits arrived in groups. I knew from experience they'd spend the entire afternoon at their tables, and were not in a hurry to be served. Unlike the States, turnover was neither expected nor encouraged at El Molokan.

"Big fat liar," Rhonda hissed.

"Yes," I agreed, "he is." I was in slight awe at his smooth falsifying ability.

"Jeez, you two," Jan whispered. "What did you expect him to say? 'My cousin I'm sticking it to is in town, shall we invite her?' "

Despite herself, Rhonda sniggered. Surrounded by all those holiday revelers, it was hard to stay in a bad mood, even in the face of unrequited love.

Chapter Thirty

I SENT NACHO an email as soon as I returned to *Raymond Johnson* after overindulging on Roberto's chicken mole, and making a breakfast date with him for the next day: **Wanna have breakfast with us tomorrow? And is Cholo around? I think we should celebrate our successful mission.**

To my astonishment, he answered right away: **What time, and where?**

My boat, nine a.m.

I will be there.

"Hey, Jan," I yelled, "I can't believe it. I sent Nacho an email and he's coming to breakfast tomorrow."

Both Rhonda and Po Thang perked up when I said Nacho's name.

"You know, Rhonda, you really shouldn't, uh, mess with Nacho. He's... unpredictable."

"You have quite a flair for the understatement, Miz Hetta," Jan drawled. "But, Rhonda, for once in her very long life, Hetta's right. Do yourself a favor and don't even think about getting involved with Nacho, you hear?"

My boat's larder was bordering on empty, so we hit several stores in town for breakfast ingredients. We didn't have the time for a run to Costco in Cabo San Lucas, and on top of that, I knew the place would be a madhouse right after Christmas. Oddly enough, Walmart has the best wine selection in La Paz, so we stocked up on champagne for New Year's Eve, as well.

I was so grateful to Jan for staying in La Paz for that night, but she said I had a hell of a lot more to worry about than spending one night alone, and suggested I begin stockpiling cat food.

We were up early preparing for our breakfast feast and by eight, we were all set. Meanwhile Rhonda changed clothes and re-combed her hair every ten minutes. Jan's patience was soon tested, and she barked, "Oh, for cripes sake, Rhonda, who are you primping for? Roberto's in lust with the nanny, and Nacho is like the last person on earth who cares what you look like. Hell, he's got the hots for Hetta, and look at *her*."

That little reality slap propelled me to my cabin's full-length mirror. I looked like a bag lady in yoga pants and Jenks's favorite, but threadbare, sweatshirt. I took a shower, blow-dried my hair all poofy, and put on a little makeup, then chose to slip into one of the silk caftans we bought in Cannes. Since one size fits all, Jan and I had lost track of which one belonged to whom.

I emerged to find both Nacho and Roberto sitting in the main salon, talking to Jan as she cooked. We'd ditched the eggs Benedict when I was able to score fresh snapper filets, and we were serving them with a savory polenta, creamy béarnaise sauce, and those wonderful pencil-thin asparagus grown in the Baja.

The wind had all but disappeared, so we retired to the sundeck to take advantage of the perfect morning. We just were sitting down with mimosas when Cholo jogged up the dock. "Sorry, I had to work this morning."

"We didn't know you were coming. What a nice surprise. No problem. Jan always cooks enough for an army, or in your case, a navy."

He gave me a look under his eyebrows. "I never said I was *in* the navy."

Ooops, he had, but obviously he didn't want Nacho to know it. "Oh, that's right. You are an undercover agent or something. "

"Hetta," Nacho said, "you might want to quit while you're ahead."

So, I did.

Sort of. "Roberto, your mom tells me you're thinking of opening a French restaurant in Puerto Vallarta."

He shook his head in dismay. "My mother cannot keep a secret."

Nope, but evidently you can.

Cholo looked confused. "But, you are in the Mexican Navy."

Nacho grinned. "It helps to have a grandfather in high places. What does he think about you giving up a military career for opening a new restaurant across the Sea?"

"He is not pleased."

"Why not open one here in La Paz?" Jan asked.

Because he doesn't want Mommy and Daddy to know he's humping his cousin?

"There is not enough tourist money to support a five-star establishment here. The peso is down against the dollar, and La Paz is more of a working person's town."

"Five star, huh? That's wonderful. Good luck and we'll have to come over and check it out when you open. Have a name for it yet?" Jan asked.

"My backer thinks it should be called Chez Cannes, because we will specialize in fresh seafood, and Puerta Vallarta is on the Mexican Riviera."

"Seems appropriate."

We chatted through our snapper and polenta, enjoying the camaraderie we'd established in Cannes, now that the competition was over. Nacho seemed quite content with the way things turned out, even though we fought him every step of the way.

Rhonda had turned her full attention on Cholo, who didn't appear to mind one bit.

Roberto was the first to leave. "Even though I do not work the lunch crowd today, I apologize for eating and running, but I must prepare tonight's menu. So good to see everyone again, and please, come down to El Molokan. Jan, that fish was *perfecto*. I might steal that dish for my new restaurant. I shall name it *Huachinango de la Jan.*

Jan actually blushed at the compliment.

As soon as Roberto left the cabin, I whispered to Jan, "Follow him."

She didn't even hesitate, just grabbed her hat and fanny pack and headed out. Po Thang protested being left behind, but if you're going to shadow someone, you sure as hell don't need a pesky pup who associates the shadow-ee with food.

If Nacho wondered why Jan took off so suddenly, he kept it to himself. To me he said, "Perhaps I could interest you in a short fishing trip? The day is so beautiful, it would be a shame to waste the rest of it. And perhaps we can replenish your fresh snapper supply."

I started to say, "No thanks, I have to wash my hair," but there was something about the way he asked that changed my mind. "Oh, why not? Just give me a minute to change clothes and pack a cooler. And how about we stop on the other side of the Magote and search for nautilus shells? It's that time of year."

Cholo turned to Rhonda. "It seems everyone has somewhere to go. How about I give you a tour of La Paz? Not the tourist part, but where the real people live."

Her cheeks flared. "Uh, sure, why not?"

Dawg House, my smaller but extremely seaworthy nine-foot panga I use as a dinghy, was still in her chocks on top of the aft deck cover, and a pain to get into the water. I was pleased when Nacho said his swanky fishing boat was all ready to go. I mean, *Dawg House* is fine as a shore boat, but is open to all elements, whereas Nacho's super-panga has a roof and a toilet. No contest.

We barreled out of the harbor and, because it was high tide, took the shortcut between the end of the Magote peninsula and a sand bar that has been the demise of many a boater who doesn't pay close attention to channel markers.

Once we cleared the tricky cut, I took the helm while Nacho brought out the fishing poles. At the sight of them, Po Thang's tail went into overdrive. He dearly loves it when a big old slimy fish hits the deck and he gets to chew on it. I had a feeling he was in for a tooth brushing later.

"Slow down," Nacho shouted over the whine of the high-powered outboards.

Once we glided to a stop, he opened a beer and a bag of chips. Po Thang stopped nuzzling a fishing pole and cozied up to the human with food.

"Hetta, I have a job for you."

"What, you want me to fetch you some salsa?"

"No, I mean a real job."

"No problem. Overpay me and give me bigger weapons," I said, meaning it as a joke.

He lifted his shirt and removed a small handgun from a belt holster. Handing me my Taurus .380, he said, "With regards from your boyfriend, Jean Luc."

"He's not my...oh, never mind. Taury!" I cooed, petting my little gun. The French government had confiscated it while busting a would-be terrorist on the Canal du Midi, and I thought I'd never see it again. Never mind that I'd planted the gun on that rat, hoping against hope they'd hold him due to some very strict French gun laws. I knew at the time he was up to no good, but had no real idea what kind of no good; only later did we learn he was a dyed-in-the-wool terrorist. Jan and I just thought he was a money-grubbing gigolo out to steal Rhonda's inheritance before we could.

"And," Nacho handed me an official-looking document and something that looked like a credit card, "here is your Mexican permit to carry."

"Who do I have to kill? You do know this gun is only effective at close range, right? I try not to get that near anyone who just needs killin'."

He grinned. "Hetta, this is not a license to kill."

"Rats."

"Let's drift and bottom fish, and I'll tell you what we want from you."

An hour later we'd snagged four good-sized red snappers, and I had a new job. I made a mental note of Nacho's GPS reading so I could come back another time and raid his secret fishing hole.

While I was filleting a snapper, I said, "So, just to be clear. I am the only one on this job? No Jan? No Cholo?"

"Just you."

"Why is that? You know you can trust them."

"Of course. The problem is, you are the only one of our group who had not yet returned to Mexico until the day before yesterday. Everyone else involved in the rescue has been here since before Christmas."

"And that is important why?"

"The ransom money we paid for Juanita is showing up in Mexico."

I almost filleted my finger. "What? You marked the money? How?"

"If I tell you, I shall have to kill you."

"Har, har. How much has shown up, and where?"

"Here in La Paz. Only about twenty thousand."

"Nowhere else?"

"No. At least as far as we know."

I was picturing that skiff I'd lowered into the water off Cannes. It was packed to the gunwales with over three hundred pounds of twenty-dollar bills, wrapped in plastic like marijuana bales so they'd float. I remember thinking how compacted three million can get when vacuum packed: there were twelve bundles, a little over six inches wide and four feet long. If we could have snagged even one, it would be worth a quarter of a million.

"Did you guys mark all of them?'

"Every single bill. It was a long flight from Mexico to Cannes."

"So, where in La Paz are they showing up?"

"Vista Hermosa."

"Vista Hermosa? You're kidding me?" I pictured the dirt-poor part of town, well hidden from a tourist's eyes. Poverty rules, tarpaper shacks dot the dusty hillsides, and although they have a stunning view (thus the name, Beautiful View), sanitation is nil, no electricity, and water is trucked in. This is where children have no shoes and go to school hungry. And where, every year, gifts are given by the community to those kids. "Let me guess. Jolly old *Papa Noel?*"

Nacho nodded. "How'd you know?"

"Before I left for France I was recruited to help drum up money and gifts for them. It's a big deal every year."

"Bigger this year. Twenty-dollar bills were distributed with the toys, fruit, and clothes. When local merchants started depositing them in their bank accounts, our phone lines lit up. We are trying to keep a lid on the story, but it is only a matter of time before someone asks where all this money came from."

"Like you are."

"Exactly. We are afraid the kidnapping story will get out somehow. El Jefe isn't concerned with the money itself, only about what will happen if the whole story somehow is unearthed. Right now, it's still a feel-good mystery Santa story."

"Except this Santa/Robin Hood snatched the young granddaughter of a prominent Mexican businessman, held her captive, and tore a hole in her ear before getting a three-million-dollar ransom."

I grabbed the last fish from the cooler and got into a tug of war with Po Thang. I won, but only after offering up one of Nacho's chips in trade.

Nacho removed his Tostitos from my reach. "Here in Mexico, men like El Jefe do not report this type of crime."

"Makes them seem less macho?" I snarled. For some reason, this type of cover-up in the name of not seeming vulnerable made my blood boil. All it does is embolden these bastards.

He looked startled, then nodded slowly. "I had not thought of it that way, but you could be right. At any rate, we want Santa bagged. Quietly."

"I wonder where the rest of the moolah is."

"My guess is that it is being laundered as we speak. It will show up, but certainly not in Mexico, and it might take months."

"How does that work, exactly?'

"Offshore investments. Building large hotels in the middle of nowhere is one way. You've seen them all over Mexico."

"Sure have. You can fire a shotgun through the lobby and not hit a soul, but they show fully booked. I've gone into one for lunch. Dining room empty, huge and impressive menu, but they are out of everything. And try to order one of those wines from their list? Also strangely not available."

"Exactly."

"So, our only hope is to track down who added the marked twenties to all those packages for the kids."

"It is our only clue."

"Looks like I'll have to re-volunteer. Several groups are still planning more events and gifts for Three King's Day. Same people running the show, so if nothing else I can maybe get a list of past volunteers. My guess is they have an appreciation lunch or something for everyone after the dust settles, as well."

"That is my thought. Shall we go look for nautilus shells on the beach?"

"Sure. Po Thang would love a run, but after that I'm looking forward to a cool drink and a soft bed for an afternoon lie down."

He leered at me.

"*Alone.*"

Chapter Thirty-one

I AM TERRIBLE at keeping secrets. Especially from Jan, of all people, but Nacho was adamant about me not sharing what I was being hired to do. Perhaps a little more than insistent; I distinctly remember the words, "Great bodily harm."

Since Rhonda and Jan were staying for New Year's Eve, I convinced them to join me in volunteering to wrap packages, put together fruit and popcorn bags, and the like, for the onslaught of kiddies who would come into downtown La Paz for Three King's Day.

The Christmas event was held out at Vista Hermosa, but Three King's Day included a broader spectrum of needy kids, from even farther afield.

Jan was already an old hand in these endeavors, as she was a part of Chino's family now, and they made certain families in poverty-level fish camps all over the peninsula received gifts and food on special occasions. As she told us on the way to sign up, "You cannot imagine the gratitude and joy on these little kids' faces when you give them a bag of oranges and a cheap toy. Or the older ones a pair of tennis shoes. It will break your heart."

I felt a little guilty that I was being paid to do what the others were doing out of the goodness of their hearts, but hey, a gal's gotta do what a gal's gotta do. However, to assuage my guilt some, I had a fat wad of 100 peso notes in my pocket to add to the packages.

I recognized many boaters among the busy volunteers, as well as many local business men and women. Even my favorite fish taco lady, Maria, was there, feeding us worker bees.

Wealthy Mexicans have not, in the past, been noted for their charity to their impoverished countrymen, but that is changing; even Carlos Slim was finally convinced to share his wealth, and is especially involved in making the internet available and educating people to work in the industry. Scoffers consider that a little on the self-serving side, but hey, whatever works.

And, admittedly, I have been a little lax in the do-gooder thing; I can be generous to a fault, according to my parents and Jenks, but not in any organized manner. I figured working to give little kids joy would do me some good, and if I made money, as well? Charity begins at home, as they say.

Looking at the smiling people filling bags, chatting about their Christmases and making sure each package was exactly equal so no child drew a short stick, it was hard to imagine that any of them had some kind of connection to a kidnapping for ransom. But someone did, and it was my job to ferret them out.

I volunteered to make up the packages for the older kids, as I figured a tween or teen was much less likely to just hand over a hundred pesos to their parents. My contribution was for these kids to use as they wished, something many of them had never been allowed to do. Luckily, those bags were not filled as yet; they were concentrating first on the little ones.

Jan joined me, while Rhonda was put in charge of toddler packs; baby food, diapers, and other necessities. After witnessing beautiful beaches littered with filthy diapers, I questioned the wisdom of doling out even more disposable nappies, but then again, most of these people didn't even have running water, much less a washing machine.

Jan, black marker in hand, labeled the package I'd just handed her: **BOY, SIZE 5** ,for the sneakers inside. Each one contained—besides those athletic shoes donated by Walmart—soccer socks, a toothbrush, toothpaste, hand sanitizer and a bar of soap. I could just imagine the look of dismay on an American yuppie puppy's face if handed such a gift but was assured the Three King's Day kids would be delighted. On a long table, another woman, a boater I knew, sorted the sacks by shoe size. On another table were fine mesh bags of oranges, hard candies, and caramel corn.

During a break, I sauntered over to one of the harassed-looking organizers.

"Wow, there must be fifty volunteers here today. Is that the norm?" I asked.

She blew a stray blonde hair out of her eyes. "Just about, take twenty or so. On the sixth we'll have twice as many, thank God."

I stuck out my hand. "Hetta Coffey, I'm a boater."

"You boaters are a godsend every year. You aren't worn down like some of us who live here year-round."

"So, when did you put together the Christmas packages and give them out?"

"Lemme think. Christmas is always a blur. Between Club Cruceros, and all the other organizations that have events far and wide, I lose track. I know blankets were handed out before Christmas. Some of these kids sleep on dirt floors without one. We start working December first to assemble all these donations, and try to hand them out just before Christmas. We used to do it Christmas Day, but got some flak from church groups."

"I heard you took loads of packages up to Vista Hermosa on December twenty-first this year. So, when were those assembled?" Realizing I was starting to sound like someone with an agenda, which I was, I added, "I'm just trying to get my calendar set for next year."

"You'll be here? Great. We started assembling Vista Hermosa gifts on the fifteenth, and were working right up until the day we handed them out. We shouldn't have waited so late, but we had that unseasonable storm which messed up our schedule. But, I guess you know that, since you're a boater."

"I was in France. Just got back."

"Lucky you."

"Do you keep a contact list for volunteers? I'll be happy to put my name on it."

She hollered for another lady and waved her over. "This is Hetta, and she wants to sign up for next year."

"Praise the Lord. Okay, follow me, I have the list in my pickup."

The older woman, who said she'd lived in La Paz for thirty years since her husband died back up in California, led me to a battered Nissan truck and rummaged around in the front seat, which was chock-a-block with all kinds of paper. "My office," she said with a laugh. She saw me eyeing the jump seat area, which was crammed full of silver soccer balls still in their boxes. Waving a hand in that direction, she sighed. "Another day. Another delivery."

I was starting to get a serious case of the guilties. These women were tireless in their efforts to add a little comfort to the indigent, and I was...not. My Mother Teresa moment was quickly erased when she handed me a three-ring binder, said, "Find the right page, give me your email address and name, and then put it back into the pile. I gotta get back to my post."

Taking my camera from my pocket I quickly located a divider labeled *Vista Hermosa, Christmas*, and started snapping pictures of the ten pages of volunteers, hoping they came out. I was just putting the book back inside when someone said, "Can I help you?"

I whirled around. "Jeez, you scared me. Donna asked me to sign the volunteer list. I was just putting it back."

"Oh, you must have gotten here late. We have a sign-up sheet near the gate."

"I signed that one. I guess she wanted me on next year's list."

"Great." She introduced herself. "I'm security, so to speak. You would not believe the people who try to sneak in and pilfer stuff. Not that you look like a soccer ball thief."

Little did *she* know.

After my scare at almost getting busted taking photos of their volunteer log, I went back to work beside Jan, and by five or so we made up the last packages. "I'm plumb worn to a frazzle, Hetta, and I have writer's cramp. We gotta go spring Po Thang, and I'm going to stretch this numb hand around a big old margarita or something."

"You've got my vote. I'll walk el dawg, if you'll mix the drinks." I looked around for Rhonda and saw her headed our way. She waved and we signaled for her to meet us at my pickup.

Once we were headed for the marina, Rhonda said, "That was so fulfilling. I've done tons of volunteering—well, we teachers are kind of volunteered whether we want to be or not—but this was great. I can't wait for Three King's Day."

"Yeah, well, I can't wait for a drink. And we still have to decide what we're doing tomorrow night. El Molokan? Stay on the boat? What?"

"Oh, I forgot to tell you. I'm going out with Cholo."

"What?" Jan and I said.

"Sorry. He sorta invited me to a homegrown celebration in the hood. I think it will broaden my horizons."

"You'd better not broaden them too far with *him*. We don't even know who he is. Who are his people?" I demanded, then added, "Oh, hell, I sound like my mother."

"Mine too," Jan said. "You go ahead and have fun. I'll stay with poor Hetta."

I bit back the retort that remark screamed for. After all, my best friend was giving up her New Year's Eve with the man she loves to be with me, so I certainly didn't want to sound like the ingrate I normally am.

Chapter Thirty-two

AFTER OUR DAY of do-gooding, the three of us dragged our exhausted, dusty, and sweaty selves back to the boat, looking forward to a hot shower and a cold drink.

I was surprised that Po Thang didn't set up a howl when he heard us coming down the dock—that dawg has better hearing than a bat—and I soon discovered why. He was nowhere to be found.

"Crap, the little turd must have escaped somehow while we were gone," I grumbled. "And I'm too damned tired to go find him."

Jan raised a shoulder. "He'll come back. It's dinnertime."

"True, that. I'll put out an AWOL call on the radio, but first I need a *Margarita Grande. Pronto*! Get to work, barkeep."

Jan said something rude and I went to my cabin to wash a layer of dust off my face and change into warmies, for a slight evening breeze over the water was cooling things down rapidly.

I took two steps into my cabin, did an about-face and rushed back into the main salon. "Okay, everybody pack up and abandon ship!" I commanded.

They both looked alarmed, and Jan asked, "What's happening? Are we takin' on water or somethin'?"

"Nope. Jenks is here! His bags are on my bed!"

Jan fixed me with a look. "Hetta Coffey, I told Chino I couldn't make it back for New Year's Eve because I didn't want to leave you alone. And now Jenks shows up and you dump me like five-day-old fish? That is just *so* wrong."

"Oh, come on. Look on the bright side. You don't have to listen to me sing Auld Lang Syne, and you still have plenty of time to beat feet to Mag Bay tomorrow and join Chino and *familia*. And Rhonda, you can just stay in La Perla Hotel until Jenks leaves. And Jan comes back."

"Who says I'm *coming* back, my not-so-steadfast friend?" Jan demanded, a look of disdain painted on her comely face.

Jan and I clown around a lot and trade insults, but her disapproval is something that really gets to me. "You know, you're right. I'm a self-centered, lousy friend and I apologize. Never mind, you two stay here. Jenks and I will move into La Perla."

Jan laughed. "Gotcha, Hetta. I was just messin' with ya. Far be it from us to disturb Hetta's love nest, right

Rhonda? Especially since she'll be springing for our hotel rooms."

I gave Jan a hug. "You're the best." She grabbed my shoulders and gently pushed me to arm's length.

"Yes, I am. Now, go do whatever you did to yourself the morning of our breakfast party, before that man of yours returns. While you make yourself beautimus, we'll pack some jammies and toothbrushes. *And*, call La Perla to book the most expensive rooms they have available."

"If they have a penthouse, book it! It's the least I can do in return for your selfless acts," I said over my shoulder as I rushed to my cabin. I had not properly unpacked since I arrived back in Mexico, and still had one suitcase full of new French wardrobe items like black silk underwear and other lacy unmentionables that I'd never even worn. Yippee!

When I emerged thirty minutes later, dressed in yet another of those colorful gauzy caftans Jan and I bought in Cannes, I felt downright glamourous. With my hair fluffed up, a little makeup applied, and that gorgeous, flowing caftan caressing my body, I made my grand entrance to the main salon, only to find it devoid of people and dogs alike. Voices drew me to the sundeck, where Jan, Po Thang, Rhonda and a beaming Jenks waited.

I rushed to plant a big smooch on Jenks at the same time Po Thang body-blocked my progress, demanding he be petted first. I shoved him aside and was reaching for Jenks when, from behind me, I heard, *"¡Caramba!* Café. You look *fantastico."*

What in the hell was Nacho doing here?

Jan and Rhonda left for the hotel after we all enjoyed one of Nacho's signature *mojitos*. He'd made himself right at home, finding everything he needed in my galley and outdoor bar. He had, after all, spent several weeks on board with me and Jan, and was our every-night bartender. If Jenks took exception to Nacho's familiarity with my boat, he didn't show it.

I, on the other hand, was more than a bit put off. "Thanks for the *mojitos*, Nacho. Now get off my boat."

He grinned and winked at Jenks. "See what I have to deal with? It is even worse when you are not here."

Jenks wisely refrained from replying.

"And yet, here you are. One might wonder why," I grumped.

"I shall soon depart. But first, the three of us have a little business to take care of."

"What business?" I wanted to know.

"The ransom bills."

I looked at Jenks, and he nodded.

"Hey, I thought you just came to spend New Year's Eve with me. You're here to work?"

Jenks reached over and gave me a tight hug. "I did come to see you. Nacho is just conveniently paying my way." His blue eyes twinkled with amusement. "They wanted to pick my brain on the marked bills; I've had a little experience in that field."

I didn't even waste my breath asking who *they* were. "Well, then, whoever *they* are, *they* just paid for a suite at

La Perla, since you obviously cannot work with Rhonda and Jan hanging around, right?"

Nacho sighed and nodded.

"And, since we seem to be working together on this, Jenks, maybe you can enlighten me. In the movies, the bank robber opens a moneybag and gets hit in the face with a red cloud that sticks to him and the loot like seagull poop. How do you discreetly mark so many twenties in the covert world?"

"Can't tell you, Red. Something new."

"Can they trace every single one of them?"

"Another secret, and way over my pay level," Jenks said. "I'm really here to take a look at one of those bills to verify a couple of things, which I've already done. Meanwhile, since you're on the snoop payroll, have you found out anything yet?"

"Yes. I took photos of the volunteer roster today, but haven't even had time to see how they turned out. You guys want to take a quick look so Nacho can go his merry way?"

"She's such a charmer," Nacho said as we moved to my office, and my new all-in-one desktop with a fabulous 24" screen. It was a Christmas gift to myself; I could now work on the computer without reading glasses.

I sent the photos from my phone, and mentally patted myself on the back when they turned out both sharp and in focus.

"Excellent work, Café," Nacho said, looking as though he was about to settle in and check out the list.

"Not so fast, *amigo*. I'll send them to you as an attachment. Three's a crowd, if you get my drift. *Feliz año nuevo, hasta la vista, y que te vaya bien*," I said, as I grabbed his arm and man-handled him onto the dock.

At the rate I throw people off my boat, I'm obviously not expecting any nominations for hostess of the year.

Jenks and I didn't get around to checking out the volunteer list until the next day. We'd spent a wonderful, quiet evening on the boat, enjoying each other's company and a meal I threw together from the freezer. We agreed that was far better than going out like the rest of the amateurs, so we planned to do the same for New Year's Eve.

Jan and Rhonda showed up around ten the next morning to gather more belongings, so our list checking was interrupted until almost noon. "Do you know any of these people?" Jenks asked me. "If we can flat out eliminate some names, that will help."

"A few boaters. I can't see them being involved in a kidnapping in France."

"It'd be a stretch. Highlight their names. You keep the master and start a whittled down group. Take it one name at a time, that way you don't get what I call suspect-hypnosis; getting overwhelmed by the sheer magnitude of possibles, and going into a trance. How many names are there, total?"

"I counted eighty-three."

"Just read their names and addresses and try to remember something about them, but don't overthink it. This is only the first round."

"Sure would help if Jan and Rhonda were in on this. They met more people than I did."

"When is the next volunteer meeting?"

"January third."

"Take photos and get names to go with them. Tell them you're making an album or something. Then send me the data."

"Okay…hey, wait a minute, what do you mean *send?*"

"Sorry, honey. I'll be winging it back to Dubai on the second. Duty calls."

"Well, crap. In that case, shut down that damned computer and let's go for a boat ride. Finding out who salted the gift packs isn't a matter of life and death."

I would later question the wisdom of that statement.

Because *Raymond Johnson* hadn't been out of the slip for almost three months, Jenks gave her an extra diligent going over while I ran out for fresh dinner and breakfast goodies. Jan had put several lobsters in the freezer, but Jenks wasn't a big fan, so I splurged on a good-sized filet mignon from the best butcher in town. They specialized in Sonoran beef, and since I knew it was a little too lean for his taste, I decided to use it for one of his favs, beef Stroganoff.

While the weather was Chamber of Commerce perfect, Jenks also went online to make sure we didn't get any nasty weather surprises along with the New Year.

We'd only be out one night, but the Sea of Cortez can be a bear when ill winds pin you against a lee shore, and the nearby anchorage we chose has ruined many a cruiser's evening.

Chapter Thirty-three

BALANDRA, ONLY ABOUT twelve miles from the marina, is one of my favorite places in the Sea of Cortez because of the incredible white sand bottom and clear turquoise water. However, we no longer knew whether we'd be allowed to anchor there, even for a few hours, as permission to do so appears to be at the whim of someone who doesn't seem to know either. You gotta love Mexico.

Our other nearby choice was at the southern tip of Espiritu Santu, which can get pretty rolly if the wind picks up. Quite naturally, when it does, it always hits around two a.m., right after any glimmer of moonlight disappears. We put out a radio call when leaving the marina and learned from a boat near there that the seas were flat calm, no bumpy stuff.

"What do you think, Hetta? Want to chance it?"

"If it was just me and der dawg, or Jan, I wouldn't do it. But, it's past noon and there is zero wind. And, with

Capitán Jenks on board? Sure. Together we can handle anything."

"Yes, we can."

"Let's hope we don't have to, at least tonight. I say we have a toast to seal our deal with Mother Nature," I said, fetching a bourbon for him and a mini-split of champagne for me.

We were rewarded with a fabulous, thankfully uneventful, and very romantic evening. Isn't it funny how, when you are with someone you love, all the hype about New Year's Eve becomes incredibly unimportant? We ate on deck in our warmies, saw a glimpse of fireworks from several locations near La Paz, and declared it officially midnight on New York time.

The euphoria of such an idyllic night began evaporating the moment my eyes opened the next morning, and I remembered Jenks would be long gone in a little over twenty-four hours.

Meanwhile, we had work to do, so we beat feet back to the marina, fired up the computers, and set up a system for vetting the volunteers. Jenks has access to all kinds of information-sorting programs—Stealth Stuff, as I call it—that I certainly don't, and neither does Nacho, because he called for Jenks's expertise. Or it could be, what with this being Mexico, Nacho doesn't trust his own resources in a country where corruption is a way of life.

I figure if he had to put me on the payroll, he must be desperate. Note to self: ask for a raise.

By the time we finished crunching data, it was cocktail hour. We'd been so absorbed with our computers I hadn't noticed that whitecaps were frothing the bay.

"Looks like we dodged a wind event bullet," I told Jenks when we went out on deck to enjoy the sunset.

"I ordered that weather yesterday, just for you."

"Wow, you must have *some* pull."

His eyes sparkled, and he gave me that crooked grin of his I love so much. "Better you don't know about my contacts in high *or* low places."

"Probably. So, Mr. Bond, what's your take on the ransom money showing up right here in La Paz? I mean, someone kidnaps a girl in France, demands three mil from her rich Mexican grandpa, he delivers it in non-sequential twenty-dollar bills as requested, we get the girl, everyone goes home, *et voilà*, some of the marked bills practically beat us back to Mexico."

Jenks shook his head. "Those odds are uncommonly high. I can run it for you if you want."

"Nah, I guess we just have to follow the money. Somehow."

"I honestly figured the Russians for the deal, but then again, everything leads back to Russians now if you believe the media. Makes me downright nostalgic for the Cold War days."

"Spy versus spy. It sure made for great movies. Refill?"

He handed me his glass. "Rocks. Not shaken or stirred, Miss Moneypenny."

"Your wish is my command."

He stood and pulled me close. "In that case," he whispered into my ear, "hold off on that drink."

Rather than sulk the rest of the day, after I dropped Jenks at the airport early on the second, I threw myself into my new job of trying to connect the ransom money to someone involved in the Christmas packages in a poor Mexican neighborhood. As I always do, I started drawing charts, beginning with a timeline.

At the top of the page, I made a box and labeled it: **Juanita snatched/disappears**. Inside the same box I added, ***Last seen boarding yacht in Cannes? By whom?***

I balled up that sheet and aimed it toward a wastepaper basket for two points, but it was intercepted by Po Thang, who proceeded to rip it into tiny pieces. Who needs a paper shredder when you have a golden retriever? I ignored the mess I'd have to clean up later and went back to the task at hand.

Starting over, I re-drew the **Juanita snatched** box to the far left of the sheet, created a right-side column next to it, and divided it in half.

Under **WHAT WE KNOW FOR SURE**, I had nothing to add, because I didn't know anything about those first few days. I did, however, make a note to myself to discuss these events with Nacho.

Below **WHAT WE *THINK* WE KNOW**, I wrote: Last seen boarding a large yacht in Cannes. Not confirmed by me. Note: who debriefed Juanita?

I left a few boxes below that entry empty, hopefully to be filled in later, so the next event was: **Team Hetta Arrives in Cannes**. Kept in dark and fed fertilizer.

I sat back and let out a scream, which scared the bejesus out of my dog. He yelped, then barked while running in circles.

Which is exactly what I was doing. I had only begun to analyze the events and was coming up with too many unknowns.

Persevering in the face of abject ignorance—something I've been accused of often—I finally arrived at the last box, denoting the day I arrived back in La Paz. That one I could fill with great authority and knowledge: I didn't bring the money from France, and if I had managed to snag it, I sure as hell wouldn't have given a bunch of it to some kids for Christmas. I was the only one I *knew* was innocent, so I started a new list of players: *anyone* who was even marginally involved in the rescue mission. The list was long, for I even included people like Prince Faoud and his yacht crew. There had to be a connection, however remote, to the volunteers we were investigating.

Staring at the over-abundance of empty boxes and question marks on my charts and lists confirmed only one thing: I didn't know squat!

I sent Nacho an email: **We need to meet. ASAP!**

Before he answered, Rhonda knocked on the hull and I quickly stashed my handiwork and invited her to join me for a glass of something on deck. My neck was stiff, my head hurt, and I realized I hadn't eaten all day, so

I grabbed some chips and salsa to ward off an alcohol overload.

After a half glass of Chardonnay while listening to Rhonda natter on and on about her *fab*ulous New Year's Eve with Cholo, my headache had worsened. So, when she suggested we go to La Perla for dinner, I readily agreed, hoping to get away from her after a quick nosh.

We'd barely been seated when, by some miracle, Cholo just happened to stroll by. Surprise, surprise.

It was plainly obvious he was just as smitten with Rhonda as he was her. I had never seen him smile so genuinely and often. I'd noticed back in Cannes that when he did smile, he was not only more handsome, he was devastatingly so.

"You know," I said after about five minutes of their billing and cooing, "I'm really not all that hungry. I think I'll go take Po Thang for a nice evening stroll and maybe pick up a fish taco. I hope you two don't mind."

Evidently, they'd both gone deaf.

When I pushed my chair back and stood, I finally got their attention.

"Hetta, did you say something?"

"Never mind. I'll see you tomorrow. Jan should be back to the boat by ten, then we have a meeting with the Three King's Day people at one.

"Oh, yes. I'd forgotten. See you in the morning."

They both protested me leaving before I'd eaten dinner, albeit half-heartedly.

I hate it when love is in the air, and so is the love of my life.

Chapter Thirty-four

PO THANG AND I shared fish tacos at my favorite stand near the marina. It was unusual for her to be open during the evening, but it was still the holiday season, and most local vendors cash in while they can. The summer months are unbearably hot, and street stands don't do well.

Also, she was providing tacos for the volunteers, so I thought I'd eradicate a duality of feathered vertebrates utilizing one stone.

My twofer paid off.

"Maria, I have a question," I said, while she deep-fried fresh-caught *cabrilla* strips in a flour and masa-based batter called capeador. She adds a dollop of mustard as her secret ingredient. The result is a puffy coating to die for, and the best fish tacos in town.

Maria doesn't speak English all that well, but she understands and answers in Spanish that is spoken slowly enough for me to understand. "*¿Si?*"

"Will you cook for us tomorrow when we meet to plan for the *niños?*"

"*Sí. Siempre.*"

Always. Okay, that's good.

"Are there new people helping this year?"

She thought about that while she scooped out the fish and folded it into a nest of two corn tortillas for each taco. Since I was the only person at her stand due to the early hour, she fried my fish one piece at a time, so they'd be fresh and hot on this chilly evening.

"*Sí, ustedes y su amigas.*"

Me and my friends? We're the only new blood?

"Only us?"

It took a while, but by the time I'd ordered, she'd cooked, and we'd eaten four tacos—two for me and two for Po Thang—she'd clarified that we were the only new *gringas.* There were a couple of Mexicans who'd volunteered for the first time.

"Do you know them?"

She shook her head.

"Can you describe them?"

One was a *rubia,* the other a *morena,* and they both looked rich. Hmmmm. The blonde should be easy to spot, but the dark-haired, dark-eyed one? Not so much. She said she would point them out to me the next day.

Jan arrived at the boat early, we got her moved back into the guest cabin, which she now had to herself; Rhonda'd called and said she was staying on at the hotel. Gee, I wonder why.

Since Nacho refused to contact me when I asked him to, I made a management decision to bring Jan into the inner circle. I needed help, and she was my comrade in arms. What's a girl to do?

After I told her the whole story, she said, "Lemme get this straight. Nacho hired *you* to ferret out who stashed some marked ransom money twenties in kids' Christmas packages?"

"Yep."

"And, you weren't supposed to tell me? Why?"

"Because you were in Mexico when the twenties started showing up. That put you in my top twenty suspects."

"Hoo-boy, that's rich. I'm on your suspect list?"

"I had to start somewhere."

"Yeah? Well here's a fresh start for ya. Take me off the list."

I ran a yellow highlighter over her name on the printout. "Done. Happy?"

"Somewhat. Now, put me on the payroll."

"I'll split what I get from Nacho with you. How's that?"

"You've got me. Keep that marker out and let's see if we can knock off a few more. Rhonda?"

I shook my head. "Not yet. She's sleeping with a suspect."

"Cholo? A suspect?"

"Under my present criteria, yes. He was in France, and then in Mexico at the same time as the money started showing up."

"Give me that list."

I handed it over and she gave it a quick once-over. "Wait a minute. Nacho's on here?"

"No one is above suspicion."

"That's rich. He hires you and you put him on the suspects' roster. I love it. Okay, Chica, let's get to work."

We massaged that list until a quarter to one, and managed to eliminate ten more names before driving down to the park for the meeting.

We got an unexpected break on arrival; everyone was wearing name tags and to make things even better, the tags included nationalities. We filled ours out, quite naturally identifying ourselves as Texans. We worked the crowd, using my previous story of putting together an album as an excuse to snap photos of everyone we could.

Typical of Mexican timeframes, the organizers finally got everyone assembled and seated by one forty-five. Jan scanned the crowd for blondes, while I parked myself near Maria's taco stand and asked her about various volunteers. She gave me the scoop on everyone she knew, and I sent text messages to myself as I cleared them as suspects.

Since the attendees outnumbered my volunteer list by almost double, we had our work cut out for us when we returned to the boat.

With not a peep out of Nacho, we did what we could, using the info we already had. Luckily Rhonda went off with Cholo somewhere for the afternoon, so we were uninterrupted. After about three hours, Jan stretched and said, "This is crap. We gotta think outside the box. Throw what we *presume* to know out."

"As in?"

"I dunno. How about, there wasn't any money in those bundles we gave the kidnappers? Ever think about that?"

"Nope."

"So consider this. Since we never actually saw the cash, what if there wasn't any in those bundles you lowered off Odyssey?"

"Wow. Let's say the kidnappers cut into one of those bundles and found newspaper or something. That would explain why they came after us once we got Juanita on board and made a run for Cannes. Jan, you are a freakin' genius! The fact that they came after us after the exchange has been bugging me. Okay, so I *did* try to swamp them, but that's because I was afraid they'd do us in once they had the cash. What if there *was* no cash in those bundles?"

"Or never left Mexico?"

"Nah, Nacho said the bills were marked by his people en route from Mexico to Cannes."

Jan snorted. "And Nacho, of course, is the poster boy of fine, upstanding citizens."

"That bastard! I'm calling Jenks, right now."

"Not so fast. We need to analyze this turn of events before we jump to conclusions. Wine!"

We moved to the aft deck with a bottle of red, my charts, the volunteer list, and my sketched-out timeline.

Everything but the wine was useless if our newly hatched suspicions about Nacho proved true.

Playing the devil's advocate, I said, "On the other hand, Nacho hired me and Jenks to investigate how some of the money showed up in Mexico. He ain't no Eagle Scout, but he isn't stupid, either. There's no way he'd let that kind of evidence get loose here in La Paz."

"Hmmm. I guess you're right, And, honestly, I don't think Nacho would try to double cross Jenks. Us? Yes. Jenks? He'd have to be a complete imbecile to cross Jenks."

Jan was right about that. I had a feeling the man I loved would make a very dangerous enemy, and surely Nacho knew that. "So then, if Nacho didn't take the loot, who did?"

"Someone with ties to La Paz."

"And besides you, me, and Rhonda, only three others were in Cannes and now here: Cholo, Roberto, and Sascha. We don't even know who Cholo really is, but, I don't think he's our guy."

"Well, then, that's that. He can't possibly be guilty, because Hetta Coffey, that megastar of sagaciousness, says so?"

"Smarty pants. My money, or rather El Jefe's money, is on Roberto and Sascha."

"Bad as I hate to admit it, I think you may be right. But how? Crime of opportunity? They went to meet Grandpa's plane. The money was right there, on the plane, they had the time, and no one was looking?"

"So, maybe the money never left the plane? All they had to do was stuff it in their suitcases and wait for the others to return with Juanita. That was taking quite a chance on their cousin's life, don't you think?"

"Yes, I do. But…oh, hell, Hetta, I just remembered something. Something I didn't think important at the time. When I followed Roberto, like you told me to the day we had everyone over for brunch, he didn't go to work. He made a beeline for those condos," she pointed to a tallish building, "over there. He let himself through the security gate with a key, so I couldn't follow, but I watched him go up three floors and enter a unit with a key. I figured he'd just gone home on his way to work, but now we know where he lives."

"Good to know, in case we need to toss the joint. I say let's head for El Molokan right now, and then if necessary, raid the thief's lair when we're sure he's at work."

"Alleged thief."

Chapter Thirty-five

JAN, PO THANG, and I set off for dinner and fact-snoopery at El Molokan. As I hoped, Roberto was busy in the kitchen and his parents were acting as hosts. We were ushered to the patio because of Po Thang, and found ourselves on our own because of a chill in the air.

Roberto's dad brought a propane heater outside, and his mother sat with us while we enjoyed the house special, watermelon Margaritas. Oddly enough, the Mexican drink was made with Midori, a Japanese sweet musk-melon liqueur, then mixed with real watermelon juice, lime and tequila.

"¡*Fabuloso!*" I told our hostess. She beamed and told me it was her idea after making a trip to Tokyo.

"Do you travel that often?" Jan asked.

"Oh, we did at one time. But now? It is difficult to get away for more than a few days, and since our house is right there," she pointed toward the hill above the restaurant, "we have no peace."

Pay dirt! "Oh, my. It really is a shame that Roberto isn't going to stay in La Paz, now that he is leaving the military. Especially since he lives so near to your home now."

"We will miss him. However, we will keep his room ready, just in case he changes his mind."

Jan pounced. "He lives with you?"

"Of course. He is a single man, where else would he live?"

I suppressed a smile and didn't dare look at Jan.

We called Rhonda and arranged to have dessert and coffee with her at La Perla on the way home.

Jan didn't waste any time. "Rhonda, I've been thinking. I know you're considering buying a yacht, but meanwhile, why don't we look at condos down here? You have the money, and it may take a while before you get that boat."

"What a great idea. Where?"

My turn. "Well, if I could afford it, I'd get one in a building near the marina. Great views, great location. Someone told me the ones right next door are fairly cheap and come fully furnished."

"How cheap?"

"I think you could find one for around two-hundred grand."

"Really? How do I get in to see one?"

Jan finished her coffee. "I'll handle it. I'm sure someone'll be available tomorrow."

"Super. God, I love my new life."

Our real estate agent turned out to be a woman I'd met while playing Mexican Train. We had coffee in the area in front of the condos and asked questions while looking at listings.

"How about rentals? Can I rent it out when I'm not here?" Rhonda asked.

"Yes, but only long-term. The residents don't want weekend partiers."

I knew how to translate that: no Mexicans. It is no secret that in Mexico, no one wants to rent to Mexicans, because they bring in too many people and leave the place a wreck. During spring break and *Semana Santa*—Easter Week—many Mexicans close their restaurants, and marinas shut down their launch ramps.

"How about security?" I asked.

"Oh, it is very good. You have to have a key to gain entry into the area, and there is a night guard."

Jan sucked in her cheeks. We'd seen many of those guys snoozing away in the wee hours. "Are the condos alarmed?"

"Not that I know of, but these days it's easy enough to put in a system. Are you ready to have a look?"

"Yes, but I think Rhonda would prefer to be on the end. It's quieter there." Jan gave a Vanna White arm wave at the bars and restaurants where we were sitting.

"Then that's where we'll start."

"I cannot believe Rhonda bought a condo! All I wanted to do was check out the building and security system."

"Maybe she's making a love nest, Hetta."

"Probably. I gotta admit, the condo has a great view and cool furniture. And on top of that, she can move right in. The owner said, since she wrote a check for the full amount, there was no reason not to."

Jan looked at my ship's clock as it dinged. "You ready to roll?"

"Yep, and we need to get going. Roberto will be leaving El Molokan in an hour, and he just might make tracks for his secret bachelor digs."

"Shall we take the balaclavas?"

"Nah, we just gotta look like gringas."

Getting into the building wasn't what we expected. We brought our lock pick set, but as it turned out, someone left the gate unlocked and we were inside and up the stairs to the third floor in a flash. We'd already scoped out the unit Jan saw Roberto enter with a key. A credit card slipped the lock like a hot knife through butter.

"We're in," Jan whispered.

"Let's make it fast. Look for anything incriminating."

"Okay. One. Two, Three."

We rushed inside to find all the lights on and a white-faced Sascha wielding a huge kitchen knife.

"That incriminating enough for ya, Hetta?"

The three of us were sitting in the living room when Roberto came home. He took one look at Sascha's tearstained cheeks and stopped short.

"Sascha? What's wrong?"

"They know, Roberto. They know we took some money from the plane."

He looked confused. "The plane?"

Jan growled, "Yep, you're busted."

He sank into a chair and put his head in his hands. Sascha rushed over and threw her arms around him. "Hetta saw us kissing at the Christmas fair. And then someone told them they saw me slipping money into the children's Christmas packages, so they put it all together, since we were the only ones alone on the plane with the money."

Jan and I, when we made the accusation, had to tweak the story some to cover the fact that the bills were marked, but Sascha folded like a cheap lawn chair once she realized we had her dead to rights.

He looked bewildered. "You told them we took money from Grandfather's plane?"

"Yes, *mi corazón*. Our fate is now in their hands."

"What will you do?" he asked me.

"I should slap you. By shorting the kidnappers, you almost got me, Jan, and your cousin, Juanita, killed."

"We are sorry," Sascha said. "We never considered the danger. When everyone left us alone on the plane with all that money, we just...."

"Stole some. How much did you get?"

Roberto was still scared speechless, so Sascha told us, "Only half of one bundle. That's all we could take in such a short time."

"That's a hundred-and-twenty-thousand dollars!" Jan said. "How did you get it home to Mexico?

"Like I said, in our suitcases. We used our clothes to refill the bundle."

Roberto, whose eyes had been glued to Sascha, finally found his voice. "What now? Will you turn us over to the police?"

Jan and I had this discussion when we figured out who we thought took the money. We exchanged a look and Jan nodded at me to take the question, but I had my own question. "What are you going to do with all that money?"

"We agreed to anonymously give some of it to charity, and use the rest to open our own restaurant in Puerto Vallarta. Roberto and I cannot remain here together. Our families are what you call old school Catholics and they will scorn us. My mother will be devastated, and my grandfather...."

"...will disown you?"

Surprisingly, both Sascha and Roberto broke out laughing.

"What's so funny?" Jan asked.

"He already has. Our grandfather has made it clear he is leaving nothing to the family. Any of us. He is a self-made man and believes family money is the key to failure. Each of us have a copy of his will, just to make sure we all know this. So, he has already disowned us. I am worried he will shun my parents, and that will be very painful for them."

"So, you are in the shadows. How long have you, uh, been together?" Call me nosy, but I wanted to know. Had they pulled a fast one on both me and Jan? If so, they should be headed for Hollywood, not Puerto Vallarta.

Roberto gazed adoringly at Sascha. "I, for one, have loved Sascha since we were teens. It was only a year ago that she let me know she felt the same way."

"Yes, that is true. I lived in Mexico City, and he here in the Baja, so we only saw each other at our yearly family reunions."

"January the fourteenth?" I blurted, drawing a frown from Jan.

"How did you know that?" Sascha asked.

Jan stepped in for the save. "I'm pretty sure Roberto's mom mentioned it. Something about the Russian New Year, right Hetta?"

Roberto looked at the ceiling. "God save us from my mother's mouth."

"I find her openness charming," I protested.

"That kind of charm can get you killed in Mexico," Sascha said. Then she realized how that sounded and added, "Sorry. In Mexico City one does not dare share information about family. It is too dangerous."

"You mean it could lead to something like kidnapping?" I asked.

Jan sighed. "God save us from Hetta's mouth."

After assuring the couple that we had no intention of turning them into the police, we left before I could step into it again.

"You did that on purpose, didn't you?" Jan asked as we walked back to the boat.

"*Moi?*"

"Yes, you. You want them to think we're a couple of stumble bumbles, not seasoned snoops. You did an excellent job, by the way. And that thing about how you promised not to turn them over to the police? Brilliant."

"It was the truth."

"But, you *are* going to tell Nacho, right?"

"I'm not so sure. What can *he* do? Tell Grandpa Juan? And then what? I kinda feel sorry for Roberto and Sascha. She can't even leave the condo here for fear she'll be seen, although she admitted she did sneak out and stuff twenties into the kid's Christmas packages."

"I could tell by Roberto's reaction he didn't know about her little philanthropic field trips. Anyhow, with all the money they have left they can move to Puerto Vallarta and start a new life together. They'll live happily ever after, unless Nacho traces those twenties flying out of their love nest."

"Gee, Hetta Coffey, you are such a sappy romantic."

"I have my moments."

After much back and forth, Jan and I decided not to tell Nacho I found our mysterious donor. "He'll find the kidnappers eventually. The rest of the bills will start showing up somewhere and get tracked back to the culprits. Hopefully that will happen before Sascha and Roberto use their money in PV. I say we stay out of it."

"So unlike you Hetta, but I agree. Maybe we should have warned the star-crossed lovers their money is marked."

"Not my problem. My conscience is clear."

"You don't have one."

"I rest my case."

Chapter Thirty-six

JAN WENT BACK to the whale camp, Rhonda moved into her new condo, and Po Thang and I settled back in on *Raymond Johnson*.

I unearthed the list of boat jobs left to do. I swear someone sneaked on board while I was gone and added items.

After spending an entire morning cleaning out the aft lazarette, I made a trip to the dumpster with moldy stuff that had accumulated there for the past two years. "Po Thang, did you hide this in there?" I asked, picking up a life jacket and shaking it at him. The stuffing was oozing out through what suspiciously resembled fang marks.

As he does when I use that tone of voice, he looked guilty. I figured this was a ploy; if you always look guilty, humans can't tell if you are or not.

"Never mind, let's get this stuff into the dumpster and we'll take a walk." The W word set his tail on spin cycle, and he raced for his leash.

I overloaded a dock cart and was struggling to push it up the ramp when my phone rang in my pocket. Ignoring it, I made it to the gate and was jockeying to open it without dumping the load of junk when Nacho materialized next to me.

Dropping everything, including Po Thang's leash and my grip on the dock cart handle, I caused several things to happen at once. The cart wheel ran over Nacho's foot, and my dog took off after another dog, a resident stray.

The cart tipped over, scattering crap all over the ramp, and into the water. Nacho cursed in two languages, Po Thang howled as the stray lunged for him, and several boaters rushed up to see what all the commotion was about.

"Nacho, dammit, you scared me."

"I scared you? You have broken my foot!"

"Good," I yelled over my shoulder as I went to Po Thang's rescue. By the time I got there, he and the stray were playing. I grabbed his leash and yanked him back to the mess I'd left.

The boaters, once I told them I was headed for the dumpster, were picking through the debris for useful items, and Nacho had limped to a bench overlooking the marina.

"What the hell do you want, Nacho?"

"A report. You have had two weeks, and I have heard nothing."

"So sue me. I ain't got nothing for you. Nada. The volunteers on my list are all clean." That was the truth.

"I suppose you still expect to be paid?"

"Yes. I did the work. It's not my fault I was operating in a vacuum. You haven't returned a single one of my calls or emails."

"What did you want?"

"I had some questions, but they aren't important, now. And by the way, I quit."

"Fine." He reached into his pocket and handed me an envelope. "Here is the money I promised."

I took it and turned to walk away, then stopped dead in my tracks and did a one-eighty. "Not so fast, *Ignacio*. That was way too easy. What are you up to, and where have you been?"

"None of your business. But I do have a piece of information you might be interested in."

Curiosity killed the *gato*.

"Buy me a beer."

"So, you're telling me the big tomato is offering a fifty-grand reward for information leading to the kidnappers?"

"Yes."

"I noticed your careful wording. Nothing like, 'for information leading to the *arrest* of the kidnappers' stuff. I'm assuming grandpa is majorly pissed and wants a piece of them."

"That's my guess."

"You're not mad that I didn't track down whoever was spreading marked bills around here?"

"So few showed up. Less than two hundred of them, each one spent in small stores by children or their parents and then eventually deposited in local banks by merchants. Some might be still floating around, but no activity lately."

Good. Roberto and Sascha are playing it cool.

On one hand, I wanted them to get that restaurant and new life in Puerto Vallarta, but once that money started showing up in PV, it was only a matter of time until their grandfather's investigators put two and two together. I'd like to be a fly on the wall when he found out his grandson and grandniece had pulled a fast one on him.

"Why are you telling me this?"

"You have time on your hands and inside information to work with, so why not? We all know how you like money."

"I'll think about it. I'm sick of this case."

"You have forgotten the kidnappers tried to kill you?"

"No. Is that what's got grandpa's knickers in a twist? That the jerks came after his granddaughter after he'd held up his end of the bargain and paid the ransom?"

"Perhaps. And there was the ear thing."

"What's in it for you if I solve the case?"

He grabbed his heart. "You wound me, Café. My motives are pure. I only want justice for that poor girl."

"Yeah, right."

Nacho talked me into staying for dinner, and afterward I took Po Thang for a short walk and then returned to my boat.

My empty boat.

I watched a movie to kill time, but it was still too early to go to bed.

Moving out on the aft deck, I had a drink.

Still restless, I cleaned out the fridge, tossing away leftovers way past their expiration date, even for my four-footed garbage disposal unit.

That task finished, I figured I'd earned a glass of wine.

Back out on the aft deck, I made it two.

Checking the clock, I decided it was permissable to go to bed and read.

On the way to my cabin, I stopped at my desk to read my email and Facebook. After sharing a post or two of cute puppies, I shut down the computer and stood to grab my Kindle when I knocked over a fat folder marked, "Juanita."

Picking up my charts, timelines, and printouts, I was drawn, like a moth to the flame, right back into the details.

Oh, okay, that fifty grand reward had something to do with it.

It was two a.m. when I said to Po Thang, "Take a look at this." I pointed to the picture of Juanita's torn ear that I'd magnified. "What do you see?"

He opened one eye, saw there was no food involved, and went back to sleep.

"Useless hound. It's times like this when I really miss Jan."

Knowing full well Jan wouldn't answer her phone at that time of night, I settled back to continue reviewing everything I had on Juanita's kidnapping. As Jan and I realized during our earlier searches, there were so many details we *didn't* know.

Zooming out from the bloody earring photo that accompanied the ransom note, something caught my attention I'd never noticed before. We'd hacked Nacho's computer, so we had the email attachment with what was probably a cellphone photo of the original email. Not the best situation, but having my new large screen helped.

Little by little, I zeroed in on the area around the earring, and I realized what we had assumed was a smear or shadow on the plate wasn't.

It was mid-morning in Cannes, so I picked up the phone and made a call, then paced until I received a reply. After I hung up, I did a little victory jig, turned on the stereo system, selected "I'm So Excited" by the Pointer Sisters, and danced around the cabin.

Finally roused from his beauty rest by my antics, Po Thang quickly threw off the bonds of Morpheus and joined me in my dance routine.

After thirty minutes of boogie-woogie, celebrating, and then downing a split of champagne direct from the bottle, I dropped onto the settee, where Po Thang joined me, even though he was normally banned from couches. I cuddled up to him, whispered, "We're in the money, honey," and fell into a self-satisfied sleep.

Chapter Thirty-seven

MY DREAM OF getting that fifty-thousand into my bank account took a dive right after I woke up and reality set in. I was a loooong way from cashing in on my suspicions. Now I was pretty sure I knew *who* was involved in Juanita's kidnapping, but there were major holes in my theory. As in, about a million unanswered questions.

Which called for brain food: breakfast enchiladas, refrieds, and tortillas.

While Po Thang and I waited for our breakfast at the Dock Café, I called Rhonda to make certain she was home, and alone, before I visited her at the condo. I wasn't positive she and Cholo were, as they say in Texas, shacking up, but I still didn't feel comfortable sharing any information with her that might get back to Team Nacho regarding my investigation into Juanita's kidnapping. Especially now that I was hot on the trail to fifty large.

While Rhonda fetched me a cup of coffee from her kitchen, I surveyed the place for signs of Cholo, but nothing was obvious, so I took the direct approach.

"So, Rhonda, how's it going with you and Cholo?"

She lit up. "He's just the most amazing person, isn't he?"

"Yes, I guess so. For such a *young* man."

If she took that as a dig, she didn't show it. "He's not as young as he looks, you know. I think. We haven't discussed it, but he did mention he can retire with full pay in ten years."

"Full pay here can't be that much, but he can get another job and be pretty well set. Well, for Mexico."

Note to self: Check retirement requirement in the Mexican Military. Is Rhonda now part of his retirement plans?

I decided to get to why I was really paying her this visit. "So, have you seen Roberto or Sascha lately?" She now knew that the kissin' cousins shared a little love nest in her building, but since she was distracted by Cholo, she didn't seem to mind much.

"I've spotted her twice. She wears a wig, scarf and oversized sunglasses when she leaves the building, and Roberto actually stopped by here one morning to say hello, but I think he was really feeling me out to see if I was going to rat on him and Sascha."

"Who to?"

"Cholo?"

"It's only a matter of time until those two run into each other here, right?"

"I don't see Cholo all that often, and it's usually during working hours for Roberto.

"And Sascha? When does she leave?"

"The two times I've seen her, it was around noonish, I think. Why?"

"Just being nosy."

We talked about how the sale of her mom's house was going, furniture she was shopping for, and an impending visit she planned with Jan and Chino at the whale camp. She'd put her boat search on a back burner.

I glanced at her clock and saw it was just before noon, so I left and snagged a table at a small café on the quay in front of the condos. From there I had a good view of the entry gate.

Unfortunately, I didn't have time to take Po Thang to the boat, so when I saw the bewigged Sascha leave, I couldn't take a chance on following her.

The next day, however, I was back at that same table, without Agent Dawg, to engage in a little stalking. I picked my spot carefully, because the day before I noticed she scanned around her before she took off at a fast clip.

I was finishing my coffee when, through the plant I was seated behind, I watched as Roberto came out through the condo gate and headed towards town, and most likely El Molokan. Ten minutes later, Sascha, disguised like the day before, also left.

Luckily the malecon is a busy place between twelve and two, so I was able to lag a block and a half behind her with no danger of being spotted. Once the shops shut down at two for their two-hour siesta, that hustle and bustle along the waterfront walkway comes to a halt.

Unfortunately, Sascha veered off the malecon and started taking small side streets, winding her way toward the center of town, so I had to catch up or lose sight of her.

When she took a sharp right through a gate and turned to close it behind her, I ducked behind a delivery truck. After I heard the gate clang shut, I dared to sneak a peek. I was debating whether to hang around or return to the boat when a window opened on the second floor, Juanita leaned out, Sascha threw her a kiss, and I heard a buzzer.

What was Juanita doing in La Paz? I could have sworn Nacho mentioned she'd gone to the States as soon as they returned from Cannes. Curiouser and curiouser.

On the way back to the boat, I turned over in my mind what I knew for certain versus what I *thought* I knew and realized I needed help.

I called my *numero uno* sounding board.

"What's the haps?" Jan asked when she answered her phone.

"Can you come back down here? We need to put our heads together, and just maybe figure something important out."

"No can do. Too busy up here. Whales everywhere."

"Big bucks can be had."

"I'll be there tomorrow."

Since Jan was coming, I changed the linens and cleaned up her room, then dropped off laundry at the wash, dry, and fold service at the marina, and by then it was time for a sandwich and an early bed in anticipation of some serious snoopery.

I rose early, took Po Thang for his walk, then decided to make a grocery run for goodies. I knew she was probably already fed up with fish at the camp, so I got steaks, hamburger, and the makings for chicken Alfredo.

After unloading the dock cart onto the deck, I climbed aboard, slid the door open and braced myself for a furry onrush, but Po Thang wasn't in the main cabin.

"Hey, you bum, wake up! I bought you some chicken."

I heard him whine and my heart stuttered. Thinking he'd hurt himself somehow, I followed the noise to my master cabin. The door was open, but I didn't see him until I stepped down into the room.

He wasn't alone.

Roberto held his leash, and Sascha and Juanita stood on either side of him.

"Hey, everyone. Family reunion?"

"Very funny," Sascha said. "Get this boat ready to leave. And don't do anything stupid." She waved a huge kitchen knife in Po Thang's direction, and he, thinking it a game, lunged for it. Roberto, thank goodness, jerked him back.

"Sascha, be careful!" he scolded in Spanish, then looked sheepish and added, in English. "I mean, if you kill him, she won't do what we say. He is our insurance, right Hetta?"

Sascha looked as though she was going to light into Roberto for criticizing her, then shrugged. "Yes, I guess we do need him. For now. Hetta, do what we say or I start removing his body parts. Understand?"

"Yes. Where do you want to go in my boat? I didn't fill my fuel tanks before I left for France. I'm low on diesel," I lied.

Sascha looked at Roberto and asked if that was a problem. He said he wasn't certain. All three of them started arguing at once. Their Spanish was so rapid I really couldn't figure out what they were saying, but certain words jumped out: *cuerpo* (body), *ancla* (anchor), *pinche pendejo* (effing a-hole). I had to agree with the last one, because they attached it to Nacho.

My translation: We have to sink the bodies unless we want Nacho on our tails.

Juanita called the bickering to a halt by asking me a question. "We'll discuss this matter soon, but first I want to know how Hetta figured out the kidnapping was a hoax." They all turned to look at me.

"I didn't."

"What? Then why did you follow Sascha to my apartment?"

"Your grandfather has offered a large reward to anyone who can identify the kidnappers, and I only knew that Sascha was somehow involved."

"How did you *know* that?" Juanita demanded. For a teenager she had all the makings of a first-class bitch.

"The photo with that bloody earring on a white plate. It was barely visible, but when I enhanced the picture I noticed a design on the china and recognized it as the corner of the hotel owner's family crest."

"You know the owner?"

"Yes. The Baronnesse de Montesquieu is a close friend." My pants were warming up, threatening to burst into flame, but I was stalling on my feet, maybe getting them riled with each other so I could take advantage of the diversion.

It was working; Juanita glared at Sascha. "Very careless, cousin."

I threw more fuel on the kindling. "The baronnesse checked out a few things for me and guess what? The house doctor had treated a young lady for an injured ear, which she told him got caught in her hairbrush. He referred her to a plastic surgeon, but in the meanwhile he placed a couple of stitches. If you look closely at that photo, you can see a stitch. Which one of you geniuses came up with the Getty kidnapping angle?"

Both Juanita and Sascha shot disapproving glances at Roberto.

Boy, how would I love to play high-stakes poker with these three.

"You do know that, so far, you have not committed a crime, right? If I were you I'd just take the money and run."

"If *you* figured out what we did, someone else might."

"But they didn't. I did. And since I wanted that fifty grand for myself, I didn't tell anyone. And, how about this? You give me the fifty and I'll keep this among ourselves. No harm, no foul and no one the wiser."

"Or, we can just tie you and your mutt to an anchor and dump you in with the sharks," Sascha said with a sneer.

"Did anyone ever tell you that you resemble Vladimir Putin?"

Sascha lashed out so fast she took me by surprise. Her slap was more like a punch that landed on the side of my head, knocking me onto my bed.

Po Thang went nuts.

Lunging again, this time he escaped Roberto's grasp and went airborne, landing a four-paw plant onto Sascha's shoulders and back, knocking her on top of me. I appreciated the gesture, but as she fell, I couldn't help but notice that gargantuan knife coming at me.

Thanks a lot, dawg.

But, like I always say, it's the thought that counts.

Chapter Thirty-eight

TIME SLOWED.

I watched in horror as that butcher knife arced downward, right for my forehead.

At the last second, I managed to move my head, and Sascha buried the knife deep into my eight-hundred-dollar mattress. Rather than relief, I felt red-hot anger: there was no way I could replace that mattress in Mexico!

She gave up trying to pull the knife out of the foam, and opted to push herself up with the other hand, using my stomach for leverage. For once, I was thankful for my lifelong antipathy for sit-ups, Pilates, and planks. Her hand sank into my jelly-belly, and she rolled sideways onto the bed, landing face up. I heard a loud thunk as her head connected with the corner of my teak built-in bedside table.

Sascha went limp., I scrambled to my knees and grabbed the knife by its hilt with both hands, but was unable to dislodge it. Where is King Arthur when you really need him?

Juanita, seeing what I was up to, latched onto one of my wrists and twisted that arm, grabbing the knife's hilt in the process. We were arm wrestling when Po Thang, not sure what to think of all this commotion, opted to chomp down on Juanita's ankle. She screamed and let go of the knife, but Roberto moved in.

He had better luck, and had just pulled it free when Juanita, for some reason, gave him a karate chop to the back of his neck, took the knife from his limp hand, and said, "That's enough of this crap. Hetta, if that dog makes another move toward me, I'll bury this thing in his eye, you hear me?"

I took hold of Po Thang's tail and gave it a hard yank. He turned and looked at me like, well, like someone had just killed the pet dog.

"Sit and stay!" I commanded.

Roberto was still out, but Sascha was moaning and calling for Juanita. Juanita moved to her, leaned over, said, "It is alright, my love, I have them under control," and planted a passionate kiss on her lips.

Whoa! I sure hadn't seen that one coming.

While Juanita guarded me and Po Thang, Sascha threw water in her face, dabbed at the bloody bump, then went topsides and returned with a twenty-foot length of line I keep on deck. "Will this do?"

"I think so. Tie up Roberto while he's still out, *corozan*, then let Hetta lash that damned mutt to him."

"Call me clairvoyant, but am I picking up on a double-cross here, ladies?" I asked.

"Shut up, you *pinche puta.*"

"Hey, I've never charged for sex in my life!"

"What part of shut up don't you get?" Juanita spat.

"The part that says, 'Hey, Hetta, why should you take these two Lizzies out to sea so they can dump your ass overboard?'"

That seemed to stump them for a moment. They shared a stare, then Sascha asked, "Lizzies?"

"All girl street gang…before your time."

Keep 'em talking, Hetta.

Roberto moaned and moved. "Get him tied up, fast," Juanita ordered.

"So, how long have you two been planning this little charade? Or maybe I should ask, how long have you love birds been pulling an end run on poor Roberto?"

"None of your stinking business," Juanita said as she watched Sascha tie Roberto up.

Grannie knots?

Just as Sascha tied the last bow and stepped away from him, his eyes popped open. "Wha…what happened?"

"Your so-called girlfriend karate chopped you. I guess *her* girlfriend and she have no further use for you. By the way, girls, where's the money?"

"*¡Cállate!*"

"Yeah, yeah, I know, you keep telling me to shut up, but I am not starting *Raymond Johnson* until two things happen. You tell me where the money is, and you let my dog off the boat."

Juanita motioned for Sascha to attack.

"Tsk, tsk, Sascha. You knife me, boat don't leave. You guys have a backup plan?"

Juanita's eyes narrowed. "We might tell you where the money is because you won't be around to spend it. The dog? You start the boat, and we'll see."

"Sounds reasonable to me. You do know I have to leave this bedroom in order to do so, right?"

"Of course I do. You think I'm stupid?"

I sure hope so.

"Let's go. Hey, Roberto, did you know that Sascha and Juanita are kissin' cousins? In my country, that makes Sascha a child molester."

Juanita shoved me up the steps. "For the record, I was the one who seduced her. Now, move."

I walked through the main salon and moved toward the stairs to the aft sun deck and flying bridge. "Stop right there! Where are you going?"

"Topsides to start the engines. I can't light them off from down here," I fibbed.

"Okay, then, but no tricks." She raised her voice. "Sascha, if you hear anything at all out of place, kill that dog."

"I will," Sascha yelled back, but her voice held no resolve.

Yippee! Of all the half-Russian lesbian nannies in the world, I get one who might be a dog lover? With any luck at all, Po Thang was doing his best hang-dawg eye-beg right about now.

At the steering station, I removed the canvas cover, then sat down in the captain's chair, made sure both throttles were pushed all the way forward and the gears all the way back. I hit the START button on the port engine, and nothing happened.

"Juanita, I think my battery bank is dead. I haven't started the engines in quite a while, you know." *Except for going out to Espiritu Santu a few days back, but who's counting?*

"I don't believe you. I said no tricks or the dog dies."

"Get real. Do you think I'd do something that would get my dog stabbed?"

"I think you're a stone bitch and I'm going to count to ten. If those engines don't start, I'll tell Sascha to finish off your dog *and* Roberto, you hear me? One. Two."

"Wait! Wait! I see the problem. The ignition switches are turned off. Hang on a minute, I'll have her going real fast."

"Amazing how that happened," she said, sarcasm dripping from her red-lips like blood after a vampire kill. *How does an eighteen-year-old get so cynical. Oh, wait, she lives in Hollywood. Probably a Twilight fan?*

"Can I just ask one question first?"

"Oh, for God's sake. What?"

"Why Roberto? I thought he was your favorite cousin. And Sascha? I saw them sucking face in an alleyway a few days ago. You just looking to make your little *ménage à trois* into a twosome?"

"I guess you aren't as smart as Nacho says you are. Yes, Roberto was useful. We needed him."

"And now you don't."

"Start this damned thing."

"Your wish is my command." I hit the BOTH ENGINES START button, something I never do, and Juanita was about to find out why.

Raymond Johnson's big diesels roared and when those props bit in, my boat, had it not been still tied to the dock, would have shot backwards across the waterway, smashing into a boat docked there. As it was, I heard what sounded like a gunshot, the boat slewed to one side, and I figured I'd yanked at least one cleat from the dock, but the other bow line and the aft lines, although groaning loudly, seemed to hold.

I was hanging onto the steering wheel, the only reason I didn't go flying myself. As it was, my arms were almost pulled from their sockets.

Juanita had much more to worry about.

When the forward cleat, still tied to my high tensile dock line went airborne, I saw it coming and ducked. It barely cleared my seatback and nailed Juanita. Even over all the noise I heard her scream and then drop like a rock.

Killing the engines while in gear and full throttle made an ominous sound that I figured was going to cost me a fortune in parts one day soon.

I glanced at Juanita, whose face was a bloody mess, but she wasn't my problem at the moment. The boat was still tossing in the slip, but I'd been on her long enough to weather just about any storm, so I bounced off railings and furniture and made my way below, making a quick stop at my desk.

Rushing down the steps to my cabin, I found Sascha, Roberto and Po Thang in a pile, thrown against the aft bulkhead. Po Thang was howling in fear, Roberto was out cold, and Sascha, just as I reached out, got her bearings and slashed out with that damned knife.

I had to get her away from my dog and Roberto before she stabbed one of them. "Sascha, put down the knife and listen to me. So far you haven't done anything wrong. All you guys have to do is give back the money, and you are home free."

"That's easy for you to say," she snarled. "You have your big boat and your rich boyfriend. Juanita and I have nothing. The family will disown us both for being lesbians, and we cannot make any decent livings here in Mexico. We will live like peasants."

"What do you want me to do?" I asked.

"Where is Juanita?"

"She's nursing a headache. Even if she survives, I don't think she'll want to."

"What do you mean?"

"Her face. It's sort of split in half. Go see for yourself." Then, because lying for a cause is justified, I added, "She's asking for you."

Sascha looked undecided for a second, then raised the knife high over her head with both hands. "Screw her *and* you."

"Stop!" I yelled.

She didn't.

When seconds count, the cops are only minutes away.

As her arms arced down with the knife point slashing toward my dog's head, I raised my Taurus .380 semi-automatic and shot six rounds at her fists and the knife. I saved one in the chamber for good measure, on the off chance she somehow was counting shots and stupidly thought I was done. However, thanks to my laser, I managed to do enough damage to deflect her aim and make her drop the knife harmlessly onto the bed. As I lit up her temple with my beam, she got lucky and fell over on her side, cradling her arms.

Chapter Thirty-nine

SASCHA REPEATEDLY SCREAMED at the top of her lungs, Po Thang's howl increased a couple of decibels, Roberto's eyes flew open, and I pocketed the gun.

I pushed Sascha out of the way, grabbed the knife, and quickly cut Po Thang free of Roberto. Po Thang took off like a shot, up the stairs and off the boat. He'd done the same thing when someone set off fireworks nearby one night.

I let him go and checked to make sure no blood was spurting from Sascha's arms. Satisfied I hadn't hit an artery, I pushed her into the head, and slammed the door. Roberto managed to sit up and realized he was bound with ropes. "What about me?"

"Jury's still out on you, Chef. I have to go check on Juanita. Scoot over and lean up against that door. I don't want Sascha to get out, and believe me, neither do you."

Evidently he remembered enough about the situation to say, "I must agree." Inching over, he leaned his back against the door and dug his heels into the carpet.

"Good boy. If you cooperate, we'll try to figure out how to get you out of this mess. I promise."

"Thank you. I fear I have been played for a fool."

I couldn't argue with that.

Juanita already had help, as people were all over the dock and boat, alerted to trouble by the brouhaha. One boater was feeling Juanita's pulse while another wrapped a towel around her ruined face. I heard a siren close by so didn't bother calling 9-1-1. That girl was going to be looking for a really good plastic surgeon in the near future, if she lived.

I turned to go find Po Thang when I heard him bark and spotted him and Jan on the dock. "Well, good gawd a mighty, Hetta, what on earth have you gone and done now?" my friend asked. She let go of Po Thang's collar and we ran to each other, meeting in the main salon.

I hugged him, felt wet, matted fur, and when I pulled my hands away, they were covered with blood. Lots of it. I let loose with a string of expletives and started looking for wounds, but Jan, now by my side, said, "It's not his. I already checked. But you? You look like you just got dragged down a dirt road behind an ornery horse."

Looking down at my hands and clothes, I saw I was pretty bloodied up myself, but so far as I knew, none of it was mine, either. Jan handed me a roll of paper towels. "Get into my cabin, change clothes, and wipe that blood spatter off your face and arms before the cops get here. Whose blood is all this?"

"Mostly Sascha's. Damned Rusky brought a knife to a gun fight."

Before I went into Jan's cabin to wipe down and change clothes, I sent Jan to attend to Sascha and Roberto.

The guest cabin bathroom mirror revealed that I indeed resembled a dragging victim, and that I also had blood splatters in my hair from that cleat hitting Juanita while I had my back to her. I removed what I could, thanked L'Oréal for my recent touchup that now worked as a coverup, and then heard what I hoped were medics pounding onto my deck. Slipping on a sweat set Jan leaves on the boat, I went out to face the music. It was only a matter of time until the cops zeroed in on me.

Jan and Roberto waited in the main salon, sitting quietly and alone. Roberto, also cleaned up, was wearing one of Jenks's jackets and a pair of my blue jeans.

Before I could say a word, Jan said, "Military medics are seeing to Sascha and Juanita. Just sit down here with us and button your lips, no matter who asks anything."

Roberto whispered, "As soon as Jan cut me loose I made a call to Nacho, and he arrived right after the first fire truck. He took command of the…situation."

"You mean the tragic *accident*," Nacho corrected Roberto, as he entered the cabin.

Epilogue

NACHO HANDLED THE Mexican police and Port Captain when they arrived. Sascha and Juanita had already been taken to the military hospital and were later transferred by air to another in Guadalajara.

Roberto left the boat that day with Nacho and Cholo, and was back at work at El Molokan the next week.

There was a small blurb in the La Paz paper about a boating accident, in which two women were badly injured by a propeller when they fell off a yacht as it was leaving the marina. Both women, one American and one Mexican citizen, will recover, but required medical attention.

An American gossip magazine reported that Juanita, the daughter of a child film star from some obscure sitcom, was injured in a boating accident in Mexico, and would require extensive facial reconstruction.

Jan and I split the fifty-grand reward given to me by Juan Tomato, but I am spending ten of my half on boat damage, interior cleanup, and dock repair. The money I made from my French assignment, El Jefe's payment for services rendered in Cannes, and the thirty left from his reward has me feeling less like a future bag lady.

According to the internet, Don Juan de Tomato called the investigation into his Russian mafia ties a witch hunt, and without any evidence to prove otherwise, it died on the vine.

Nacho told us that El Jefe had his suspicions about an insider involved in Juanita's kidnapping because he kept three million in his safe at all times, and almost everyone in the family knew it.

However, once he was given back the suitcases containing the remainder of the marked bills, he chose not to further investigate who, why, or how it was recovered. According to Nacho, sometimes families prefer to clean up their messes internally, especially where the Mexican monied elite are concerned.

The prince has forgiven me for trashing his yacht, especially since El Jefe paid for the cleanup. Last I heard, the two of them were planning a fishing trip off Cabo.

Rhonda and Cholo are still an item and are looking for a yacht for when he retires. She isn't overly happy about his frequent work-related absences, but hey, welcome to the ranks of us women with retired and active duty special ops dudes.

Speaking of, Jenks is due into La Paz in a few days, and we plan to cruise Mexican waters for a few weeks before he goes back to the Middle East.

Thanks to apples, lettuce, tuna fish, and daily Mexican Zumba classes run by those tiny women with no bones, I've lost eight pounds so I can pack them back on during our vacation. Po Thang is in a snit over the lack of leftovers and has probably slimmed down himself, but who can tell under all that fluff? Hmmm. Maybe I'm not fat, just fluffy?

THE END

OTHER BOOKS BY JINX SCHWARTZ

The Hetta Coffey Series
Just Add Water (Book1)
Just Add Salt (Book 2)
Just Add Trouble (Book 3)
Just Deserts (Book4)
Just the Pits (Book 5)
Just Needs Killin' (Book 6)
Just Different Devils (Book 7)
Just Pardon My French (Book 8)

Other Books

The Texicans
Troubled Sea
Land of Mountains

Boxed Sets

Hetta Coffey Boxed Collection (Books 1-4)
Hetta Coffey Boxed Collection (Books 5-8)

If you have enjoyed this book, please tell your friends about Hetta, or post a short review on Amazon. Word of mouth is an author's best friend, and is much appreciated.

I have editors, but boo-boos do manage to creep into a book, no matter how many great people look at it before publication. If you find an error, it's all on me.

And, should you come upon one of these culprits, please let me know and I shall smite it with my mighty keyboard! You can e-mail me at **jinxschwartz@yahoo.com**

And if you want to be alerted when I have a free, discounted, or new book, you can go to

http://jinxschwartz.com

and sign up for my newsletter. I promise not to deluge you with pictures of puppies and kittens.

Also, you can find me on Facebook at

https://www.facebook.com/jinxschwartz That puppy and kitten thing? No promises on FB posts :-)

BookBub also alerts my readers when I have book feature with the, or a new release. You can follow my author page to be notified.

https://www.bookbub.com/authors/jinx-schwartz

ACKNOWLEDGEMENTS

Holly Whitman has been the editor of every one of my books, and she keeps me out of the ditch when write myself into one. The last eyes on the book before I hit the "publish" button, are Donna Rich's. Thanks Holly and Donna.

I have some amazing beta readers! I have to thank all the sharp eyed readers for catching boo-boos I overlooked. And here they are, in no particular order: Sybil Dean, Frances Moore, Carmen Repsold, Jeff Brockman, Jenni Cornell, William Jones, Wayne Burnop, Lela Cargill, Krystyna Sews and Steven Brown

Also, we have to thank Kepler Biard, our cover dog. He's is a very good boy who deserves a big treat for not eating the twenties in the money shot on the cover.

And for the cover art, we have Karen Phillips to thank.

83261775R00194

Made in the USA
Middletown, DE
10 August 2018